PRAISE FOR

"In this first novel in a projected fant[...]
ham's LGBTQ representation among th[...]
fictional cult with the patriarchy, and she compares ιπ[...]μ[...]μ[...]ιε[...]
relationships in the fantasy world with LGBTQ relationships in ours."

~**Kirkus Reviews**

"I love me some wacky plots and characters, and between the thrills and chills in *Floodlight*, this book has a lot of humorous stuff in it. Besides, there are elves and griffins and dwarves—oh, my!—who could ask for anything more? If you like the funny urban fantasies of Charlaine Harris or Jim Butcher's Dresden Files, you'll likely enjoy Birmingham's new series."

~**Jessie Chandler, award-winning author of The Shay O'Hanlon Caper Series**

"From the cozy tenderness of two middle-aged lesbians spooning each other to sleep after a long day of tax preparation to an epic battle between dwarves, elves, and humans, *Floodlight* champions the magic of the ordinary and vice versa. Birmingham is the real thing, and it feels like she is just getting started. Lucky for us."

~**Patricia Loughrey, award-winning playwright and author of** *Dear Harvey* **and** *Sonata 1962*

"In *Floodlight,* this first-time author creates a fantasy world that, if the author continues honing her craft, might be compared to the fantasy worlds of Rowling, Tolkien and C.S. Lewis. Birmingham is already ahead of these famous authors in that she is not afraid to feature lesbians and lesbian couples as her heroes. To see lesbians waging war with evil is not a new sight for gay men whose lesbian friends literally helped them survive the HIV/AIDS virus. But to the average reader who may not have ever thought much about lesbians, this will be a colorful and creative entry into a whole new world."

~**Mel White, Author of** *Stranger at the Gate: To be Gay and Christian in America* **and** *Holy Terror: Lies the Christian Right Tells Us to Deny Gay Equality*

FLOODLIGHT

BOOK ONE
THE HERCYNIAN FOREST SERIES

REBA BIRMINGHAM

Launch Point Press
Portland, Oregon

ISBN: 978-1-63304-204-9
SECOND EDITION - Revised & Re-Edited
First Printing, 2018

Cover: TreeHouse Studios

Launch Point Press
Portland, Oregon
www.LaunchPointPress.com

This book is dedicated with gratitude to my parents, who both made their transitions recently. While they didn't always understand me, they loved and encouraged me. Thanks.

~

ACKNOWLEDGMENTS

Books go through a lot of people's minds as they read the unedited version(s) of your work and tell you what they think. I was honored to have, in no particular order, Jennifer Onstott Warner, Jennifer Johnson Richey, Zach Birmingham, Judy Baker, Marta Mora, Deb & Mary Love, Billie Summerfield, Katie Cotter, Mary Artino, Dr. Tina Tessina, and the Rev. Mel White–contribute valuable feedback. Special thanks to Thea Samaniego, who once lived near the Black Forest and advised me on German phrases. Special thanks also to Professor Suzan Gridley, who first taught me "Writing is rewriting" and sent me to comma school.

This Second Edition is being published by Launch Point Press of Oregon, owned by Lori L. Lake, a terrific editor and publisher. This journey has been an epic trek, which began with telling author Verda Foster I wanted to write a book. She will be my friend forever.

Reba Birmingham
December 2018

"Art should be dangerous, darling."
~Fiona Castlebaum

CHAPTER ONE

MERRYVILLE, USA

The weirdest and most unbelievable events of my life started with a pendant and the exclamation, "We could all live in there!"

I was sitting with my wife, Mitzi, and our best friends, Valerie and Juniper Gooden, at Utopia, a local restaurant. We were seated outside getting ready to order dinner when Juniper suddenly made that observation.

I put down my drink and asked, "In where?"

"There!" Juniper pointed to my chest with a long, painted, rainbow nail. Juniper's always "matchy-matchy," as Mitzi says, her carefully coiffed red hair going well with her green eyes and creamy complexion.

My hair is, by comparison, cowlicky and never acts right when I comb it. I looked down at my Steampunk Octopus picture in a half bubble of plastic. "My pendant?" I raised my eyebrows.

Juniper smiled a mysterious smile and Valerie laughed.

"Why not?" Valerie asked. "All it takes is a little imagination." A beautiful fifty-something, Valerie's not quite as flashy as her Juniper, though her dark-blue eyes are kind and her black hair thick and silky.

Mitzi said, "Kind of like, an Octopus's Garden in the Sea." She leaned forward, letting her imagination flow. Mitzi was very animated, and her "sticky uppy" brunette hair had two beaded braids that glittered in the waning sun.

I stayed frozen. "It's a piece of plastic, ladies." All three women started studying their menus. I realized I sounded a bit too cranky.

"But I do love the Beatles," I said, finally catching the reference.

Mitzi patted my shoulder as if she felt sorry for me. She looked at our friends. "It's the end of March, tax deadline approaching, no time for playing word games."

"How are we all going to fit in there?" I still held the pendant in my hand off my chest, thinking it through.

Juniper sighed and picked an imaginary piece of lint off of her colorful caftan. "Panda, Panda, Panda, life should be magical." A dramatic sigh. "Back to the real world, I guess. Anyone have the arugula salad here before?"

I felt a bit like a killjoy and surveyed the table, allowing myself to feel warmed by my friends and the fun conversation. Why couldn't I be more like them? I hadn't had much time to be silly in my life. I tended to think of all impractical or impossible things as silly. I knew my companions had a flair for adventure and the fabulous, but they were women of great achievement, too. Valerie, a nurse, had seen much suffering. Juniper was curator at the local museum and the one to suggest a universe in a small half globe of plastic over an octopus. My wife, Mitzi, is a tour guide and values all things exotic.

Mitzi's brown eyes appeared over the menu. "I'm having the Japanese eggplant."

"Perhaps we could shrink ourselves?" I said, but the moment had been lost, my comment ignored.

"The arugula is wonderful," Mitzi said. "It comes from a local organic garden. I love this farm-to-table movement." Soon the conversation swirled around food, travel, and the latest village gossip, the pendant temporarily forgotten.

But I'm getting ahead of myself. My name is Panda, an odd name to be sure, but it could be worse. My mom and dad were children of the Sixties, and I have a brother named Brook and a sister named Puddle. The water theme seemed to have run its course—no pun intended—when they became fascinated with mammals. Somewhere in Peru, my parents left this earth while chasing the myth of a hidden Incan village, leaving the three of us with a more conservative aunt and uncle in California. Not all of us took to the Golden State. Brook is now killing it on Wall Street in the New York financial district, and Puddle, the most like our folks, lives in an ashram in India.

My wife and I live in the city of Merryville, a booming port city on the left coast with miles of urban sprawl and home of a diverse collection of immigrants, LGBTQ, and midwestern transplants. We also have a fair amount of citizens who can trace their lineage back to the Spanish land grant. Life is pretty good here for a house with a Mrs. and Mrs. We live in a mid-twentieth-century home, which could politely be described as in a state of arrested decay. Each week is like the next: work, home, work, farmer's market, work, work, and work, with maybe a movie and a couple of days to recover. The travel industry has been a bit depressed, so Mitzi has taken to helping me with my job as a tax preparer. We have a store-front business catering to the average Joe who can't figure out TurboTax. It pays the bills.

ొ

CHAPTER TWO

APRIL 1
FOWLER TAX SERVICES

When tax season is over I want to visit Puddle again." Mitzi leaned on a four-drawer file and picked idly at an Areca palm in the corner of my office.

"India's hot," I replied automatically, not looking up from the Fabishes' joint return. "Do you see a W-2 floating around for the Fabishes?"

She languidly reached to the floor in front of my wooden desk and picked up said W-2. I wondered anew at her fluidity. How did she get so graceful? Oh yeah, yoga.

"How about Bali?" she asked. This woman was relentless.

"Same thing." I peered over the top of my glasses. "And too expensive."

Sound of the calculator.

Not wanting to be dismissive, I said, "What do we have planned this weekend?"

Silence.

I sensed a shift in our conversational rhythm and looked up with my whole head.

Mitzi was frowning at a piece of mail, and she handed it to me dramatically. "Maybe this!"

I took it and read the invitation:

THIS TICKET WILL ADMIT PANDA AND MITZI FOWLER AND TWO GUESTS TO THE GARDEN CIRCLE IN HERCYNIAN FOREST.
THE DAY IS THAT OF THE DOG SUN.
CHOOSE WELL . . .

I knew that look. Mitzi was intrigued.

The light flickered. Always thinking monetarily, I said, "Did we forget to pay the light bill?" My attempt at changing the subject didn't deter my wife.

"Panda, this is interesting. I wonder who sent it? Maybe Val and Juniper want to go." She snatched the message back.

I looked down at my desk, piled with paper, and the ever-present April Fifteenth tax deadline loomed ominously in my mind. I gestured at the mess with both hands. "Go where? Listen, darling pie, let me finish these returns, and we can talk about it tonight." A pause, then my fakish smile. Again, the killjoy.

She set down the invite and picked up her purse and keys. "Okay."

Uh-oh, that was abrupt. I got a quick kiss and put my hand on her arm.

She leaned over me and picked up the invitation.

"Please don't be disappointed is all I'm saying."

She fixed a gaze on me with her warm brown eyes. "All I can say is I'll be really glad when this tax season is over."

My resolve wavered. I wanted to follow her out the door and never look back. Instead I said, "I promise, baby, we'll do something fun."

She paused, and a beat passed while she wrestled with my response. "Sure." Time froze in the way it does between couples sometimes. You notice everything; she was letting me off the hook, again. One of the things I loved best about Mitzi was her ability to see the positive in virtually everything. I shook my head as she danced out singing, "Hercynian Forest, here we come!" Her hair beads swung around, and I promised myself to think up something truly special for us to do once the work was done.

The sun set and the clock marked a few more hours. I stretched and prepared to leave. My habit before walking out the door was to go in the closet-sized bathroom and brush my hair in the dull mirror. Tired brown eyes looked back at me, but Mitzi says I'm adorable, which, as a woman over forty, is good enough for me. I put the brush on its hook and went to get my purse, wondering if she was already asleep. The SHUT sign had been turned from OPEN for hours, so I was startled from my reverie by a knock.

I peeked between the metal slats on the door and saw Lulu, our security guard, all in what my wife would call a twoozle. She shifted her considerable girth from one foot to the other and appeared to be in great distress. I put up an index finger while I searched for my big circle full of keys. After negotiating the deadbolts, thinking she had to use the restroom, I opened the door. "Hello, Lulu."

"Oh, Ms. Fowler," She put her hand on her chest dramatically. "Thank God you're still here." Lulu took her job very seriously. Her brown eyes were very wide and her curly Samoan hair fanned out on either side of her cherubic face. "I saw somethin' that don't seem right. Can you come?" Her flashlight beam went wide as her arms flailed a beat to her heavy breathing.

"Sure," I said and locked the door behind me. "Where?"

"Follow me." For a woman of size, she moved with surprising speed.

My tax office is in a strip mall, tucked in between a hair salon and a Brazilian jiujitsu place. There are bright street lights and a few anemic meshed rectangles of illumination on metal poles, which could use a couple of coats of paint from our stingy landlord. The asphalt was striped so patrons could park in front of the storefront they wanted.

Cell phone poised, ready to dial 9-1-1, I loped along behind her, thinking that ten o'clock in this neighborhood wasn't the greatest place to be.

The normally talkative Lulu was stealthy, and she suddenly stopped short, with me bumping up behind her. "What?"

"Shhh," she said. "Look"

I peered around her and at first saw nothing. The strip mall was dark, except for the feeble illumination in the parking lot. Lulu's light swept the shadows and stopped at the bushes near the end of the businesses. The beam sparkled on a jewel, embedded in a two-inch hilt, attached to a blade lying in the dirt. "What's that?" I said, and moved to pick it up.

"Don't! They may still be around."

"Who Lulu?"

"Him." Lulu pointed her flashlight on what appeared to be a garden gnome. He stood perfectly still, his blue eyes fixed on me. Stunned, I shook my head. Maybe Mitzi was right and I was working too hard.

"It's not real and he can't hurt us." This was a spontaneous mantra from childhood. I had no idea if it was true.

"Why he have a knife then?" Lulu fixed her big brown eyes on me.

"It's probably a harmless toy."

I looked at the gnome and he blinked. "What the—" His expression reminded me of a deer caught in headlights. He didn't move, but his gaze changed from me to Lulu and back to me again. Then he glanced at the little dagger and inched toward it. My mouth went dry and I tried to swallow. My rational mind told me that gnomes aren't alive, but the reality was standing right in front of me.

"You see dat," Lulu said. "Your garden gnome's walkin' jes as purty as you please."

I nodded, unable to speak. He inched closer still, the dagger halfway between us now. I took a step back and my heart pounded so loud it echoed in my ears. I thought I was going to pee my pants. Suddenly he dashed forward, picked up the dagger, and fled.

Lulu turned to me, as if doubting her own sanity." Did you see dat?"

"I'm not sure what I saw." My go-to emotional state is to shut down. "It's late and I have to go home."

She walked me back muttering, "I din want to call that in." Her radio squawked as if in reply.

"I don't blame you. They'd think you were still drinking." Why did I say that? My heart was starting to return to normal, but my mouth was running.

She got serious. "No way, Jose! You would smell it."

I remembered being drunk could get her fired, and she had a little history there. "I didn't mean I thought you were drinking. Oh, never mind. Why didn't you get the Brazilian boys?" This was referring to our strip mall jiujitsu studio.

She motioned with the flashlight to the storefront two windows down. "Closed. You the only one still here."

I looked around at the abandoned mall, and it occurred to me I'd been working way too many hours.

"Makes sense. That's about the only thing that does. Weird." Then after a beat, I said, "Are you going to be okay?"

"Oh yeah." She flashed a broad grin. "Now that I seen the little fella, I can take 'em."

"You sure? You want me to call anybody?"

She shook her head vigorously. "Oh hell to the no. Who you gonna call? This what I do—I protect! That jes threw me a little is all." She gave me a little back hand wave as she returned to her duties.

I locked up and when I looked around she was on patrol, trusty flashlight in hand.

I arrived home and was met by Brutus, our Bengal cat. I'd wanted a dog, Mitzi wanted a cat, and he was the compromise. As usual, he waited in the garage and walked me inside. "Hey, Brute, How you doing, little boy?"

He looked up at me with his golden eyes, big ears, and wide nose, looking for all the world like a miniature cheetah. I got a hearty purr and a face rub on my overloaded arms as I wrestled with my key ring.

I couldn't wait to tell Mitzi about the strange visitor we had at the strip mall. It seemed surreal, and I needed my rock of sanity to bounce it off of.

The house was semi-dark. After rewarding Brutus with a treat for his comforting companionship, I laid down my folders and purse, took off my clunky shoes, and tried to tiptoe into the bedroom, where Mitzi was sleeping.

When you're trying to be quiet, everything sounds loud. I opened the dresser drawer as softly as I could to get my pajamas. "Hi, babe," Mitzi said sleepily from the pillow.

"Sorry, hi, are you awake?"

The blanket stirred enough that I could see her eye roll. Brutus took it as an invitation to jump on her chest and stare down. His dense, spotted coat made you want to run your hands through it.

"That's okay, I had to get up anyway because some lady came in all noisy." Mitzi gave him a pat.

Feeling cute, in my best Groucho Marx imitation, I asked, "What time does your wife come home?" We kissed and I sat on the bed. "Mitz, the weirdest thing happened tonight. Lulu had me go with her to check out a disturbance, and we saw what looked like a living, breathing, garden gnome. I know that sounds strange but—"

"Oh, Panda."

"What?"

Mitzi laughed. "She got you."

"Huh?"

"It's April First, April Fool's day, you tax nerd."

"April Fool's? Oh my God! Are you freaking kidding me? If so, I don't know how she could have pulled it off."

Suddenly, it occurred to me that in the weeks before April Fifteenth—the center of my universe—others did celebrate April Fool's Day and played silly jokes on one another.

"Well I'll be damned," I said, relieved. "I thought we were having a mass hallucination." I pulled my pajama top on. "I didn't think Lulu was that complex. She sure got me. I wonder how she did it."

The light snapped off and I heard a muffled voice say, "She probably got a kid to dress like a gnome. Don't know, don't care. Now come to bed."

I climbed in next to Mitzi and fell into a deep sleep from 1040-inspired exhaustion, thinking about what I would say to our night guard the next time I saw her.

❧

I awoke to pans clanging in the kitchen, a marvelous sound. The aroma of coffee wafted through the hallowed halls of our humble home. Brutus was asleep on my hip, presumably protecting me from all enemies, foreign and domestic. In a frayed kimono, Mitzi brought me a steaming mug of caffeine and said, "It lives." I must have looked a sight with my hair going in all directions. I took a sip and practically purred. Then she dropped a minor bomb. "Babe, I forgot to tell you this weekend is Juniper's Superstar Artist showing at the museum, and we promised to attend." She looked so pretty—how could she make me do these things?

I groaned. "What day?" I asked, knowing this was work-every-day-through-the-fifteenth season. I pulled the blanket over my head.

Mitzi uncovered my face and kissed it. "Don't be like that—she's our best friend. Besides, the event is going to be really interesting. Saturday night she's showing an installation called Floodlight!" She motioned to the newspaper folded neatly on our quilt. "The notice is even in the paper."

"Oh, I've heard of that." I picked up the cup and leaned to blow steam off the hot liquid. "That lady from New York who lights up dark places and films what she finds."

Mitzi settled in with her favorite pastime, Sudoku. "I know. Her show is called, Floodlight, yep."

"Sounds kind of dangerous."

Eye roll and sigh. "You are so dramatic."

"Moi?"

"Aren't you the one who came home last night babbling about dwarves?"

"Garden gnomes, and there was only one."

"Thank you for the clarification. That's so much saner."

Our house phone rang. While Mitzi went to answer it, I opened the paper and searched for any reference to the Saturday event. Page three in the *Weekend Edition* had a full spread on Juniper's celebrity artist, the current darling of the art world.

MERRYVILLE MUSEUM TO HOST FIONA CASTLEBAUM'S "FLOODLIGHT!"

The art world has been buzzing since Fiona burst on the scene two years ago. Her first, and now infamous, project involved Paris alleys. "Let's throw some light on it and get at the truth!" The truth, it seems, is that alleys are the highways of criminals. In France, Castlebaum caused a sensation with her images of the seedier side of the City of Lights when she exposed the child sex trade. Faces were clear and some notables were literally "caught in the act."

It's true, Interpol cops have become art lovers. But not everyone is a fan of her work, and in fact, she has had death threats. Castlebaum laughs them off. "Of course art is dangerous, darling."

Mitzi called from the living room, "It's Babs from the office. There are several walk-ins."

"Dang, I was hoping we could have a leisurely breakfast together. I didn't even finish this article." Mitzi soon returned with an "Egg in a Nest," one of my favorites.

"Go," she said and handed me the toast. "It's good to be so popular."

"Why, Mrs. Fowler, if I didn't know better, I'd say you were trying to get rid of me."

"Oh sure, my girlfriend will be over shortly. If you want to stick around and do manual labor instead of taxes, I'm redoing the garden so we can have our own garden-to-table veggies."

Our backyard was going through a rough transformation. A number of attempts had been made to turn the clay soil.

"Is that why it looks like a war zone?"

"Ha-ha, I'm going to fill in the holes but have more research to do. Do you know the Hercynian Forest does exist? It's also called the Black Forest and is located in Germany."

"Uh-huh." I pulled on my socks. "Didn't you go there once?"

"Oh, yes! The forest was awesome, but apparently I didn't do the right tour. Let me read to you from Google: The Black Forest region is supposedly blessed with a rich mythological landscape, said to be haunted by werewolves, sorcerers, witches, and the devil in differing guises." Her brown eyes fixed on mine as she delivered the last line, "Helpful dwarves try to balance the scales."

At that, I caught the twinkle in her eyes. I never know whether she's teasing me or getting one of her wild ideas. Part of our relationship is that she keeps me guessing . . . I guess. Although weekends should be for rest, at this time of year I have to use every moment to stay on top of tax season.

"Well, the more I work, the closer we get to our next trip." I grabbed the egg and toast and gave her a quick kiss. "But I'm thinking somewhere warm might be nice. Cabo San Lucas?" She calmly smiled and went back to her research, which always makes me nervous. Our friend Juniper says the most dangerous thing in the world is a woman quietly sitting in the corner smiling.

Great. The Black Forest has *dwarves*. That Lulu—she got me good.

Upon arriving at the office, I had no time to muse over unexplained events or what my lovely wife might be up to. A smiling longshoreman came in with an untidy shoebox of receipts and statements and thrust it at me, as if to say, "Here, fix." I have many different clients, but they come in two sizes: "anal" and "hot mess." He was in the latter category.

Babs kept the coffee going all day, and after seven p.m. we turned the sign to SHUT.

She said, "I'm leaving now. Do you need anything else?" She looked as tired as I felt. She had already worked too much for what I paid her.

"No, thanks. Do it all again tomorrow?" I asked, our standard joke.

"If I don't win the lotto tonight," she said. We both laughed as if it hadn't been said a hundred times before. Babs tended to her elderly father, and I knew her night shift at home was about to start after her care worker left. I made a mental note to ask Valerie about home services that might be available for him.

This night no unexpected knock on the door occurred and no Lulu as she didn't start her rounds until nine-thirty p.m. I was getting out early for this time of year. I decided to stop by the French bakery— run by Mexicans—on the way home for a little dessert surprise for my long-suffering spouse.

Fowler Tax Services had no parking garage, and as I pulled away from a curb where I'd parked, two streets away, I noticed a piece of paper flapping under my windshield wipers. "What now?" I said aloud.

Since the side street was quiet, I stopped and got out, thinking it might be a ticket. Instead, in the same eerie script as the invitation that had come in the mail yesterday, the paper said:

THE WITCHING HOUR

I made a note to check into mental health services for Lulu—or me—balled it up and threw it in the back of the car.

The weather this week had been gorgeous, which is another reason we're so attached to this place. I put the top down on my smart car. Needing to be grounded, I punched the numbers for my favorite nurse on my car Bluetooth and called my pal, Val, who answered on the third ring. "Whatcha doing?" I said, navigating around bicyclers.

"Trying to save our orchids. It got a touch too hot this week." I could picture her in her and Juniper's back bathroom. Covered with windows, it doubled as a very suitable, makeshift greenhouse.

"Well, it is the dead of spring. I see you're still healing—only flowers, not people, this time."

"Ha-ha, true. I can't believe you're not at the office. Is this a holiday?" Sounds of a water spritzer.

"Knocked off early. I don't want Mitzi to forget what I look like. Are we all set for Saturday? Was Juniper able to get us on the list?"

"Yes, darling, she remembers the little people," she said in her best Gloria Swanson voice.

I winced inwardly about little people—shades of dwarves and gnomes. Last night's adventure with Lulu came to mind.

Valerie laughed her musical laugh. "But of course. But, babe, I gotta tell ya, this is the hottest ticket in town."

"No kidding. How did Juniper do it? I read the article this morning, well, at least some of it. Her event will be a crazy mob scene."

"I know. Juniper's down at the museum right now seeing to all the details—security, media, parking."

"The devil is in the details they say."

"You're right, love. Be sure to check in around seven. Your names are on the list."

"Cool. I feel like a celebrity."

"See you, babe."

"Ciao, bella!" When did I start talking like this? Oh yes, after Mitzi made me take Italian with her.

I would prefer to stay home and sleep next Saturday, but Mitzi was so charming and excited about the event, her enthusiasm was contagious. Truthfully, life has to be about more than work, and this was not an opportunity to be shunned. Juniper had taken over the local art museum a year before, and her events were all the buzz. While the former curator showed respectable, if predictable, art shows, Juniper had an eye for the off-center and trending. How she snagged an artist of Fiona Castlebaum's stature to appear at our modest museum was nothing short of amazing.

Along with my early arrival, the pastry did the trick. I left my briefcase in the back of Sweetpea, my smart car, and Mitzi and I spent the evening talking and watching recorded *Modern Family* episodes. Our favorite thing to do is to laugh together, and lately there hadn't been enough time to do that.

"What all did you do today? Are we ready to plant?" My feet were curled under me as we sat on the couch and ate our éclairs.

Mitzi reached for another delicious mini-delight. "No, actually today was kind of bizarre. Remember we were just talking about the German trip I took during undergrad?" She stuck out her tongue to catch a drip of cream. "I got a call from Madame Dresser, who financed the whole thing for my college."

"Doesn't she live in New York?" My hands were sticky, and I was wishing for a damp cloth but didn't want to move. Brutus licked some cream off my finger.

"Yes, and other places. She's got to be a hundred and not very sociable. I was really surprised. She said she wanted to see me this weekend. She's 'schvinging through Los Angeleeees' on her way back from Asia. I don't know how she even found me."

"Isn't she royalty or something? What does she want with you?"

I ducked as Mitzi threw a pillow at me.

"So I'm not good enough for royalty to come calling?" she asked playfully.

"Babe, of course you are. I mean, you're royalty to me." Yes, I'm a total suck up. "Did she say what was on her mind?"

"Kind of. She wants to see my pictures from that trip. I told her we could digitize them and email them, or I could have copies made, but she wouldn't hear of it. She's coming out to California anyway for something. I dunno. We talked. It will be fun to pull those photos out. Remember when we used film and had to get them developed?"

Madame Dresser wasn't the only one getting old. Something else niggled right at the edges of my mind. My stoic and pragmatic gut was tingling. Too many strange things had happened this week, but I didn't want to rain on Mitzi's parade. She loved the exotic and unusual, and this certainly fit the bill. "When do you see her?"

"She's coming here Sunday, before she leaves for Baden-Baden," Mitzi said, imitating the old woman's thick German accent, "to take in the Schpa." I smiled. The spa.

"Well," I said, "I guess we need to break out the white gloves and give this place a good cleaning." Surveying the tchotchke-dotted living room, I saw that would be quite a task. We looked at each other and simultaneously laughed. Not a bit of dusting was going to happen. Every time we traveled, some precious find came back with us, and the result was, um, eclectic, but us.

The rest of the night was pretty ordinary, and we ended it spooning as the moon rose over our little place.

CHAPTER THREE

FLOODLIGHT GALA

Saturday, we arrived at the museum at seven on the dot and stood in a line before the check-in table. Mitzi waved and hugged her many acquaintances as I stood there smiling when appropriate. I hoped I didn't nod off during the show.

On the open green space in between museum buildings, a stage was set up for the local politicians to blah blah to us, the captive audience. Hundreds of conversations took place at the same time, and it took Garcia, the MC, a minute to calm the excited crowd.

Garcia, Juniper's right-hand man, said into the mic, "Ladies and gentlemen, before we enter the exhibit, we have a proclamation from the mayor and the city council member for this district. First, we will hear from Gary Smithers, our city councilperson."

Ugh! This man was the closest thing our liberal city had to a right winger. He limply grabbed the mic and blathered on about the importance of art. Yawn. Most folks continued grabbing canapés and chatting among themselves. A clique from Smithers' office who would normally never be caught dead at an *avant-garde* event clapped at all the right pauses and frowned at people not paying attention. Mr. Smithers, while not fully endorsing Ms. Castlebaum's work, at least mustered some enthusiasm for art in general.

Mercifully, his stint was short, and he handed the mic with two fingers to Garcia, an openly gay young man, who announced, "Without further ado, our mayor, Tom Reed."

Mayor Reed fairly knocked the curly-haired MC out of the way, grabbed the microphone, and launched into his standard fare: "This is a proud moment for Merryville. Our fair city, under leadership of the current administration, has attracted business, reduced crime, and now it can add, is becoming a cultural beacon!" His comments were bombastic but, to give him his due, effective.

Juniper was fighting an eye roll. She'd never been a fan. Here he was, practically taking credit for Fiona Castlebaum's installation, and we knew the only "art" at City Hall was a very old, white-bread series of pictures about our founding fathers. I surveyed the crowd, noted the usual suspects, and saw Phillip, a writer from the Fishwrap—our affectionate term for the local *Merryville Bee*. PRESS: Check.

Society maven Charlotte Windingle—you could find a Windingle building on almost every block in Merryville. MONEY: Check.

Up and coming museum board member and Juniper nemesis, Linda Chicolet, who was busy pressing the flesh even though the mayor was still talking. NARCISSISTS: Check.

A number of those who simply can't stand to miss an opportunity to see and be seen and knew somebody to get on the list. Oops—I guess that was me and Mitzi, too. LOCAL NOTABLES: Check.

Then there were people I didn't recognize, some dressed pretty quirky and artsy, but that was to be expected—right? Fiona Castlebaum was from another country, Ireland I think, and I could only describe these folks as foreign.

I felt a rib nudge, got a pay-attention smile from my wife, and tuned back in.

The Mayor continued loudly, "Yes, art is good for business!"

The crowd roared, but my ADD (Squirrel!) drew me back to surveying the people.

I'd done taxes for many of the locals and smiled to see that Merryville cleaned up pretty good.

Valerie wended her way through the crowd and brought us a couple of sparkling ciders. "Isn't this great?"

I nodded. "Thanks for the drink." Mitzi leaned over to gossip in whispers with Valerie about Linda Chicolet, who must be green with envy at Juniper's artistic coup. As the mayor droned on, I noticed a heavy police presence, which made sense given what the article said this morning.

The mayor said, "And we hope this is the first of many such events, placing Merryville squarely on the national map for artists." He closed with his usual "let's say it together." The crowd joined in for a rousing "Paris! London! New York! Merryville!" This time I saw Juniper cough and look down, Valerie whispered, "She hates that." We all giggled and watched as Juniper took the microphone. She looked dazzling in her evening gown and trademark red hair, expertly coiffed. Photographers' lights flashed. Diamonds sparkled at her earlobes. She did a little throat clear, and you could feel the crowd lean in.

"No one was more surprised than I," she said, "when Fiona herself called last November." The crowd reacted with a cheer. This was the most famous celebrity most could remember in Merryville since Snoop Dogg. Juniper stood there until you could hear a pin drop, then continued. "This event puts us on the world stage."

Another cheer.

"We've been working with Ms. Castlebaum for the last four months to show her work as well as our fair city"—a glance at the mayor"—in the very best light, pun intended. You all know the stories, and they'll be covered in a short film once you're seated. Without further ado, I give you Fiona Castlebaum."

Juniper looked to her left, and we were all puzzled, as the star of the art world was nowhere on the stage. The air was chilly now that the sun had gone down and the wind blew in from the ocean. The crowd murmured, and those on the dais looked left and right as if the artist were hiding among them. Was this real or part of the show? Juniper whispered to Garcia.

Suddenly all the lights went out. The police looked to be on high alert until, a beat later, floodlights lit up the bluff. Over the loudspeaker, we heard what I presumed to be Fiona's lilting voice: "Follow the light, children. Come see what's in the bushes, only a stone's throw away." The crowd roared, loving the unexpected. Ushers appeared with flashlights to safely guide the audience past the stage and to the railing over the back of the green space. Cops relaxed.

Lit below was an area that most locals didn't even see anymore because it had become part of the landscape. Fiona Castlebaum was on a cherry picker that rose up from the beach below to the level of the crowd. She wore a shimmering gown and a headset worthy of Madonna. "I give you, *a hidden world*," she said dramatically.

The crowd gasped as the many floodlights exposed the bluff in excruciating detail, revealing hundreds of feral cats fleeing in different directions. Trash littered the underbrush, including abandoned bowls from people who fed the colony, and one homeless man blinked at the intense light.

Fiona's voice continued. "When I come to a town, I want to see its underbelly, sometimes its benign neglect, sometimes pure evil. Merryville is no different." Jaws dropped and I saw the mayor and Smithers making their way through the crowd toward the parking lot. No way were they going to be a part of this unscripted embarrassment.

"Paris, London?" she said mockingly, her voice blaring at the crowd. "Try Calcutta." Now the crowd started to mutter and become agitated.

A spotlight painted her face as she floated above the crowd, otherworldly. "This is a little taste of what I do. More will be revealed. Right now you have seen hundreds of cats, breeding unchecked, using the bluff a stone's throw away from your beautiful museum as a litter box. You see a human being living there, in that filth." Her ice-blue eyes glittered dangerously. "And I'm just getting started."

Like many others, I was paralyzed. What would happen next? The feeling was unsettling and, I imagine, what made her so effective.

She turned a spotlight on Juniper: "In agreeing to have me here, you gave me artistic freedom, and for that I thank you." Juniper looked betrayed as photographers snapped the surreal scene. Fiona addressed the crowd. "Trap, spay, and release. Go to the dark places, find the human beings there, be creative, but take care of the problems in your city." She shaded her eyes. "Where is Mayor Reed? Can we find the mayor?" she said mockingly. The cherry picker lowered her onto the grass by the invitees, who were now confused and a little bit frightened. As she alighted, a spotlight searched out the mayor and caught him getting in his car. He turned and seemed torn whether to stay or flee. He acted like he hadn't heard her, and the car door closed. Moments later, the vehicle sped off.

Police radios crackled, and we all seemed to be released from whatever spell was upon us.

Fiona's microphone was working well as she strode through the crowd toward the museum. "All those with courage and a desire to know the capital 't' Truth, follow me." Pandemonium ensued. Many followed her, raised their drinks, and shouted in an anarchic thrall. Many headed to the parking lot, women with purses held close to their bodies, husbands with protective arms around them.

"Girl knows how to thin out a crowd," Mitzi whispered to me. We watched the defections as some of the more-conservative members of the board followed the mayor out. Linda Chicolet looked delighted as we heard her explain to another, "I told you this was going to be a disaster."

I heard more than one say variations of "crazy" and "how insulting."

"This ain't New York," one said ironically.

"Nope, still Iowa by the sea," I said to no one in particular. The police seemed nervous and added to the tension of the departing crowd. Valerie said nothing but looked grim.

The light followed Fiona to the entrance of the art museum, cum theater, where she turned, pulled herself to her full height and said, "Time for the show, enter if you dare!" She walked into the exhibit/theater, and the remaining folks surged behind her, apparently fascinated, not sure if this was an art show or a car wreck.

Phillip was on the phone off to the side, uploading pictures to the *Merryville Bee*. He was open-minded and an animal lover. I felt he would be fair. Mitzi grabbed my hand, and we followed Valerie to her frazzled wife.

When we caught up with her, Juniper was talking to Dick Mortimer, chairman of the museum board. "Of course, we knew what we were getting—this is what she does. It's art for goodness sake. Don't leave. It won't look good."

His eyes narrowed. "We're well beyond not looking good." He favored traditional art shows and hadn't voted for Juniper to take over the chief curator position. "We'll speak Monday." He turned on his heel, lips so firmly pressed they were white. He seemed to have another thought and spoke over his shoulder in a fierce whisper, "If we lose one quarter as a result of this—well, we'll talk Monday, be sure of that."

He stomped off to meet Mrs. Windingle, the museum's biggest patron, who clutched a glass of wine and looked a bit dazed.

Uh-oh. All three of us eavesdropped intently and tried to look like we were having our own conversation.

Dick opened his arms like he was just so sorry. "Mrs. Windingle, I hope you know this was a surprise to us, too. We really appreciate you underwriting this event."

The older woman silently looked at him, eyebrows raised. He went on. "I assure you, we will be back to the normal classic art we made our name on. This," he said and motioned to the pandemonium, "is an aberration."

After a pause, Mrs. Windingle said, "Dick, I give to art because I love art. Artists allow us to see the world in ways we don't otherwise. You of all people should know that." With her very white teeth and cultured voice, I found it difficult to know what was behind her words. Her intent was clarified momentarily when she turned to our friend and gave Juniper a big smile. She clasped her hand in both of hers and said, "It's about time someone paid attention to the feral cats and homeless. I didn't expect it to happen this way, but good on Fiona! I'm going in." Then, to Dick, she said, "Lighten up." She whooped with laughter and her entourage followed suit.

Dick mouthed to Juniper, "This isn't over," before leaving with Linda Chicolet and others of a more conservative vein. The police presence did nothing to calm fears, and all those uniforms made the situation seem more dangerous than it was. Some probably left, not sure of their safety. Every time it seemed things were calming, Fiona's voice boomed from the loud speakers, "That's right, no one is safe, people of Merryville."

Dick walked over to try to catch some of the departing patrons. I shrugged and turned toward Juniper. "Shall we?" I indicated the tent.

She looked a bit overwhelmed but said, "Might as well, it can't get any worse."

Inside, the energy was insane. A DJ was set up in the entryway with two turntables blasting music.

The little theater was packed, but there were fewer folks than had been on the lawn. "How are you doing?" someone asked Juniper as we sped by.

She flashed a smile. "Well, the overcrowding issue is resolved. I just hope I have a job on Monday."

Little did Juniper know, this was to be the caption under her picture in the *Merryville Bee*, but I'm getting ahead of the story.

Mitzi and I worked our way into the middle of the seats and glued our eyes on the screen, not sure what would come next. As the lights dimmed, the planned fifteen-minute-intro movie, which had been in the museum's script, began. The basics of Fiona Castlebaum's life were recounted: born in war-torn Ireland, raised in the slums of New York, and her arrival as darling of the avant-garde art world years later in Paris. Her projects were always surprising, fresh, and poked power or evil with her insightful commentary and a "bath of light." Her goal: always to leave the places changed for the better.

After the short film, the screen rose into the ceiling and the back wall, which was only a curtain in the makeshift theater, parted. The exhibit itself consisted of picture after picture of deeds of the dark thrown into the light. Many had quotes about the power of light attached to them. The display was weird and utterly compelling. Wasn't that the famed, married football star with a groupie in a compromising position outside the downtown arena? How about our mayor, still blinking from the light, posing with a dead deer at the NRA convention? Many of these images were already known, but the local stuff was new.

The crowd was subdued, and a lot of alcohol was consumed as we wandered the walls. "This is very different from last year," was all I could say. Mitzi and Valerie were talking about the quality of the photography. Juniper, consummate actress, was mingling and seemed to be enjoying herself. The series on cats and the homeless really was astonishing. Cats at the marina, cats in the garbage when we sleep, pictures of cats on death row at our Merryville "No Kill" shelter. It made you want to weep. A final series showed homeless people at the base of our new courthouse being shooed away before the official day began.

The hour got late and the crowd naturally dwindled. We sat with our friends as we did an autopsy on the night and ate leftover canapes. I said to Juniper, "Did you have any idea she wasn't on the stage when you introduced her?"

"Panda, that would be no. The spectacle is part of her process, not to say. She simply shows up and does her thing. I must admit the cherry picker was new."

"Where is she now?"

With her inimitable timing, Fiona swept through the museum doors, followed by a coterie of foreign-looking people and a few of Merryville's more adventurous.

Juniper got back on her heels and approached the woman, who had apparently finished what must have been a very amusing story.

Juniper stood there, and for a second I thought she might slap Fiona, who looked much older close up.

"You couldn't have told me about the cherry picker?"

In the beat that followed, we overheard departing guests still talking about the dramatic opening.

"Did you see the look on the mayor's face when the spotlight hit him? Priceless."

"You're welcome." Fiona laughed and went out to her waiting limousine.

The next morning, the headline of the *Merryville Bee* screamed: *Merryville Called Out on its Feral Cat and Homeless Problem,* and the inset with Juniper's picture was all about *Trouble on the Board at the Merryville Museum*

"Did you see this?" I held up the article. "Juniper is described as 'the embattled curator.' "

"I know. Linda Chicolet is probably drinking champagne and celebrating. Are you on your way to work?"

"Yes, you coming with?"

"No, remember I'm expecting Madame Dresser today. I'm about to get up and dig out my grad school photographs."

I got to the storefront about nine on, yes, a Sunday, and proceeded to do what I do. Babs was still having her weekend, and I could be alone and do my workaholic thing.

By lunchtime, I'd finished the Fabishes and was on to my next project when the phone rang. Valerie said, "Have you seen the headlines?"

I was typing with the phone wedged between my right shoulder and ear. "Yes, I'm so sorry. How's Juniper doing?"

"She's depressed. The board wants to see her tomorrow."

"That can't be good."

"Probably not. The *Monroe County Register*'s headline is: MERRYVILLE, the new CALCUTTA."

I groaned in sympathy.

"Hey, where's Mitzi? I've been calling your house all morning."

That figured: my wife and Val were the usual exchangers of community gossip, not me. They know my head is in tax season. I've been told during this time of year I'm not very fun—sticking to the facts and all. Not great at multitasking, I absentmindedly said, "She should be home. Did you try her cell? She was meeting there with Madame Dresser, an old acquaintance."

Valerie sighed. "Maybe she's turned off her phone. I don't want to be a stalker."

"She doesn't do that. Let me try her. Now you've got me wondering. She usually at least calls to see if I'm hungry."

"Aaah, the famous Panda stomach clock. Speaking of that, I better go and bring my own madame a tea. She's really distraught."

"Oh, man, please give her hugs. Tell her after the fifteenth we can plan a trip somewhere—would do us all good. Mitzi's been chomping at the bit to get on a plane."

Val rang off and I tried our home number, then Mitzi's cell, then the home number again, to no avail. The clock and my stomach said one-thirty p.m., later than my usual lunch hour. I looked at the pile on my desk and decided it would still be there when I got back. I locked up and checked for gnomes. Seeing none, I chuckled to myself and drove the six blocks to our home.

Mitzi's car was in the driveway, and I was annoyed that she'd probably gotten sidetracked with her exotic guest. Annoyance turned to puzzlement as I noted the front door was open. "Mitzi! You're going to let Brutus out." I locked the door. The cat was nowhere to be seen either. Damn. I bet he got out. "Mitzi!"

Then it hit me. The house was way too quiet. I heard a faint meowing and followed it upstairs. Brutus was in our bedroom closet and fairly lunged at me when I opened the door. "Brutus, baby, what happened?" The bed was still unmade, which sometimes happens on a weekend, but that tingle I felt the night before was turning into a serious alarm. Had Madame Dresser come and gone already? Did they leave in her car for lunch? Why didn't Mitzi call and tell me that?

I forced myself to calm down, but it was hard with the cat circling my legs and meowing loudly. I wish I could speak cat. I returned downstairs, and the disarray told a story. The kitchen table was covered with shoe boxes. It appeared Mitzi had at least looked for her old Germany photos. The coffee pot had turned itself off, which happened after hours of being idle, and the two cups on the table were cold. Two cups . . .

I walked our block in the neighborhood, questioning anyone who was home. No one had seen my wife other than to give a wave while getting their morning paper. I tossed the house for a note, thinking she probably went out and I was being an idiot. That's when I saw it. A note all right, but not written by any hand I knew.

ॐ

APRIL 12
THE WITCHING HOUR

It couldn't be Lulu this time. She didn't even know where we lived. Something was seriously wrong. I picked up my cell and called 9-1-1. The conversation went something like this:

"Nine-one-one, what's your emergency?"

"It's my wife. I think she's missing. I arrived got home and she's not here."

"Your name?"

"Panda Fowler, nine Thistle Drive. You have my phone number."

"The name of the missing party?"

"Mitzi Fowler, my wife."

"How long has she been missing?"

"Well, uh."

"When was the last time you saw her?"

"This morning."

A beat. "Ma'am, is she an adult?"

"Yes."

"Is she disabled, mentally or physically?"

"No."

"You need to give it twenty-four hours before we can take a missing person's report. Go to the station if she doesn't come home by then."

I could tell by the change in tone that the operator didn't think this was an emergency.

"But I think there's been foul play."

"Why?"

"I found a note when I got here. Someone left one like it on my car and mailed one to my office."

"What does it say, Ms. Fowler?"

"It's an invitation of some sort." I realized how I sounded. "You know what, I'll call after twenty-four hours have gone by."

"I think that's a good idea."

No way could I explain this to anyone but Val and Juniper. My next call was to Juniper's cell. It rang and rang then went to voice mail. The message box was full. Next I called Valerie, who answered.

"I tried Juniper's cell, but I couldn't leave a message."

"She's not answering today. It's been rough after last night, the phone was blowing up and we finally shut it off."

"Sorry to intrude, but I've got an emergency here. Mitzi is missing."

"What?"

"It's a complicated story. Can you guys come over? I hope I'm being ridiculous but . . . just come."

In less than ten minutes, Juniper's Citroen roared up our driveway and parked behind Mitzi's Miata. It took longer than ten minutes to tell them about the original invitation, Madame Dresser, and Brutus being locked in the closet. Both women kept interrupting with questions and more than a few "are you sure she just hasn't . . .?" inquiries.

By now it was three o'clock, and still no word from Mitzi. I found her cell phone in the house next to her keys, so I saw no point in calling. I knew something bad must have happened. She always had her cell phone with her. In fact, she was the first person I had ever known to own a cell. I could tell Jun and Val were worried, too.

Valerie got a sketchpad from their trunk and spread the paper on the dining-room table. "Okay. What do we know?"

I needed this approach. My head felt like a popcorn popper of ideas going in too many different directions. Brutus stood in my lap and swirled his tail over my neck and chin. He was showing solidarity but had pent-up energy. I knew how he felt because I wanted to do something, but what? Val had offered a way to organize.

I said, "Mitzi was supposed to be home today showing pictures to Madame Dresser. I don't know exactly what time because I was working today."

Juniper shot me a look then wrote: *Madame Dresser to meet Mitzi.*

"Who is Madame Dresser?" Valerie asked. "I don't recognize that name."

I stood up to go into the kitchen and get the pictures, and Brutus jumped on the pad to sniff the marking pen. "She's an old German woman who financed Mitzi's anthropology class to Germany when she was in grad school."

I didn't find many pictures. They took up a third of a box, once I figured out which box. The photos appeared as though Mitzi hadn't touched them for years.

"Weird, nobody looked at these today. Did Mitzi fall for a ruse to get her to meet this woman?"

Val looked at a photo closely. "Are we sure it really was Madame Dresser?"

My heart sank into my stomach. "Oh my God, I told her that lady must be a hundred by now. But why would someone pose as such an obscure figure from the past?" A beat while we all thought. "Wait, the call came in Friday."

Juniper said, "Get her cell phone. Let's see if her number is on it."

I smacked my head like the V8 commercial. "Why didn't I think of that?"

Juniper patted my hand. "You're worried, dear." I was touched that both dear friends had put aside their current crisis to help me with ours.

Valerie scrolled through recent calls and reported, "Okay, you've called her forty-seven times." She laughed. "And there's a number in the 510 area code."

"That's her mom." Oh crap, what was I going to tell her mom?

"Any out-of-country or New York area codes?" I grabbed the phone before I could stop my impulse. "Here's one. I'm calling it. Two-one-two is New York, right?"

Juniper nodded. She'd gone to college there.

After a brief wait, I heard a cultured voice say, "Four Seasons."

"May I have Ms. Dresser's room please?"

"One moment." A pause. "Ms. Dresser is not a current guest of ours."

"Can you tell me when she checked out?"

"And you are?"

"Mitzi Fowler," I said without hesitation. "Did you have any messages for me?"

"One moment."

The voice returned. "Actually yes, it wasn't picked up apparently. Madame Dresser said, 'I would love to see the pendant you were given by your mother, the one you showed me in Germany. See you Sunday.'"

I wrote it down to make sure I got it word for word. God bless expensive hotels. The No-Tell Motels on Pacific Coast Highway wouldn't have bothered.

I'd put it on speaker, and the girls crowded around so they could hear it all.

"Is she talking about that octopus pendant?" Valerie asked.

"Maybe, I guess." I held it away from my body and looked at it as if it could speak. "Mitzi never got the message, so I wore it today like I always do."

"Who is this Madame Dresser?" Juniper snapped her fingers and pointed to the sketchpad. "Everything you know "

"Mitzi met her when she paid for a trip for her semester abroad."

"Did she pay for any of the other students?"

"I don't know! I don't know. It was before I met her. It was just a story from college. I must think." I grabbed a handful of hair and shook my head.

Valerie, the healer, said, "I'm making tea. Do you have Chamomile?" She rooted around in the cupboard.

Images popped into my mind. "The note. There's a note in the back of my car. Let's get the weird writings all together."

"Meanwhile," Juniper said, "I'm going to look through these pictures for this Madame Dresser."

Pretty soon, I located the original invitation, the balled-up note in the back of Sweetpea, and the note waiting for me at home today. We put them side by side on the table.

THIS TICKET WILL ADMIT PANDA AND MITZI FOWLER AND TWO GUESTS TO THE GARDEN CIRCLE IN HERCYNIAN FOREST
THE DAY IS THAT OF THE DOG SUN
CHOOSE WELL . . .

THE WITCHING HOUR 12 APRIL.

APRIL 12 ER HAT TENTAKEL UND SIEHT AUS WIE EIN RIESIGER AGGRESSIVER OKTOPUS.

"Only some of it's in English. It's clearly sent to me and Mitzi, so someone is behind this. How could I show this to the police though? They would send the padded truck and take me to Metro Hospital." I sat down hard, frustrated. "Wait, some of this isn't in English, but Oktopus must be octopus. Maybe my octopus pendant is valuable and this lady was coming to steal it."

"The pendant!" Valerie quickly got on Google translator. "Here's what Mr. Google says."

Juniper raised her eyebrows. "How do you know it's not Mrs. Google?"

I looked back and forth between my dear, exasperating friends. "Girls, focus."

"Okay. Here goes. It has tentacles and looks like a giant octopus. Aggressive."

"That's it?" I said, no closer to understanding its meaning. "Other than the fact that Mitzi gave it to me and it has an octopus on it, I think we're facing a dead end."

"But Madame Dresser specifically asked Mitzi about it." Juniper added that to the list.

Brutus meowed, and once again I wished I knew what he wanted to say. The clock ticked in the background as we all feverishly thought. Valerie sipped her tea and leaned on the stove.

Juniper was quiet, sitting at the kitchen table and staring at the photos then the paper pieces. When she finally spoke, we all jumped a bit. "Okay, put it together this way. This ticket will admit Panda and Mitzi Fowler and two guests to the Garden Circle in Hercynian Forest. Period. Then, The Witching Hour is midnight, right?"

"What about the dog sun?"

"I'll Google that, too." After some typing, Val read from Wikipedia: "Wow! Sun dogs typically appear as two subtly colored patches of light to the left and right of the sun." Juniper and I crowded around her and looked over her shoulder. "Also called phantom sun or mock sun. The etymology of sun dog largely remains a mystery. The Oxford English Dictionary states it as being of obscure origin."

"There's an understatement." I missed Mitzi. She would have had lots to say. As a researcher of everything, she deprecatingly referred to herself as "a storehouse of useless knowledge," but it was what made her such a good tour guide.

Val said, "Holy crap, the next one is scheduled to appear April twelfth—that's Friday!"

I sat up as these bits of information started to gel. "Okay, so we know when, if we take them all together. April 12 at midnight. This must be the day of the dog sun."

Juniper looked me in the eye and smiled. "And we know where."

Valerie glanced at me and Juniper. Clearly both of us were having the same idea. "Oh, no. No, no nonono."

Juniper looked at Valerie. "We need to go to the Hercynian Forest at midnight on April twelfth. That's not very long from now."

"No, this is some kind of joke," Valerie said. "Come on, guys, this sort of thing doesn't happen in real life. You know how crazy you both are, right? Mitzi is going to come waltzing in after having a late lunch with her friend, and you're going to look like lunatics. Tea?" She poured us Chamomile in floral cups that Mitzi loved. Tears welled in my eyes. Was I losing it? This was way too much for Lulu to be behind.

"Besides," Val said, "there's no sun at midnight, silly girls." Val was so rational.

I put my fist to my mouth and willed my mind to focus. "Maybe we should give her a few hours more."

Juniper turned back to the sketchpad. "What else do we know? Is there something you're not telling us?"

I'd never been able to keep a secret. I told them about seeing the fleeing garden gnome at the office.

"Was it a dwarf or an elf?" Juniper asked, all serious.

I've always heard the joke about true friends helping you bury the body and never speaking of it again. I didn't plan to test that theory, but I was happy they didn't think me crazy. Valerie might tease about us being lunatics, but only to guide her more fanciful friends back to reality.

"I don't know. It looked like one of those little statues in the garden, but bigger. I thought it was weird when Mitzi read about the Hercynian Forest, where it says helpful dwarves try to balance the scales, whatever that means. The Hercynian Forest is actually the Black Forest in Germany, so called because it's so dense and dark in there."

They both looked at me, surprised at my knowledge. "Mitzi," was all I said.

"Have you talked to Lulu since?" Juniper was back on it like a Schnauzer, refusing to be sidetracked.

"No, she comes in at nine-thirty p.m."

"Then tonight you need to go talk to her. Somebody must have paid her to leave those notes." Valerie still refused to entertain the possibility it wasn't a hoax of some sort.

Juniper added to the sketchpad, "Dwarf or elf?" Eye roll from Valerie.

I grabbed a clump of my hair in frustration. "It's going to take hours and hours to catch up on my tax work. Do you know what time of year this is?"

"Yes, terribly inconvenient of Mitzi to disappear," Juniper said.

My eyes filled with tears and I crumpled. Juniper put her arm around me.

"Okay," she said. "Here's the plan. You go to the office, work your ass off making 1040s, or whatever, in case we need to go"—she looked at a very disapproving Val—"somewhere before the fifteenth. And talk to Lulu when she arrives."

"Will one of you stay here and see if Mitzi shows up?" I asked in a tremulous voice.

They clasped hands and plunked down on the couch almost in unison. "We both will," Juniper said. "It'll be nice to escape our ringing telephone at our house for a while."

I left, thanking the Goddess for such good friends and glad to have a plan. You can put one foot in front of the other when there's a plan. A big part of me held out hope that Mitzi would come home or call or something, and this budding nightmare would end.

CHAPTER FOUR

FOWLER TAX SERVICES

Back at the office, I couldn't concentrate on work and spent the time Googling Madame Dresser. I didn't know her first name. Why didn't I listen more closely? Did Mitzi give me these details? I couldn't even name one student who went to school with her fifteen years ago before I met her. I couldn't call the college today because it's Sunday. Beyond that, what was this all about? Would Mitzi have left the country without saying something to me? I called home, and Valerie answered.

"Find anything?"

"Nothing yet, but we're going through the pictures. Do you know what this gal looked like?"

"No, other than female, German, and she was no spring chicken fifteen years ago. Hey, will you go upstairs and make sure Mitzi's passport is still in her bedside table?"

A few minutes later, Val returned. "Yours is, but hers isn't."

"Dammit! I should be calling the airlines."

"Check your credit card."

"Of course! Call you back."

None of our cards had been used, and I wondered if the mysterious Madame Dresser had paid for yet another trip to Germany. Why? Mitzi wasn't even German. As far as I knew, she was Euro mix of some sort— I guess German could be in there. Stomach rumbling, I hunted around for food and found old popcorn and a power bar. It wasn't yet dark. Even in the worst of times, Panda must be fed and my meager supplies wouldn't cut it. As I walked down to the corner market, I saw a flash in the periphery of my vision.

I walked slower and pretended to tie my shoe. I yawned and stretched as I turned my head toward the bushes. The trees were manicured right up to the planter by the wall, where several bougainvillea had enthusiastically and colorfully filled in the spaces behind the broken border. The arrangement was kind of pretty, if haphazard, and some of the feral cats Fiona had railed about lived in the little tunnels created by the thicket. I saw movement—and a touch of green fabric.

Everything that had gone sideways seemed to happen here, at the office. This was where the first invitation had come. This is where Lulu and I had sighted the . . . whatever it was. I was so tired of being baffled and being the target of unseen and unknown forces, something snapped.

Perhaps it was my desperation or anger driven by hunger, but I suddenly ran toward the bushes and jumped in, ready to tackle a tiger if need be. Thorns tore at my sleeves, and I connected with what at first appeared to be a child, who was as startled as I was. It was the garden gnome, as I'd taken to calling him in my mind.

Before he could react, I put my hands in his underarms and lifted him to eye height. He was heavy. Neither of us spoke. His little hand tried to reach his dagger and his feet kept kicking out. He was strong for his size, but no match for this Rambo tax preparer whose mate had gone missing. Soon the dagger was mine, shoved into my back pocket.

It was four o'clock on a Sunday when I said words I never dreamed would leave my mouth, "Are you a dwarf or an elf?"

His little, perfectly-shaped mouth opened, and he said in heavily accented English, "Dwarves get all the credit. I'm an elf. Will you put me down now?"

"Not a chance." Not trusting the little fella, I body hugged him and marched back to the office. He squirmed at first, then he went limp the way cats do, but no way was I letting go. Here was concrete proof of . . . of . . . of something.

I unlocked the door with one hand, placed him in a desk chair opposite mine, and said, "Talk."

He was elven, all right: fine features; little pointed ears like in the fairy tales; sunburned cheeks; and bloodshot, water-blue eyes. His soft hair was blond like straw, and he looked very tired and disheveled.

I felt sorry for him at this point. He was so small, and his exposed skin was covered with scratches from the Bougainvillea.

"Do you have anything to eat?" was the first thing he said, an elf after my own heart.

"Do you like popcorn?"

"Anything, I'm starving."

"Me, too."

When the microwave was busy doing its thing, and the shock had lessened a bit, I handed him the power bar and asked, "Do you know where my wife is?"

"Maybe."

I grabbed his shirt. "Where? Don't play games with me you little . . . elf!"

"Easy, easy. I know who took her, and maybe where they are, but I can't say for sure."

"Don't make me stick you with this." I took his weapon out of my pocket and shook it at him before putting it on a top shelf, out of reach. He looked suitably cowed.

"You weren't supposed to see me."

I never took my eyes off him as I backed up to get the popcorn. As he tore into it, I called my home number again.

"Did you find out anything?" Juniper asked.

"Sort of. You guys need to come to the office. Now." My voice was strangely calm. "Will you ask Val to bring a first-aid kit?"

"What's wrong, are you hurt?"

"No, it's only a couple of scratches."

"What if Mitzi comes home?"

"I don't think that's going to happen, but just in case, leave her a note."

The strange little fella and I sat there eating popcorn together until he said, "Do you have any water?" Not trusting him not to bolt, I handed him an unopened bottle I kept under my desk. He drank from it greedily. It was about now I noticed he was a bit smelly.

"I thought elves were clean."

"We try to be, but all this travel makes it kind of hard. I've been living in a bush for a week." He paused. "You weren't supposed to see me."

"I get that. Who are you?"

"Ekkehard, most call me Ekk."

"My name is Panda."

"That's a weird name."

"Really? That's the first thing that comes to mind from an elf named Ekk? Okay." This whole conversation was surreal. I was in such shock, I still wasn't sure whether or not I was hallucinating. "Where are you from?"

He didn't answer, and kept shoving popcorn in his perfectly defined mouth, his eyes straying to the top of the shelf. I admit I was fascinated by his little mouth, chewing.

"Germany?" I guessed.

"The Hercynian Garden."

"Are you really an elf?"

"Yes," he said, bits of popcorn clinging to his lips.

"How could you even travel in that get up? Come on, who paid you to dress up like that?" I reached forward and tugged on a pointed ear.

"Ow. That hurts."

The girls knocked on the door. Again, I backed over there and didn't take my eyes off him for a second.

They came in talking but became silent after laying eyes on my new acquaintance.

"Ladies, this is Ekkehard, Ekk for short."

Val walked in slowly and put her bag down with one hand, the other traveling to cover her mouth. "Great Spirit in the sky!" I guessed this was the Native American version of, "Oh my God."

"He was about to tell us what happened to Mitzi," I said. With my own scratches and bits of bougainvillea in my hair, I probably looked as crazy as this whole thing sounded. "He's an elf and he's here from Hercynian Garden."

"In Germany," Juniper said, looking incredulous.

"In Germany," I repeated.

Val finally spoke. "I need to say this out loud for my own sanity. Officially, this day cannot get any weirder."

I turned to Ekk. "Where's Mitzi?"

"My dagger will tell the story."

Having believed way more than six impossible things today, I calmly retrieved it and inspected it closely. "You want to stab me now? I'm really not in the mood, little elf."

He shook his head. "There's a device on it. Move one of the rubies. It's really a button. There's a holograph that explains things."

"From whom?" I asked.

"You'll find out if you look at the holograph."

I touched the biggest ruby, which slid easily. A projection of a tough-looking woman in battle garb appeared in a pre-recorded, three-dimensional message like I'd only seen in sci-fi films.

"Greetings. My name is Heloisa. I'm a guardian of this place. There's a war that has gone on outside the edges of your world for eons. There are many legends. Volkort the Necromancer, tales of werewolves, and others. This enemy, called Wolfrum, is worse, and has spilled over into your world. He leads a twisted religion that requires the death of anyone who will not convert to it. At first it was subtle, but then beheadings began. Whole villages of peaceful griffins were rounded up and enslaved or killed. Our coalition is that of all the free creatures, elves, unicorns"— Juniper smiled widely at that—"griffins, both mixed and pure, friendly dwarves—there's a split—and others."

Her manner of speaking was a bit frustrating.

"The people were not wary enough and accepted the enemy's story of being followers of a peaceful way. When they had sufficient numbers, they took over. Many elves are enslaved, many have died. We need the help of our distant descendants, who have powerful abilities that are still dormant. I sent Ekk to you because of his special skills. We need anyone who carries even a drop of griffin blood to help us, or the world will be lost, ours and yours. The octopus is safety—when all else fails. Unfortunately, Odilia, the one you know as Madame Dresser, got to Mitzi first. Time is short. We are learning your ways, but we had no time to contact you sooner. If you will help us, come. We need three humans to help Mitzi, daughter of Ehrenhardt, to form the sacred pattern that will extend protection we have had for centuries. Ekk will tell you what you need to do next."

We all stood, transfixed, and stared at the place the Barbie-sized hologram had been.

Valerie said, "That was just like Star Wars—remember Princess Leia?" She started to panic. "Can this be real? I feel like I must be dreaming."

Ekk quietly got up off his chair and pinched her.

"Ow," she said. "Why did you do that?" She rubbed her arm.

"That's what they said to do in the human manual if someone thinks they're dreaming." He pulled a tiny pair of gold-rimmed glasses out of an invisible pocket and fit them on his diminutive nose. He looked so sincere.

"The human manual," Juniper repeated thoughtfully, and a smile tugged at her lips.

All three of us laughed, the kind where you tip over to one side and tears run down your face. I know I snorted. Joni Mitchell said it best. "Laughing and crying, you know, it's the same release." But again, I digress.

Resigned, I asked Ekk, "When do we leave?"

"Tomorrow morning, if you can. There's no time to waste. Before you get to the battleground, you need to be properly briefed."

"If you're so organized, why the hell wasn't somebody watching Mitzi?"

"I don't know what happened to Mitzi. We're so low on cross-world travelers, but Heloisa sent one of our best guardians to watch over her." His lip trembled. "The guardian hasn't checked in. In fact, she has disappeared, too, so no food no water for me. The one you call Dresser probably got to Mitzi first. I'm sorry."

"But why Mitzi? My wife's a completely human woman from California, I assure you. Her mom lives in Stockton." As if this was proof of her non-griffindomness.

"Have you ever met her father, Dr. Schadt?" Ekk used Mitzi's maiden name.

"He died."

"That's what they probably told her."

The clock dinged six. I sat down hard. "I don't know if I can take any more."

"Panda, your wife is half griffin and has access to very powerful magic, if we can get her to remember." Ekk was frustrated, hungry, and tired.

"Guys, gals," Val said, "as fun as this is, I think I need to go home and lay down. Some of us have to work tomorrow. Juniper has to report to the board of the museum, and I'm on overload. Let's get Ekk to Panda's house to clean up." She stretched out one of his short arms. "And dress some nasty scratches."

Val is so practical.

"Oh my God, this is the busiest time of the tax year. I can't leave."

Juniper nailed me to my chair with a look.

"Of course I can. It's just so ingrained." In twenty-three years, I've never left before my work was done. Again the killjoy. Trying to backtrack to our lighter mood, I said, "Perhaps elves will come in and finish my work." I tried not to think of my pissed-off clients when I put in filing extensions for all of them. At least "Mongo," the client with the shoebox, wouldn't care.

Ekk fairly squeaked out, "Yes, they will. At least, this one will. You didn't ask what my special skill is. I'm an accountant." He cracked his knuckles. "After a couple hours sleep, I'll be ready to roll."

"Where did you learn how to do California taxes?" Juniper asked.

"The Internet has revolutionized both our worlds. Lots of your movies are really quite popular in the realm."

"Let me get this straight. I'm supposed to turn over my files to an *elf*?"

"An enrolled agent elf." His broad smile was reassuring.

"Honey," Val said. "You're willing to get on a plane to Goddess knows where to get your wife back—who's been kidnapped by an evil man named Wolf something—and enter a realm of the Black Forest. Oh, and you need to find out whatever secrets Mitzi's family has been keeping. And your problem is letting someone else do a couple of 1040s?"

I smiled sheepishly. "It's not someone else. It's an elf."

"An enrolled agent elf," Juniper added, smiling.

"It will be fine," Ekk said. "Let's come back after I have some food. I'm fading."

"We're all tired," I snapped.

"Uh-oh." Val pointed to his hand, which was now translucent.

Literally, he was fading.

"We require food from your world to stay connected to it."

I grabbed my keys. "Everybody. My house."

Val nudged Juniper, imitating me. "Stat."

It was dark by then, and no neighbors noticed three humans with an elf in Juniper's oversized bag.

Back at the house, the three of us moved as if previously coordinated. I ran bathwater, Juniper cooked, and Valerie inspected Ekk's wounds.

He ate two grilled cheeses and drank several sodas, confiding he wasn't supposed to but they were so good.

While he bathed, I washed his stinky little clothes, which dried extraordinarily fast. I was accepting of anything at this point and thought, of course they do.

Cleaned up, with several bandages here and there, Ekk was fully solid again. It was a question of time.

"Where is Mitzi and where are we going?" I asked.

"She landed at Frankfurt, unless they went through Zurich, then took a car to the entrance of the Black Forest."

"That sounds so civilized," Val said. "Kind of like a tour."

"Yeah, World Spree," I said flatly.

"It gets different after that, trust me," Ekk said. "From there, you'll be taken to our version of your 'safe house.' More instruction will follow. This is all I know other than Mitzi is alive and will be, until April twelfth at midnight. I was trying to invite you all, but that didn't work."

"The invitation was so fragmented."

"I kept fading out. It was hard to get food. And that enormous woman with the torch kept hunting me. She's the reason I haven't eaten or slept except for a few hours during the day."

"Lulu, the formidable." I giggled. Val was online, seeing about tickets to Europe.

"Economy?" she asked.

"Yes," I said as Juniper said, "No."

"Economy." Val turned in our computer chair. I could see Ekk in the background petting Brutus.

"Hey, guys," Val said. "I can't leave for a couple more days. Mr. Dodd is failing." Neither Juniper nor I argued with her. She puts her clients, who are on hospice, first. I couldn't ask her to do more. My God, she was ready to fly halfway across the world on the word of an elf. "I'm making your reservations for tomorrow, after Juniper meets with the board at the museum. We're doing this right. I plan for us all to come back and have careers after this."

No one could disagree. In the silence, we heard Ekk say, "Two? What happened then?"

I ran to the couch and sat next to him. The look in Brutus' eyes was one I've never seen. It was as if he was fully aware. I turned to Ekk. "You can talk to him?"

"I speak to cats, but not really well. It's more of an image thing that comes in my mind."

Juniper was overjoyed and loving all these new possibilities. I worried she might decide to stay in the Hercynian Garden. "What did he say?" Her eyes were bright.

"A woman and a dwarf came here this morning and took Mitzi. They didn't hurt her, but she drank something and it looked like she was sleeping."

"That's all?"

"Well, he likes the stuff you feed him from the purple bag, and he was really mad about being locked in the closet by the dwarf. That's it."

Cats.

∾

The next morning Juniper dressed in her most businesslike attire, a blue-and-white-collared shirt with blazer, white pants, and blue-and-white spectator pumps. Her hair was in a perfect updo, and you'd never know she'd been cavorting with otherworldly creatures the day before.

As she approached the Craftsman structure that housed the museum, she saw workmen removing banners that had announced the Castlebaum exhibit.

She parked her Citroen in the usual spot in front of the museum. Her loyal assistant, Garcia, intercepted her at her car before she could walk through the front door.

"Ms. Juniper, don't go in!" he said, breathless. "The whole board met last night. They're waiting to gang up on you in there."

Juniper appreciated his loyalty and hugged his shoulders. "Don't worry, I've got my big-girl panties on." She pranced up the steps like she owned the place.

Garcia followed her up the stairs. He'd been her biggest supporter since joining the staff upon Linda Chicolet's recommendation. It was, in Juniper's opinion, the one good thing she'd done. They walked up to the big, wooden, antique desk together. Mona, the receptionist, appeared to be nervously awaiting Juniper's arrival. "The board wants to meet with you in the conference room," Mona said. Then in a quieter voice, she added, "I've been asked to say." She lowered her eyes.

What nastiness there must have been prior to her arrival.

Juniper righted an earring, a habit when she was thinking, and turned to Garcia. "Is Lucas Windingle or Maribel Martine there?" They were her biggest supporters on the board.

"No. I think that's why they called the meeting now. Neither one will be back in town 'til next week." Garcia fixed her with big brown eyes. "This is much worse than when we tried to introduce the Gay and Lesbian exhibit."

She had to smile thinking of that upheaval. "Uh-huh, thanks."

Juniper walked to the end of the mahogany hallway, squared her shoulders, and strode in to the board room. Dick Mortimer was seated at the head of the table and didn't get up. Linda Chicolet was to his right. Several invertebrates—Val's not so affectionate nickname for them—were present and very few friendly faces.

"Please, have a seat," Dick said. "The board has called a special meeting."

Juniper took a deep breath and said, "Dick, board, glad you're all here, because I'm taking a well-deserved, two-week vacation. Starting today. The museum calendar, including Floodlight, is set and this is a good time." She could tell they were irritated at her acting as if she called the meeting.

It appeared that Dick wasn't about to let her steal his thunder. "Miss Gooden, I called this meeting to tell you it's a good time for you to leave—but not for a vacation."

"It's Ms." She looked around. "How about waiting 'til you have a full board?"

The table was polished and oval, and the shiny reddish wood showed more than a few reflected faces looking sheepish.

"I agree," Jason Drake, a reasonable board member, said. "This is a topic for the full board. Let's put it off until next week when Maribel and Lucas are back."

Dick shot him a poisonous look. "We already went through that yesterday." Then to Juniper, he said, "Not even your deluded supporters on the board can save you now. After the disaster Saturday night, I must do the only responsible thing and—"

"Throw me under the bus?"

"No, show this town the museum responds appropriately to an upstart curator making a mockery of Merryville and its mayor."

Several heads nodded.

"But Mrs. Windingle at the Floodlight event said—"

Dick cut her off. "She'll come around. Her support of the museum is unfailing, and I think she was just being gracious Saturday night. There's no excuse for your lack of control of the exhibit or the artist."

Linda added, "And there's also an out-of-budget bill for the cherry picker. Had no idea those things cost this much, did you?" The false empathy was nauseating as she tried to hide her smirk.

Garcia opened his mouth, but Juniper put up a hand for him to let her speak.

"I see." She took another moment, brow furrowed, and then looked up. "Just to be clear, are you firing me?"

Cynthia Snively, human resource tool of Linda and Dick said, "Of course we'd rather you resigned. It would look better for both you and the museum." She looked like a caricature of sadness.

Juniper jumped up. "No, I don't think I want to do that. Either put me down as on vacation or fire me. Let me know. I have a plane to catch. Anything else?" She sounded like she was dismissing them.

The board erupted in comments such as, "This is impertinent," and "The gall."

Dick rapped his gavel for order. "You can go, Juniper. We're releasing a statement to the press. Ms. Snively has your check. The board has spoken."

Juniper walked the hall back to reception, and Garcia and Mona hugged her silently. They all had tears in their eyes. There was nothing to say.

Back at the house, Valerie met her at the door, bags packed.

"Did you get the books?" Juniper asked.

"Yep, three copies of *Eat Pray Love*, but why?"

"You'll see."

❧

Ekk and I went back to the office at five a.m., the better to avoid prying eyes and to get a jump on the work ahead of him. My clients are more than the sum of their files. I really feel I have a duty to treat each and every one like they're the only one. It was difficult to turn them over to anyone, especially an elf from another world.

"Here's the first one, David and Margie Mendez. No kids, but he has an S Corporation."

I sat in the chair next to Ekk and watched him work with growing amazement. First, he was neat and orderly. He sharpened his pencils and organized the paperwork as he should. By seven-thirty a.m., although tired, I was feeling much better about leaving. I had only one more thing to do.

I called Babs, the one and only employee besides me, at home, and said, "Hi." The idea was to head her off at the pass. I really should have thought this out better before dialing.

She said a slow, "Hi," probably because it was very strange for me to call her at home when she would see me in about forty-five minutes. We always got to the office early before seeing clients.

"What's up?" she asked.

"You won't believe this, Babs, but we're ready to close a few days early this tax season. Go ahead and take this week off."

Silence on the other line, then she said, "April Fool's was awhile ago. Have you been drinking?"

"No. I need to leave town today, so I worked through the weekend."

"Okay, I'll come in the office a bit early and—"

"No!"

"Does someone there have a gun?" she whispered. "Just say tomatoes so they don't get suspicious."

I laughed. "No, Babs, no tomatoes, and you really deserve some time off. In fact, I forbid you to come in this week."

"Have I been replaced? You know I really need this job." I heard a sob.

Oh God. "Stop, come in now if you must, but hurry. I need to bring you up to speed and then jump on a plane."

Twenty minutes later, I heard the bell on the front door. Before I could prepare her, Ekk came out of our office kitchen area wearing a knitted cap to cover his ears, with two mugs of hot coffee.

"Oh my Gawd!" Babs said. "How cute! I'm sorry, you're kinda elf like."

Babs was very honest, if not too tactful.

Ekk turned red.

"Babs, meet Ekk. He's an enrolled agent and is going to be here for a couple of days working but can't be seen by our clients, okay?"

"Sure." She nodded conspiratorially, then said to Ekk, "Ya'll like to be called little people, right?"

Ekk put down his coffee and, correctly reading the situation, said, "Sure."

"Ekk is here because obviously the final returns need to be completed and sent in. You meet with the clients for any last-minute changes. If anyone asks, tell them I stepped out. Don't be fooled by appearances. Ekk is very capable. Things will be back to normal in a week or so. Any questions?"

Whatever I was expecting, it wasn't "what temp agency did you use?"

༃

I Ubered down to the airport. I easily spotted Juniper in her multicolored clothes, sunglasses, and white pants. She stood in front of the International Terminal. She greeted me with a big smile and hug. "Here, take this," she said, and handed me a book.

"*Eat Pray Love*?"

"Yes. We're on a mission to save the World and Mitzi. We can't raise any eyebrows." At my look, she added, "Nobody pays attention to middle-aged women reading books like this."

I looked at her getup and compared it with mine—jeans, a blue-and-white jumper, and athletic shoes. "Sure." We did look pretty harmless.

I rolled my carryon inside and got in a crowded line that snaked around like a ride at Disneyland and led up to the Lufthansa ticketing window.

Juniper wagged a well-manicured index finger in front of me. "Uh-uh," she said and walked over to business class. Curious, I followed.

"Val upgraded us last night."

"How did you win that one?"

"Safety. Rightly or wrongly, people in business class are watched over more. There may be bad guys after us."

"Okay!" My mood brightened. The thought of spending fourteen hours in steerage hadn't been appealing.

"Besides, we might die and then we'd have spent our last hours being miserable."

I looked at her again, my smile fading, but she was already smiling and walking up to the ticket agent.

TSA was a breeze. Between our ages, the books, and upgraded seats, we were shooed through. I wished for the thousandth time that it was Mitzi and I going on vacation.

We walked toward our gate, and I found myself staring at every person in the airport.

"Stop that," Juniper said without turning.

"Stop what?"

"You aren't acting like a carefree tourist. Here, let's go into the bookstore."

In the store, I hunted for something I hadn't already read. There were books Mitzi would have loved, and it made my eyes sting. What were we doing? Would we get there in time? Ironically, it was while I was paying attention to shopping that I noticed a fellow who looked familiar. He was dark and foreign, much like the folks at the museum event a couple of days before. Had they been following us even then?

Flipping a magazine, I asked Juniper out of the side of my mouth. "Do you recognize that guy over there? I think he's following us."

"No," she said out of the side of hers, mocking me, then laughed and pretended to hit my arm. "Stop it."

"I'm going to the gate," I said, and decided to read *Eat Pray Love*. Val was due to follow us in a couple of days, and along with everything else, I was hoping things were going well for her and her elderly charge. After a couple of minutes, I heard a commotion behind me. Security was handcuffing the strange man, who was shooting daggers at me with his eyes. Juniper came over and sat by me. "Strangest thing. He was overheard talking about a bomb. They don't take kindly to that kind of thing at the Aero Puerto."

"Did you . . . how . . . whaa?"

"I reported him. Close your mouth, darling. Of course, they're going to believe the middle-aged business class traveler, clutching a copy of *Eat Pray Love* over that of a suspicious looking young man with a German accent." She fanned herself. I grinned and shook my head.

"I told you he was following us."

I used the next fifteen or so hours, when I wasn't fitfully sleeping, to make a mental list of things I needed to find out. Where was Mitzi? Who had her? Was she being tortured while I lay on this flat bed thirty-five thousand feet in the air? What was she eating? How were the taxes going? Could Babs keep a secret? I had to remember to call Mitzi's mom, too. She'd left a message, and it was strange for the two of them to go more than a week without talking. Did my cell phone even have international calling? Did I have enough clothing? Was it warm enough? It went on and on.

When I did sleep, there were nightmares. Images of a great, dark cloud rising up from the Black Forest, and then it split into a million dark birds headed for all four corners of our planet. I woke up in a sweat and stared at the plastic ceiling.

Talking to Juniper was hard because each first class sitting area was semi-private and only for one. We would have had more of a chance to plot and plan in economy. When I did get up, Juniper was chatting with the flight attendant and checking out the Duty Free. I probably would have enjoyed the flight more if my other half wasn't in danger. As it was, I used the time to rest. We would need to hit the ground running once we landed.

ᕙᕗ

BADEN BADEN, GERMANY
APRIL TENTH

Forty-five degrees Fahrenheit is cold, but the Celsius sign at the airport said 7.222, which somehow seemed even colder. We landed first in Frankfurt, and then took a local puddle jumper plane to the Baden-Baden airport, which catered to the upper-class spa crowd like the erstwhile Madame Dresser. After retrieving our luggage, I went into the bathroom and changed into a fluffy parka, previously worn only once, that my sister sent me from Tibet. It had a paisley pattern and was many shades of Indian orange.

"Wowzers!" Juniper twirled me around. "That's some jacket."

"It's warm," I said, feeling very conspicuous. "Now what? Stand here and look like cheerful tourists some more?"

"Now we wait." She seemed to be enjoying this. "I've always wanted to see Germany."

"Being extorted into someone else's war is hardly seeing Germany. It's like being in the middle of someone else's bad divorce."

"Well, if you believe that Heloisa hologram, it's our war too, or soon going to be."

"True." I rocked on my heels and tucked my arms in my armpits.

Fairly soon a Volkswagen Touareg pulled up, and a sturdy man jumped out and apologized in thickly accented English for being "the late." We piled in and were whisked off to parts literally unknown.

CHAPTER FIVE

BACK IN MERRYVILLE

Hello, is this the police?"

"Yes, our non-emergency line, how can I help you?"

"It's my neighbors, the Fowlers. They're both women who are married to each other. That's legal now, I guess. Something's not right over there. I mean, not the fact that they're gay. I guess society needs to adjust. It's something else."

"Do you want a welfare check, ma'am? Any reason to believe there's a need for police involvement?"

"Well, I hate getting in other people's business, but there have been some strange comings and goings of late. I got up this morning at two-thirty. Sometimes I can't sleep with Frank's snoring, and I saw Panda Fowler leaving alone with luggage. I haven't seen her wife for days."

"What's the wife's name?"

"Mitzi Fowler."

"Maybe they went on vacation."

"I don't think so. My neighbor told me Panda Fowler was going around the neighborhood a couple of days ago asking if anyone had seen Mitzi."

"Ok, we'll send a car around to check on it."

In an unknown location, Mitzi pounded on the rough wooden door. "Hey! It's freezing in here. Somebody answer!"

All five-foot-six of her was vertical and super pissed. After waking in this cell, she realized that Madame Dresser, who probably wasn't Madame Dresser at all, had drugged her.

At first, the woman seemed nice. She was shrouded in scarves and could have been the lady she met all those years ago in grad school. She seemed in a hurry and became irritated when Mitzi wasn't wearing the pendant her mother had given her as a child. But then she smiled again and hugged her. Once inside, Mitzi took her to the kitchen and made tea. The tea! She must have put a sleeping draught in the tea, the old witch.

Mitzi beat on the door again. "I know you can hear me. Let me out, now!" She kicked the door for good measure, but it only made her foot hurt.

She heard jangling keys. It reminded her of Panda and the ridiculously huge circle of keys she kept. She said it was a key ring that had belonged to her granddaddy who was a janitor. Feelings caught in her throat that she had no time to deal with. She let her anger burn away anything that would deter her from getting out of here.

"Hey!" Bang, bang, bang.

The Tourareg was fast, and the driver expert. Before we could speak further to him, an elf turned and introduced herself. I hadn't seen her at first because of her diminutive size. She had a cherry blossom face. That was my first impression. I didn't know why, other than the woman's cheeks were rosy red.

"I'm Elsa and will be guiding you through your orientation."

"This is like a World Spree adventure tour," I said to Juniper, having had a thoroughly satisfactory trip to Vietnam a few years before with that organization.

"I'm Juniper and my rather stunned friend is—"

"Panda, yes I know. We've been expecting you."

With that, she turned and sat facing forward. We could no longer see her but could hear her cheery voice.

"There has been some pretty intense fighting where we're going to enter the forest, so tonight you'll be staying at the hotel *Der Kleine Prinz*."

"Nice," Juniper said. I had never heard of it.

Elsa added, "The owners of the hotel are friendly to our cause. While there, you will be met by an operative who speaks very good English. I cannot join you, for obvious reasons."

"I want to comment on that," I said, poking my head into the front-seat area. "You speak of intense fighting, and I look around and see pristine countryside."

Elsa thought for a tick then answered, "There are many rules that we in the Hercynian Forest abide by. One is to keep the conflict hidden. Another, and this is really strange"—her accent made it sound like schtrange—"is that we can only use weapons that existed at the time of the last dog sun."

I shook my head and said almost to myself, "You're also as real as can be, I mean, since we've met Ekk."

Elsa's eyes lit up. "You met Ekk? Is he okay?"

"Yes, he's watching my tax practice." My eyes narrowed. "Why don't you know that?"

Her big eyes became watery, and she turned to the front again. I felt mean.

Her voice was still sweet. "I failed in my mission, and I'm relegated to earning back the trust of my comrades. You see, it's my fault Mitzi was kidnapped."

"What?" My head popped back in her area. The driver gave me a gruff look.

Tears rolled down her doll-like face. "The coalition sent me and Ekk to watch you both and intervene if necessary. This was a fluid situation, and we didn't know if the enemy would even reach out as far as California in your world. Clearly, they did."

Juniper handed me a granola bar, no doubt worried I was what we call "hangry." In unwrapped it not taking my eyes off of Elsa. "What happened?"

She blushed. "You and she have a nice relationship. I saw you feeding her candy on the couch."

Juniper smiled and looked sideways at me. My chewing slowed.

"Those were mini-eclairs," I said in my most dignified voice. "And?"

"Nothing much happened until yesterday. I fell asleep. Odilia's dwarf, one of the bad ones, tied me up and left me in your shed until I disappeared."

"They starved you!" I cried, a truly horrible way to go.

"Yes. And I failed. I'm really sorry."

"Do you just appear back here when you fade from our world?" Juniper asked, always wanting to know how things worked.

"Something like that. Oh, here we are. Your contact will meet you at dinner. Go to the dining room at seven p.m."

"But wait."

"I can't. Lots to do. Please go and be patient."

Before we knew it, Juniper and I were checking in to the sumptuous hotel. "I'll see you at dinner," I said to Juniper. "In the meantime, I plan to see if my phone works here."

A guest came up and asked Juniper, in German, if I were her Sherpa. My Tibetan parka was quite ethnic looking I suppose, and I didn't look like the typical spa client I guess. The English-speaking concierge intervened. After embarrassed apologies and heavy tipping, I was safely ensconced in my room, where I lay on the bed and fiddled with my phone. Without meaning to, I fell asleep on the soft comforter and began to dream.

ᘐ

BACK IN MERRYVILLE

Detective Potts was having a slow day. When the call for a welfare check came through, he said he'd take it. All the black-and-whites were out in the field, due to the annual Merryville Flower show and the Mayor's Skeet Shoot going on simultaneously this weekend. Besides, it was a nice day and he wanted to get out of the office and smoke.

The grizzled veteran drove down Thistle Drive to number 9. He parked and, before getting out, decided to run the address to see if there had been any past domestic disturbances. Not expecting anything really, he enjoyed a cigarette, his guilty pleasure. His cop instincts went on high alert when a record of a 9-1-1 call popped up, from two days before.

Potts ground out his cigarette and gave the home his full attention.

Mitzi sunk to the stone floor and was really freezing when she heard a key turn in the lock. Pale light filled the cell, and a thickly muscled dwarf appeared in the doorway and said, "*Folge mir*," which in English meant, "Follow me." Somehow, she understood.

She didn't need to be asked twice. She jumped to her feet and followed. The dwarf led her down a stone passageway and into a castle-like structure. The temperature gradually warmed until she was deposited in a room with a roaring fireplace. There were weapons on the wall and floor-to-high-ceiling red drapes. It smelled of old cooking odors and like it hadn't been dusted in a considerable period of time. A rustic wooden table with seating for a dozen was set with pewter dishes. Only one person sat at the head of the table.

At first she didn't even see him. In his brown robe and utter stillness, she thought him part of the landscape. Only now, as he took his hood down with skinny, white, blue-veined hands did she say, "Hey, will you tell me what the hell is going on?"

He flinched at "hell" and motioned her to sit beside him. She did.

"Your mother said you were fiery."

Whatever Mitzi had been expecting, it wasn't that. "Who are you? What do you know about my mother?"

"I know a great deal about you, young woman. A great deal."

"I was drugged, kidnapped, and apparently you or someone brought me here. I want to know why. By the way, where is here?"

He sighed an old man's sigh. "You are in the dining room of Der Schwarzvald Castle, high in the mountains of Germany."

Mitzi blinked. The cold, the architecture, all fit what she'd been experiencing.

"How did you get me on a plane unconscious? Surely Homeland Security would have been all over that."

"You were brought here in a somnambulant walking state with your caregiver." He said this without irony or guilt.

"A zombie? You made me a zombie? Let me tell you something, sir. People will miss me. People will come to get me. The trail can't be that hard to follow. Let let me go right now, and I'll forget this ever happened."

"You are hardly in a bargaining position, Ms. Fowler, or, let me call you by your real name, Mitzi Winters."

Mitzi started to speak, but the old man waved his hand and her lips wouldn't part. She was going to say her maiden name was Schadt.

"I've heard enough from you right now. It's time for you to listen. You are the child of an abomination, a griffin and a fairy contributed sperm to your mother, the surrogate. Apparently you are part magical creature, although you look human like your mother. I need to know how infected you are and if you can even be saved."

Mitzi thought the man was crazy. He kind of sounded like some of the fundamentalists back home, except for the part about magic. She stared at him in horror, a sinking feeling in the pit of her stomach.

Several monks entered the room. Most were young men, but a couple appeared to be dwarves, same brown robes, chanting in German. Somehow, Mitzi understood them.

"Begin the awakening," the still unidentified man with the white hands said to the assembly. In harmony, the masculine voices chanted:

"Wolves are always followed by ravens"

"Scavenging for the kill"

"Eat fast, ravening wolf"

"Ravens follow five and twenty"

"Cleansing the world of unworthy prey"

"Taking out the weak"

"Consuming the meek"

"Wolf-Raven cycles this world to the next"

Mitzi jumped up. Everything within her told her to run. She had a strange sensation in the pit of her gut as the monks sang. Strong arms held her, and the voices rang out again and again with the same awful song.

HOTEL DER KLEINE PRINZ

Having given in to jet lag, I had the same dream as before. Only this time I was near a castle in the forest that sent out the clouds of ravens. I was very cold, looking up as the sky turned black. In the distance, I heard the howl of a wolf, and a different kind of chill went down my spine. I tried to run to the castle, to people and warmth, but snow grabbed my boots like quicksand. To make matters worse, I could see Mitzi in between trees. I opened my mouth to yell for her, but nothing came out. The alarm in my room woke me, and for that I was glad.

It was a while before dinner, and I was dying to talk to Ekk or Babs or Val, but it was three a.m. at home. Instead, I used the time to dress as well as I could, given the unexpectedness of our tony surroundings.

The Prinz dining room was a study in blue, white, and gold and was the height of European elegance. I had dressed in my best white-collared shirt and wore the octopus pendant that Mitzi gave me after we'd been together awhile. It made me feel close to her. Black pants and boots completed my outfit. While not stunning, at least I felt appropriate.

Juniper entered not too much later and had on essentially the same outfit as before, only trading her sandals for boots and adding a scarf for warmth. "Any idea who we're meeting yet?" she asked.

"No, I only sat down myself a minute ago. Did you call Val?"

"Yes. She was sleepy. Her client is still alive, but she said it can't go on much longer."

"I hope not. Today is the ninth—only three more days until the deadline at midnight."

"She knows. Even if her client doesn't die, I'm sure she'll be here." She picked up the menu. "What looks good?"

Again, amazed my friend could be semi-enjoying herself, I followed suit and looked for something appetizing. Both of us lifted our heads in unison as we heard a familiar voice.

"Of course, darling, I'm here to meet two friends from over the pond. Oh, there you are!"

I sat stunned as Fiona Castlebaum air-kissed me. She plunked herself down without attempting that with Juniper, correctly reading she might get her eyes scratched out.

"You."

"Yes, me," Fiona said and motioned to the wait staff. "We'll start with the tuna and follow it with the pesto crusted lamb." She looked at our stunned faces. "You do eat lamb?"

Juniper nodded

"I'm a vegetarian," I said.

"Oh yes, that is part of the lesbian cachet in California, no?" She turned back to the server and said, "And a salad."

I was too startled to be offended. "Are you part of this?"

"The Little Prince? No, I like to eat here. The other? Yep. The Coalition we call it. And some Earl Grey, hot," she added absently to the server, handing him the menus.

"I lost my job at the museum because of you," Juniper said, still not taking her eyes off the older woman.

Fiona held up her hand, and we waited to hear what she had to say.

"We will see. When I come to town, it's always for a very specific purpose. In this case, to scope out Mitzi's people and to poke the mayor a bit. Once you were identified as a BFF, I needed to meet you, too." Her knowledge of American colloquialisms was impressive. "I had to test your mettle." Juniper glared as she sipped her water.

Fiona raised her eyebrows and swallowed. "You passed."

My moment of social paralysis ended. "Goody. You couldn't have simply talked to us?"

Clearing her throat, Fiona dropped some of her flippancy. "I wanted to see how you would act under intense pressure and I might add, you never would have believed me if I'd said your wife"—nodding at me—"and best pal"—nodding at Juniper—"is a half-magical creature and may be needed to play a part in an otherworldly war."

She was right about that. Our drinks arrived, and Juniper and I peppered her with questions. After she answered and explained some more, our food came. It was time to summarize.

"So, being an artist gives you a cover that allows you to travel anywhere and everywhere at a moment's notice," I said.

"Yes. It's been quite convenient. I must admit, though, my thirst for throwing light on uncomfortable subjects makes the work quite dangerous." She smiled a wicked smile. "But fun."

Juniper scowled.

"In fact, that was one of my bodyguards you had thrown in the grey bar hotel at the airport."

Juniper looked at me, her eyes big and innocent.

"Why was he following us?" I asked

"He was making sure you got on the plane safely."

Juniper gave Fiona a wicked smile and said, "Oops."

"Don't worry. He got out after they found nothing on him and no criminal history. He acted gay as a goose and said you misunderstood him when he said your outfit was 'The Bomb.' "

Even I had to laugh.

"I guess we're even then," Juniper said. The two women were really more alike than not. I could see them becoming friends, maybe, after much time had passed.

Fiona turned to me. "I see you're wearing the pendant. That's smart. It will give you some protection from Wolfrum's men."

"My pendant? Mitzi gave this to me."

"I assumed so. It's about a thousand years old, and the only way it's passed down is through family."

"I thought it was plastic," Juniper said, leaning across to inspect it more closely.

"Plastic?" Fiona's laugh was musical. "It probably looks like that, yes. Have you ever heard the phrase '*Er hat Tentakel und sieht aus wie ein riesiger aggressiver Oktopus?*' "

"That's not a common saying back in California," I said dryly and poured more coffee. "We looked it up online but it didn't help a great deal."

"It literally translates as, 'It has tentacles and looks like a big octopus if a bit more aggressive.' It describes an ancient guardian of the Hercynian Forest that will protect you from even the most powerful evil. See," she said, responding to my puzzled look, "even myths have myths."

"How did you pronounce that?" My fork tried to stab an olive.

"*Her sin ee in,*" Fiona said with a flourish.

"Ekk was trying to tell you that I guess," Juniper said.

I shrugged, wondering why these people all talked in puzzles. It was so much easier to be plain speaking.

"Fiona, with a name like Castlebaum, were you really born in Ireland?" I asked.

"Yes, that was one of my husbands' names, darling. He was Jewish. In fact, he was the one who introduced me to this otherworld."

"What happened to him?" Juniper asked.

"Make no mistake. Even though out of most of our sight, a war is being waged. He was killed by Wolfrum's men." She took a bite of a roll.

That shut me up. She looked sad, and I didn't pry further.

"What can you tell us about April twelfth and the ritual?" I asked, tired of all the code and beating around the bush.

Fiona looked left and right then said, "I've never seen one, but I will tell you about the legend of the dog suns as soon as we have a chance to talk privately."

A waiter placed a salad on a beautiful china plate in front of me. I tucked my napkin in my neckline, and Juniper shot me a look. I said, "What? I'm trying to keep my shirt from getting spots."

Juniper and Fiona gave each other a look and let it go.

The restaurant was full of other diners' conversations and music over the sound system.

"Okay," Fiona said quietly, "there are periods of time when both our worlds go on their merry way, operating under the rules of the last dog sun reset. It's actually kind of organized."

"Sounds like rivals meeting in a sports challenge from time to time." I forked a leafy morsel into my mouth.

"How nice if it were," she said. "Unfortunately, people die when they lose. It's all about who has power and how much."

I remembered again her husband was one of those casualties. "How does this religion fit in? Monks sound Catholic." I couldn't let it go.

"Catholics have had their Crusade period to be sure, but this is different. No mercy for anyone." She again looked around. "Wol— let's just say the evil man at the head of the cult, uses trappings of mainstream religion, but his goal is utter subjugation of both our worlds."

Juniper put down her utensils. "To what end? What drives him or them?"

"The desire for utter and complete power. They have money and they want hearts and minds. They really believe the world—both worlds— would be better off if men were in charge and women stayed home and made babies. More foot soldiers for the cause."

I gulped. "Gee, doesn't leave much room for lesbians, does it?"

Fiona motioned for more coffee. "No. Or heterosexual women who want to teach or even go to school. It's really regressive. Most of their recruits are unemployed young men and dwarves, who are fed a diet of good food and given shoes, along with this philosophy that would give them power for the first time. They haven't the life experience to understand true balance involves both sexes." She looked at Juniper and me and added, "Or maybe even three or more sexes." She laughed her throaty laugh at her challenging comment.

We ate in silence for a while. "This is about men versus women? Why are they beheading people?"

"To scare ordinary folks. They move in and start doing good, holding rallies, planting trees, and promising order and safety. Then when there are enough of them, once-voluntary observances become mandatory. It's insidious."

"Why not just speak out?" I was angry. "Protest. Write books!" My appetite went away.

"Too dangerous. It's not out in the open like that. Listen, soon you'll see and hear more that will help you understand. Tonight, your only job is to get a good night's sleep."

"Like that will happen." I stood and put my messy napkin on the beautifully appointed table.

Some monks came in the front door as Fiona popped up and dabbed her lips. "Time to go." She hustled us out the back door of the restaurant and into the lobby area. We hurried to the elevator, and Juniper and I got in.

"Oh, and don't worry," Fiona said to Juniper. "I sent a check to the museum for that thing that lifted me up from the beach. A nice touch, yes?"

The cherry picker. We laughed about that, until Mitzi's predicament intruded upon my mind. "What about Mitzi? Is there a plan?" The doors started to close, and I put out my hand to hold it.

"Yes. The four of you, together, are needed for the ritual in the Hercynian Garden. More will be revealed when you get to the Garden."

"The one you still haven't fully explained." The door kept trying to close.

"Yes, more will be revealed at the right time," she said in a serious tone. This time she stopped the door from closing. "And get Valerie here quickly. The stakes are high." The doors closed with a ding.

∾

I was all alone in my hotel room after dinner, and my mind did crazy cartwheels around the information we'd been given by Fiona. Apparently, Mitzi was being held by monks of the Black Forest who believed that the only way to save the world was to kill anyone who didn't convert to their views. Magic, in their minds, was evil and magical creatures the embodiment of evil. They also didn't like queers, Muslims, or women in leadership roles. If Mitzi was half-magic and a lesbian, I had asked, why were they not killing her, too?

"Oh they will," Fiona said gravely. "If she's not able to perform the April twelfth ritual. They can't kill her until that date has passed because of a magical protection spell that's due to expire. They're waiting for the sun dogs, a celestial sign of the transition."

After several misdials, I finally got through to Babs in California, where it was the morning of this day.

"Fowler Tax Services."

"Babs. How are things?"

"Okay. Where are you?"

"I'd rather not say. How are things there?"

"Okay, I guess. Your little friend got all the returns out, and I met with the clients when they dropped off their checks and signed. We had a couple of close calls, and once I had to stuff him in a deep drawer."

I couldn't help but smile, imagining that, then burst out in laughter when she said, "Little people can really be cranky."

I breathed a sigh of relief. "Is he gone?"

"Yes. Where do I send his check?"

"Um, hold onto it."

"One more thing." Her voice went to a whisper. "A detective came by wanting to know where you were and had I seen Mitzi. Is Mitzi okay?"

"Yes, everything's fine. We'll be back after the twelfth. It was just a quick, unscheduled trip."

"Okay. I told him you and Juniper had to catch a plane. Should I tell him anything else if he comes back?"

"Why did you tell him that?" I said, shocked.

"You didn't say not to. He's the good guys, right?"

There was no point being mad at her. I never said don't speak to the police. "What else did he say?"

"That he thought it was weird, you leaving before the fifteenth and all. Are you in Germany?"

"Yes. What else?"

"He asked me if I'd seen Mitzi myself. Panda, I had to say no. Was that wrong? What's going on?"

I sighed. "The less you know, the more you don't have to lie, right? But do text me if anything more happens, and stop talking to the police. Why don't you close up and take a few days off."

"Am I still going to have a job?" A note of terror.

I hesitated, having no idea if any of us would survive what was ahead. Wanting to instill confidence in her, I said, "Absolutely," wishing I felt like I sounded.

The next morning, Juniper and I met in the lobby. The same Touareg came barreling down the snowy road and screeched to a halt in front of the hotel. The same man who helped us at the airport loaded our bags and said, "*Mach schnell.*" I didn't have to understand German to know what that meant. Shake a leg!

The second our butts hit the heated seats, Elsa turned around. "Buckle up," she said. "It's going to be rough."

She wasn't kidding. In the backseat, as we swayed back and forth, Juniper told me she'd talked to Val, who had also gotten a visit by a Detective Potts. He seemed to know Juniper and I had left together for Germany. This was very disturbing. Why were the police even involved?

I held on as we skidded around a corner and headed out of town, directly to the forest. There were many signposts on the twisty roads, and each seemed to lead to another unpronounceable but quaint village.

The scenery was breathtaking.

The driver, who had never been introduced, looked worried and said something to Elsa in rapid-fire German. He sounded angry, but then, to me, the language always sounds like that. Elsa squeaked back in German to him, then turned to us.

"We're being followed. Hold on."

I thought we couldn't possibly go any faster, but the driver shifted into a new gear and we fairly flew over the bumps. Green and white flew by, and I wished Mitzi and I were there on vacation. Juniper opened her compact to get a look at who, or what, was behind us. "I don't see anything," she said.

She and I exchanged glances. Were these people trustworthy?

"You wouldn't," Elsa said. "These are ravens. Look up." We both went to our respective windows and saw a cloud of black drifting in front of the sun.

"Birds?" I asked.

"Not regular birds, they're Wolfrum's eyes. Give our driver a few more minutes and we'll shake them."

The driver took a hairpin turn down a slushy road, and soon we were under a canopy of trees so dense it appeared to be night. "This is why they call it the Black Forest," I reminded Juniper, who looked a bit worried. We bumped down the road, and I was grateful for the seatbelt and quality workmanship of the car.

We eventually slowed to a reasonable pace. It was impossible to go too fast as we squeezed in between trees. My knuckles were white from holding on. The big car finally stopped with a jerk, and the three of us got out. The driver left Elsa, Juniper, and me on an icy patch in an opening near a rocky outcrop. There appeared to be nothing there but more forest and some big rocks.

He maneuvered the big German car through the trees, apparently unmindful of scratches to the paint, and soon was gone. "He took off like a bat out of hell," I said.

"It's for the best. He is human only." Elsa's eyes were big and blue, like clear water.

"So are we, Miss Elsa," Juniper said. "Should we be worried?"

"Oh, now you get nervous," I said to Juniper. I was being sarcastic, something Mitzi says I do when overwhelmed.

"Are you ladies all right?" Elsa looked up from one of our faces to the other. "We're about to enter the Hercynian Forest."

I don't know what she did, but I felt a shift and became calmer. The atmosphere then became like another entity. I was aware of the smell of earthy undergrowth and the energy contained in the damp old trees.

"This is where it gets interesting," Juniper said softly. I was surprised at how quiet she was. The place had that effect. It felt like a cathedral.

I said, "I thought we were in the Hercynian Forest already."

"Well, you are, sort of, just not the magic part. That's over here." And with that, the slightly built elf disappeared.

"Holy shit, now we're really up a creek." As I started to panic, my body broke out in a cold sweat. Being miles from anywhere, with no phone reception in a foreign country, was freaking this city girl out.

Elsa popped into our view again. "Follow me. The rock is an illusion. Come on."

Juniper wrapped her scarf around her more securely, looked at me, and said, "Mach schnell," with a smile.

I walked exactly where Elsa stepped and soon felt a warm breeze on my cheeks. The oppressive darkness of the trees was replaced with blue sky and some smaller trees by a clear brook. As far as the eye could see were verdant hills, occasionally dotted by dollhouse-sized cabins.

"Our ride will be here in a moment," Elsa said, and that same imagery of cherry blossoms filled my head for some reason.

"I like it better in here," I thought, then realized I'd said it with my outside voice.

"It's okay. Thoughts are hard to keep inside here. It's part of our protection. There's magic on all the boundaries. I'm going to take you to the safe house now." A unicorn clopped up, with a normal-sized woman riding it. "Welcome to the Hercynian Garden. I'm Heloisa." She was extremely fit and wore brown-leather armor. She dismounted gracefully.

Juniper's jaw dropped at sight of the unicorn. "May I pet it?"

The unicorn nodded, and I was filled with wonder as she got her wish. Startled, I laughed and turned to Heloisa. "How?"

"In this place, the magic allows us all to understand each other. German, elven, dwarf, orc, and then the many horse and lower-form languages are spoken. Unicorns understand us but choose not to speak."

I stood there amazed. I fought the urge to take out my phone and snap a picture. Breaking the spell, our host said, "Come, we have serious work to discuss." Heloisa gave a slight inclination of her head and several things happened at once. A miniature, elf-sized, horse-drawn carriage pulled up, and I wasn't sure we would fit.

"Sorry," Heloisa said, "it's all I could get on short notice." She remounted with graceful speed, a practiced muscle memory. The driver of our carriage was an elf who looked very young. He clicked his tongue to rev up the "horsepower." Elsa was perfectly suited for the shallow bench seat. Juniper and I felt like giants as we lowered our heads and squished in. Our luggage was on the top of the contraption as we rolled down the road.

"I still don't see any indication of battle or war, Elsa." Again I scooched my butt to be more comfortable.

"If all goes well, you won't," Elsa said. "We know you haven't been trained to fight. We need the four of you for the ritual."

The trip was quiet, both Juniper and I lost in thought and looking out the wood-framed windows. We could hear the steady clop of hooved feet on dirt. We soon stopped in front of the most unusual building we'd seen yet. It had a wall around it that looked like it had grown there organically. I saw creatures of all descriptions posted at various intervals on the top of it. The gate opened and we entered. Now we began to see the effects of the war. Refugees were so crowded within, that they had set up a tent city inside. Cooking fires made our eyes sting as we alighted and followed Heloisa on foot. The young elf was joined by a dwarf who then followed with our things.

"I can pick up some of what you're thinking," Heloisa said. "The idyllic feeling you had upon arrival is magical. We use it to clean up what we can and to make a safe space between ourselves and the evil nipping at our heels."

"Kind of like a moat," Juniper said.

"Exactly." Heloisa looked pleased she'd made the connection.

My eyes must have been very round, as I took it all in.

Elven children played, as children do, chasing a ball the size of a golf ball down a break in the tents. We stopped for a moment as geese honked and a female elf guided them through. It was crowded. I'd describe it as "organized chaos." We passed a tent and heard fighting of the more domestic sort.

Heloisa stopped. "Merl, Briggard, what's the problem?" Two angry-looking dwarves were playing tug-of-war over a sack of something, but stopped when they saw Heloisa.

"There's hardly any meat to eat, and this pig dwarf," the rough-looking dwarf said and gave another swat to Briggard, "keeps stealing mine."

"Briggard, is that true?"

I blinked, fascinated by the exchange. Briggard was a smidge bigger than most in the yard.

"I was hungry."

"We all are. Save your energy for the enemy. Keep your hands off Merl's food. We all get the same allotment."

She walked forward, a leader, assured that her word would be followed.

"Where are we going?"

"I think it's time you met Mitzi's father."

Juniper and I exchanged glances. Each of us could see the other's open mouth.

CHAPTER SIX

MERRYVILLE

Detective Potts lit another cigarette. Disgruntled, he sat in his car across from Fowler Tax Services. The employee had told him that the owner, Mitzi's wife, had left the country. His own digging confirmed she had left for Germany with Juniper Gooden, which was highly suspicious. He wanted to investigate further, but there wasn't enough evidence for a warrant to search either woman's place. The employee, Babs, had acted like everything was fine, but she was nervous. This reinforced what he knew in his cop gut: that Mitzi Fowler was missing and that Panda Fowler—what kind of name was that?—had something to do with it. Maybe that other woman, Juniper, too. Not just any woman, Juniper Gooden was the lesbian who ran the cray-cray art museum that recently sucked up all the police resources for that visiting "artiste." He grunted. Typical. These types of relationships were inherently unstable. Women needed a man. Then he thought about his three ex-wives. Maybe they were all gay.

After a few hours of nothing, he decided to stake out the home of Juniper and Valerie Gooden on Lemon Street nearby.

When he knocked on Juniper Gooden's door, her "partner," Valerie, acted nervous.

"Ms. Gooden, my name is Detective Potts from MPD."

"It's Mrs. Can I help you?" she said frostily, not opening the door the whole way.

"I'm investigating a missing person, a friend of yours, Mitzi Fowler?"

"Mitzi's missing? I don't think so."

Which made his cop senses tingle.

"Who said she was missing?"

Another weird question. In his experience, most innocent people would spill everything they knew and try to help.

"I'm asking the questions if you don't mind." He hitched up his belt. "Do you know where she is, this Mitzi friend of yours?" He sniffed, damn cold trying to catch him.

"No, she's on vacation in Germany is what I know."

"Really? Who with?"

"My wife and her wife are there, too."

"Where?"

"I really don't feel comfortable standing here and answering any more questions. Mitzi is fine." She started closing the door on him, but he stuck his foot in it and handed her a card through the crack.

"I don't know what's going on, but if you want to tell me, here's my card. We're not gonna let this go until we find your friend."

"Thank you, Detective, your worries are misplaced." The door snicked shut.

Potts sat in his car, opened his notebook, and went over what he knew.

First, Panda Fowler had left the country, shortly before the most important day of the year in the tax biz, April fifteenth. Weird, but not illegal.

Second, Panda Fowler was seen walking around her neighborhood the day before, asking if anyone had seen Mitzi.

Third, on Sunday, Panda Fowler made a 9-1-1 call about Mitzi, then canceled it.

Fourth, that nut job curator, Juniper Gooden, gets on a plane for Germany with Panda Fowler.

Lesbians. Maybe Panda and Juniper were lovers. Maybe Mitzi was in the way. But that didn't fit.

If this Valerie had been left by Juniper Gooden for another woman, why wouldn't she say so? Was she in on it? Oh, wouldn't that be a big, juicy mess. He started the car and lit another cigarette.

He hadn't even put the car in drive when the front door opened. Valerie emerged carrying a book and some luggage. Holy shit! There's only one reason for her to not tell him she was fleeing the country. She was in on it. Even though he didn't know the why, no more suspects were leaving the ol' U.S. of A. on his watch. Potts reached for the radio.

Back at the castle, Mitzi wanted to bolt. Strong hands kept her in her chair, and the chanting finally stopped. "It's time for the first cleansing," the man with white hands said.

Females entered, dressed in white robes. Their faces were covered, and they bowed to the man as each passed. Softer hands took Mitzi. One of them spoke through her veil. "Wolfrum, we will prepare her for the ritual."

Wolfrum, for that apparently was his name, nodded. The women took Mitzi and departed the great room. They walked her back down the same corridor but this time took one of the halls leading in a direction other than the prison. She still couldn't speak. The women were silent as they escorted her to a place of running water. Tears ran down her face. They're going to drown me, she thought.

One of the younger women turned to her, put a finger to her lips, and shook her head no, as if Mitzi had spoken. What a strange, strange place.

HERCYNIAN GARDEN KEEP

Juniper and I, along with our two magical hosts, entered the only five-story structure on the grounds and walked along a deep plush carpet to reach what could only be described as the throne room. An enormous and strangely designed chair stood on a slightly raised platform in the center. A petite, velvet seat was next to it. Footstool? Walls were covered with what looked like the college pennants I'd seen back in Iowa, where I attended college.

"Each one has the name of a province in the Hercynian Garden," Elsa said. "There are thirteen. This one is the center of the magical world."

Truthfully, after seeing the state of the masses outside, the "magical world" didn't inspire confidence, although I didn't think I had expectations.

Very shortly, an elf bellowed, "Be upstanding!"

The soldiers who dotted the room stood up straighter, and we were led to a place in front of the dais. A griffin—Mitzi's father?—came in on all fours, one of his wings dragging on the ground.

Obviously, I'd never seen a real griffin before. Until now I believed them to be mythological creatures. My Episcopal church had a Flying Ox as a symbol on one of the banners back in Merryville. I would have envisioned that, if anything. That stylized creature didn't do this real one justice. Even though he looked somewhat broken, he carried power and dignity with him. He had a lion's powerful body and an eagle's head and wings. It was his eyes, so full of pain, however, that arrested me. He leaped gracefully to his throne, and I saw why it had such an odd shape. The tail must be accommodated. Makes sense. Funny how we focus on details like this when on overload.

Heloisa turned to us and said, "This is Ehrenhardt, leader of the free magical world. He knows who you are already."

"Good day, sir," I said, resorting to fairy tale formality.

Juniper, for once silent, gave a slight curtsy.

The griffin looked us over and rested his eyes on me. "So you and my Mitzi are married," he said with a sad smile. "I never thought we would meet."

"That makes you my father-in-law," I said, as if we were at a cocktail party.

He responded in kind. "Call me Ehren. Elsa tells me you make my daughter very happy."

"How long has she been watching us?" I asked, glancing at the little spy. She looked down.

"Don't be angry with her. She was acting on my orders." His voice was very definitely male, and carried a "don't mess with me" timbre. This was a griffin who was used to being in charge and obeyed.

"How come Mitzi didn't know you're her father?"

At that, four elves came forward with wooden chairs.

"Sit down, this may take a while," he rumbled.

We sat. It was one of those moments where you wouldn't be anywhere else in the world for all the tea in China. Kind of like when Juniper saw that unicorn.

Ehren looked off to the distance. "Griffins mate for life. When I met Frederick—"

In my head I thought-shouted, "Frederick?"

He looked straight at me with his eagle eyes, and I shrank. "Yes, Frederick."

"Frederick was brave and strong and beautiful. We lived together in this very place and ruled the magical kingdom. Frederick was a fairy, and our pairing was strong, both being magical. Griffins live for over a hundred years. Fairies"—he sighed heavily—" do not. We wanted a child to be part of both of us, but neither could carry a child. We found, Susan, Mitzi's mother."

"She was a surrogate?"

"Yes. She carried our child and lived here in the castle for a time with our new baby."

His face darkened. "Then, her desire to keep a child she had carried was bolstered by the new Wolf-Raven religion sweeping the land. Wolfrum and his monks want to rule and to relegate all creatures to roles they set out for them. Without getting into heavy theology, there's no place in their new leadership for an old griffin and a fairy, let alone two males, to live together."

I noted then the smaller seat that I had mistaken for a footstool was probably fairy sized. Frederick's seat sat empty beside Ehren.

My heart was sad for them. After he was silent for a full minute, I decided to prompt him. "So then what happened?"

"Aided by the monks, Susan left the magical world with Mitzi. I named her. It means beloved." A tear rolled down his feathery fatherly cheek. "We watched her grow from afar. Many elves were sent over the years to make sure she got what she needed."

"But you just let her go back to California? Why?"

"The peace of the magical world was no more, as the Wolf-Ravens kept us under constant attack. It was safer for her there, and I couldn't leave here. For another, nothing physically indicated that our daughter was anything other than human. At the base of it, the best interests of Mitzi were uppermost in my mind. I love her."

"Isn't her last name Schadt?" Juniper asked.

Ehren answered, "Her mother's husband's name. He was Mitzi's stepfather."

Juniper opened her mouth to ask another. There were thousands of questions I wanted answers to.

"That's enough for now. We're at war, and there's another matter that must be attended to." He made as if ready to go.

"Sir, I must know, what's being done to rescue Mitzi?"

"Go to your rooms and rest. We will speak at dinner." His voice had a definite edge. Obviously, talking about such painful things wasn't easy for him.

As Elsa, Juniper, and I arose, the front door opened and who should come running in but our old friend Ekk.

"Your Majesty!" He panted, looking breathless as he knelt before Ehrenhardt on the carpet before the throne. "The one they call Valerie has been arrested."

An angry cloud seemed to fill the room. Ehren bellowed to Ekk, "Stand and report!"

"I finished my assignment with Panda Fowler's tax business. It was successful," he said, nodding in my direction. In spite of the grave situation, I was still relieved to hear it. He continued. "I headed over to the Goodens to make sure the woman, Valerie, left in time to be here for the April twelfth ritual. She had her ticket, was packed, and was headed out to the car when a Detective Potts blocked her driveway with an unmarked car."

Juniper's fists tightened.

Ekk said, "Six black-and-white cars came, and they arrested her in handcuffs. She's being held in the Merryville jail."

Juniper erupted. "Those bastards! On what charge?"

"Silence! I must think." Ehren nodded to one of the elves with pen in hand. "Get Alexandra Stephanovsky out to the courthouse. We only have two days to get Valerie here." The elf ran to carry out his command.

"Guards," Ehren said, "take these two to their rooms."

Several other commands were given in a language we couldn't understand. Seven of what must be Ehren's advisors came quickly into the room. It was a motley crew: a fairy, three elves, a dwarf, and a couple of creatures I couldn't identify.

"I must ask you to leave now," Ehren said to us.

"Not a chance!" Juniper said. "Valerie's my wife." She grabbed my arm. "We're staying."

I wish I had a camera. Juniper faced up to Ehren, who was twice her size and in possession of talons that would make Brutus jealous. The room froze. Apparently, Ehren didn't get challenged in this way very often. It obviously took great restraint for him to dial his anger back a notch. "Of course, but do not interfere or you'll be sent to your rooms." I silently thought Mitzi may have been better off being raised in California.

ॐ

It soon became clear, however, that Juniper and I needed to go so Ehren could act. We were escorted to our rooms in the safe house by dwarves. We didn't make a fuss because the dwarves were somewhat surly. So many questions swirled in my mind. I sat on Juniper's bed while she paced. "This makes no sense. Valerie has done nothing, I mean nothing, to get arrested for."

I tried to calm the waters. "Let's look at this from the police viewpoint. Somebody reports Mitzi is missing."

"Who?"

"Well, me. I called 9-1-1 and they must have followed up. That would make sense, since a detective showed up at your doorstep asking questions about where she was. Everyone knows we're friends."

"Right. Oh my God. It must look bad that we both left the country. I didn't even think about that." Juniper's wheels were turning.

"I know. We were on a mission to save Mitzi and didn't think about how it might look to someone else." My heart sank, Where was Mitzi? "We may be in the same country, but we're no closer to saving Mitzi. Meanwhile this big deadline no one has really explained is getting closer."

We sat silent.

"Her dad is gay?" Juniper said, apropos of nothing.

"I know. Funny isn't it? I wonder if that's all she inherited from Ehrenhardt." We shared a look.

Juniper plopped down next to me. "What are we going to do about all this? What can we do?"

"And who is Alexandra Stephanovsky?" I added to the list of unanswered questions.

Back in Merryville, Potts was jubilant. He'd arrested Valerie Gooden for obstruction of the investigation into the disappearance of Mitzi Fowler. He stared at her through the two-way mirror, thinking how foreign she looked, what with her dark skin and blue eyes. Her cheekbones were pronounced, Iranian maybe. She sure didn't look German, so that bit confused him.

Someone leaked it to the press, and the story was about to get front page status, maybe with national exposure, especially on the heels of that crazy woman at the museum who had made a fool of the mayor. This because Valerie was Juniper Gooden's wife. Too good. He was basking in attention, what with Councilman Smithers calling him directly for information.

Unfortunately, Valerie Gooden wasn't saying anything more than she had already said at the door. At least she hadn't asked for an attorney. She would crack soon. She'd already missed her flight out of the country, and the squad room was abuzz with the return call he had received from Interpol a few minutes ago. He needed a celebratory cigarette.

HERCYNIAN GARDEN

Mitzi was glad to be away from the monks. Then she was led into a room filled with perfumed water. She felt she must be dreaming as her mother, Susan, was seated on a tile bench next to the woman she believed was Madame Dresser.

She tried to say, "Mom!" but her lips were still sealed.

Odilia Dresser waved her hand, like Wolfrum had done, and she could speak. "Get away from her. She's the one who kidnapped me."

The women sat there calmly, waiting for her to stop shouting.

Mitzi couldn't believe her mother just sat there, eyes downcast.

"That's Wolfrum's sister," her mother said.

"What? I don't care. What are you doing here? We need to get out of this place."

Neither Odilia nor Susan moved. They looked at each other and back at Mitzi. "I told you she would be like this," Susan said to Madame Dresser. Then she turned back to Mitzi. "Come and sit with us. It's high time we have a conversation I should have had with you years ago."

Stunned at the betrayal, Mitzi walked forward and sat with the two older women. Madame Dresser spoke first. "Everything you think you know about your past is false. This woman is your mother, but the man you know as your father was only her husband, not your biological father. Your father is not human."

Not human? The words jangled in her brain. Mitzi fought to regain control of her thoughts. "And who are you?" she asked.

"Odilia, the one who is here to save your life." She gave a toothy smile that looked more predatory than reassuring.

Mitzi sat.

"You were raised by your mother far away from this place, with the hopes that any taint from your birth would be forgotten," Odilia said in her thick German accent. "Raised by Susan and her God-fearing husband, Mr. Schadt, away from the magic you have seen. We hoped you would grow into a normal young woman. Unfortunately, that was not the case." Her voice was cold.

"Excuse me?" the very normal Mitzi said.

"You live with another woman as if she were a husband. This is a death sentence in our world."

"Who the hell are you to judge me?" Mitzi said, standing up.

"Like I said, I'm the one who will save your life—or take it." Her blue eyes were icy.

Susan began to cry and turned to the old woman. "I tried, Odilia. She was raised with a mother and a father. We took her to church. I made sure she never knew anything about this place or who her father was."

Odilia stroked Susan's hair in a parody of motherly love. Mitzi wasn't buying it.

"This is because I'm a lesbian?"

"Partly. It's also because of who your father was. Is. Also because we are at war and have been since before you were born. Unfortunately, you appear to have been born on the wrong side of the struggle."

The women who had brought her to this place removed Mitzi's clothing. Mitzi hung on to her clothes and tried to push them away.

"I would think you'd like this part," Odilia said cruelly.

"You old bitch!" Mitzi lunged at Odilia as the women clutched her and held her back. "Stop it! Leave me alone!"

Her mother sobbed.

"You have no right to hold me here. I'm forty-three-years old, not ten. I—"

With another flick of her hand, Odilia sealed Mitzi's lips again. She said to the women, "Scrub her good. Scrub the devil out of her." Her eyes narrowed. "Then deliver her to the retraining room."

She put her arm around Susan and led her out of the cleansing room. Susan's face looked worried. "We talked about this. You weren't going to—"

"Don't make me seal your lips, too, Susan. You've done quite enough damage. We let you have the child because you so earnestly promised us we would never hear from her again."

Mitzi maniacally tried to break her lips to scream at this woman.

Susan shrank under Odilia's gaze. "Don't hurt her," she squeaked out.

"You know the penalty for disobedience."

"Take me instead."

"You know that won't work."

Mitzi could no longer hear. The dwarf women pushed her head underwater and scrubbed her with wooden brushes. She wondered if this was the "schpa" Odilia Dresser had anticipated for Mitzi when she first called, seeking a reunion.

APRIL ELEVENTH

High Five! Potts took another congratulatory lap around the squad room then headed toward the interview room. He entered and Valerie Gooden was sitting at the metal table, hands on her lap, twisting her wedding ring. She looked fragile and uncomfortable.

Good. She'll be singing like a birdy with a few more hours of this, he thought. "Let's begin again," Potts said. He turned a chair around backwards and straddled it. "When was the last time you saw Mitzi Fowler?"

"Saturday, at the museum opening." Valerie squeezed the fabric on the hem of her blouse.

"The Fiona whatsername disaster?"

"I wouldn't call it that, and her name is Fiona Castlebaum," she said defiantly.

"You told me Panda Fowler and your wife went to Germany a couple of days ago."

"Yes."

"Did you know your friend Panda called 9-1-1 to report Mitzi missing?"

She shifted uncomfortably in the cold metal chair.

"I'll take that for a no. How well do you know Panda Fowler?"

"Very well. Mitzi and Panda are our best friends."

"See each other socially?"

"Yes, of course."

"Anything else?" he added suggestively.

"What do you mean?"

"You know, anything else. How close are you?" He gestured a "go on" motion.

Valerie looked disgusted, but before she could answer, the door burst open.

The woman standing there was a detective's worst nightmare. Alexandra Stephanovsky was the kind of defense attorney who not only won more than he was comfortable with, she did it in style. Today she had on Dupioni black-silk pants, a red-tailored jacket with a brooch, and spectator shoes. Her eyeglasses matched her socks and buttons. She was a semi-celeb in Merryville's legal pond.

"Hello, Potts," she said with a fierce grin.

He responded with something under his breath. "Alex."

Alexandra turned to Valerie. "I'm your defense attorney. You're not to say another word."

"But—"

Alexandra put her finger to Valerie's lips and shook her head. "That's a word." She then turned to Detective Potts. "Is my client being charged with anything?"

"Yes she is." He looked surly. "Obstruction of justice."

"Who's on the case?"

Potts sighed. "Debra Ehrlich." An assistant district attorney they both knew well.

Alexandra rapped on the two-way mirror. "Hullo, Debra, I know you're in there. Chop chop. Let's arraign her. She has places to be."

Debra's voice crackled from the ancient speakers. "Not so fast, Alexandra. We can't get her before a judge until Monday, April fifteenth."

"You don't plan on holding her in here, do you? A woman with zero criminal record?"

Debra entered the room, and she and Potts looked at each other.

Alex turned fierce, all kidding aside. "I demand a bail hearing this afternoon or tomorrow at the latest. She needs to be out to aid in her own defense. Obstruction is a cheesy offense, and you know it."

♒

That afternoon, Valerie was brought before Judge Dinwitter.

"All rise!" the bailiff shouted.

With only a glance up, the old judge said, "Ms. Stephanovsky, nice to see you. How does your client plead?"

"Not guilty, Your Honor."

Valerie stood beside her counsel as if in shock.

"People?" The judge turned to Debra Ehrlich.

"People ask the court to remand. She's a flight risk."

"This is ridiculous, Your Honor. Ms. Gooden is a home-healthcare nurse taking care of a very ill client."

Ehrlich cut her off. "She fails to mention that Ms. Gooden's wife and the missing woman's wife have left the country."

"Bail is set at fifty thousand dollars, and she's to turn in her passport."

Valerie turned to Alexandra as if to speak. Alex put up her finger to shush her and turned to the judge. "Your Honor—"

"That's my ruling." The gavel came down.

PANDA IN THE HERCYNIAN GARDEN

Once alone, I tried and tried to get my phone to work. I wasn't even sure who to call. Tinkering with my phone kept me busy. I couldn't think of anything more frustrating than being held back from doing something. I opened the window, which was more of a glass-covered slit and pretty high off the ground, and stuck my hand out to try to get a signal. Nothing. The green substance of which the entire place was constructed seemed to absorb my signal.

I did something then that I could do. I prayed.

Minutes later, the same dwarves who had escorted us to our rooms took Juniper and me to a communal dining room. Ehren was seated already, and several of his advisors were filing in. I noticed Elsa and Ekk sat together, and it finally dawned on me they were a couple. Even with everything going on, I thought how cute they were, and knew Babs would squeal if she saw them together like salt and pepper shakers.

A bell rang. Fairies and elves floated in bringing food with the most delicious smells. We hadn't eaten since early morning at the hotel. The dinner was amazing: lots of vegetables, nuts, soup, and homemade bread with a "roast beast" on a platter surrounded by potatoes. Most were drinking ale, but I chose water. I wanted to keep a clear head.

I started to ask a question, but the elf next to me said, "Not until he's ready. That is our way. Eat."

So we ate. Juniper struck up a conversation with a dwarf next to her, who seemed way too interested in her cleavage. I spent my time studying the room, which was very old and modern at the same time. It had the feel of a thousand-year-old ranch house, but was made of some material other than adobe. Its greenish cast reminded me of Play-Doh. Again, I had the sense it had grown this way, like the Play-Doh walls outside.

A fire crackled in an oven built into the wall, and if you didn't know it, you'd think this was a festive occasion. Meanwhile, I had to have some answers.

"Ehren, enough. What can we do to get Mitzi back?" A low grumbling went around the table, and the eagle-faced griffin wiped his face slowly in an exaggerated manner.

"*We* do nothing. My troops are on their way after dinner to bring her back."

The last day or so I'd been astounded with the idea of this whole magic world, jet-lagged from crossing the pond, and somewhat numb, having failed to process all that was happening to me so rapidly. I was done with being stymied. I stood and faced the head of the table.

"Whatever plans you have to rescue Mitzi include me. Anything else is not an option. She's my wife, Ehren." I threw my napkin on the plate and turned to go.

The place seemed to collectively hold its breath. A soft growl and Ehren said, "Then go suit up now. The unit is preparing to leave."

Juniper jumped up and said, "I go, too."

"If you fail, you all die," Ehren said. "If you don't succeed in getting Mitzi, you all die. Remember that."

Well, all righty then.

Elsa and Ekk scurried forward and led us to the armaments area. Elves quickly and quietly put leather armor on us and fitted us each out with daggers. We then joined Heloisa, who was giving final instructions to her troop.

"Quickly and quietly, we go to the lower quadrant of the forest and set up camp." She stopped talking when she noticed us. "What are you two doing here?"

"We're going with you."

"You, Panda, I understand are a tax person in the other world?"

"Yes."

"And you, Juniper, work for an art museum?"

"Yes."

Heloisa looked at the ceiling as if appealing to some goddess. "Stick with the dwarves in the back and stay out of my way." She turned and mounted her unicorn.

We were given normal horses, and it took a few minutes to get used to riding and wearing all the leather gear. My dagger kept jabbing me in the thigh, but it felt good to finally be doing something. A smaller gate in the back of the compound opened with a great groaning of gears. A dirt path led to the horizon.

Heloisa was in the lead, with a coterie of strange elves. We, as promised, rode between two battle-tested-looking dwarves. Their armor had scrapes and nicks that they wore with pride. All moved, as promised, swiftly and silently.

The first part of the journey through the magical "moat" area was idyllic. The grass was green, birds chirped, the sun always shined, and the feeling of peace was almost intoxicating. Soon, we moved from the magical world into the Black Forest, and it became very dark and cold. Suddenly, I was happy for all the leather over my Tibetan parka. I then noticed Heloisa's unicorn's horn had disappeared, and her steed had become a beautiful, but normal, horse. The dwarves and elves kept their shape, which confused me. It was one more thing to ask about later.

After the warmth of the Hercynian Garden, this place sucked out anything of home and hearth. Branches tore at us, the horses stumbled over twisted roots, and soon we became aware of ravens in the trees, watching our every move.

Progress was slow in some places, and we plodded along, cold and silent, until midnight. It was dark, and the rhythmic clopping of hooves made me nod off. A hooting owl jerked me awake.

"We camp here," Heloisa said softly, brooking no comment from the others. "Camp" was a moderately damp area in a clearing, where the horses champed and blew steam from their nostrils. Crude tents were quickly erected, and some of the elves disappeared into them. Soon, a fire blazed, and Juniper and I were practically in it trying to stay warm.

Heloisa pulled us aside. "Meet me one-hundred yards to the south of here in one hour," she said. Her eyes swept my appearance. "Panda, lose the neon jacket."

I nodded, too numb to speak, but the thought of losing my jacket was almost unbearable. However, if it meant getting Mitzi back in one piece then fine, I would swing a dead chicken over my head. It dawned on me that perhaps this was all a trick and Heloisa was trying to freeze us to death. Nevertheless, we had no choice but to trust her.

Juniper and I paced out the hundred yards, and soon Heloisa joined us. She tossed me a black cloak that helped my frozen condition. "Are you going to tell me—"

The warrior woman put a finger to her lips and motioned for us to follow.

We walked, it seemed, for miles, and with all of us in black, we must have been pretty hard to see, which was probably the point. Eventually, we came upon a brightly colored gypsy wagon next to a smoldering fire. After looking around, Heloisa grabbed my arm and led me to the door. I gasped as it opened quickly, and she shoved me in. Juniper followed, but Heloisa stayed outside. At least it was warm in there.

A heavily bejeweled creature sat at a table with one candle lit. "Greetings," she said in heavily Slavic tones. Both of us started a bit. She sounded like a female Dracula. "Don't be afraid. Your guardian is checking outside to make sure you were not followed."

"No worries," I murmured. "Thank you for letting us in." One must remember their manners when in a gypsy wagon in the Black Forest. I almost giggled hysterically.

Juniper reached out to lightly touch the woman's necklace, but the woman grabbed her wrist. My startled friend said, "Sorry, that's an amazing piece."

The Rom smiled slyly as she released Juniper's arm. "It's very old."

I was in that surreal numb-tired-wired place you can get and silently waited, hypervigilant. A ticking clock sounded very loud from a dark corner. I didn't think anything could surprise me anymore.

The door of the brightly-colored wooden wagon opened, and Heloisa joined us. It was very crowded in there. The gypsy said to her nervously, "Good?" Heloisa nodded. Our strange host reached into a place below her chair,. The table, upon which sat a crystal ball, tilted all the way back, revealing a tunnel with a ladder. It was dark in the hole below, and cold dank air blew out of it.

"You don't expect us to go down there?" I said.

"You will go. Now." Apparently, she did.

Heloisa confirmed it. "We need to get below quickly. Follow me." She took a lantern from the woman, lit it with the candle, and rapidly descended the ladder. I looked at Juniper, who was grim. She shrugged as if to say, "In for a penny, in for a pound." We followed.

The door snapped shut over our heads as Juniper's fingers cleared the top rung. It was about twenty-five feet 'til we dropped down to a subterranean tunnel. "Can we talk now?" I asked, exasperated.

"Yes, for the moment. I think it's safe here." Heloisa looked fierce in the flickering light, but strangely emanated safety. "I am a guardian," she said, as if she could read my thoughts. "You must trust what I'm about to say. Lives depend upon it."

"Whatever I need to do," I said. "I'm in, if it's for Mitzi. Juniper needs to make her own choices." I turned to my good friend. "It's kind of late to go back now, but I can't ask you to go any further. This is crazy."

"Our fates are linked," Juniper said. "I can see that. In times like these, there's no going back." She turned to Heloisa. "Tell us what we need to do."

IN THE CASTLE

After her cleansing, a very red-skinned Mitzi was wrapped in a white toga and taken to a bedroom. She was tired and, if she could have spoken, would have admitted to being freaked, especially since seeing her mother in this place. The room was decorated like a bordello, and at the center of it was a four-poster bed. It made her skin crawl to think this may be the retraining room.

Most of all, she missed Panda and wondered if she was—even now—coming with the cavalry to save her. Her shoulders shuddered as she thought about how far California was and how hopeless the whole situation had become. Hot tears of frustration and rage streaked down her face. Inside she felt a tingling, a warmth that felt like a flower blossoming.

It was this moment when the door opened, and her mother came in. Mitzi's spine stiffened. Talk about betrayal.

"I'm so sorry. This is all my fault," Susan said.

"You bet it is." Mitzi and her mother both started, shocked that she could speak.

"You can speak." They stared at one another. Mitzi wondered what that meant. "Did Odilia come see you again?"

"No. No one did"

"Oh my God, you're magical."

"What? No. The mute thing probably wore off." Then Mitzi got mad again. "I thought we were good. We talk every week. I mean, you didn't come to our wedding, but I thought you liked Panda. And all this? Really? My dad is a griffin? From a magical forest? Really, Mom, you couldn't have just told me?"

"Mitzi. Would you even have believed me? The monks mean well. We're trying to keep you from eternal suffering. This sin has its roots in the past. Way in the past."

"I am not a sin, Mom. And this isn't about only you anymore. You dragged me and Panda into your nightmare. Thanks a lot."

"You're right. It's quite a mess." Susan sank to a chair against the wall. "And the ritual—"

"Tell me about that. Now!" Mitzi made her demand in a tone that would not be ignored.

Susan looked surprised. "God, you sounded like your father."

"Which one?"

"Mitzi. . ."

"Spill it." Mitzi was done messing around.

"Every four generations, the treaty between worlds is ratified. It keeps a relative peace because without it there are no rules. Already there has been death."

Mitzi was exasperated. "Who, Mom? The treaty is between who and who?"

"Between the human world and the magical world. Magic is evil, Mitzi."

"Wait a minute, Mom. When Odilia or that Wolfrum guy waves their hand, they shut people up. Isn't that magic?"

"That's a gift from the spirit."

"Oh, please." Mitzi shook her head, walked to the window cut into stone, and looked out at the horizon of tangled forest. "I don't even know who you are."

"You wanted to know about the ritual, so listen."

Mitzi fixed her with an unhappy gaze.

"The ritual is from a very old story about two suns. There's a real sun and a false sun, the one who is 'dogging' the real sun. This is why they sometimes call it the dog sun. Both are chased by two wolves, who are hunting the sun and the moon."

Mitzi, a tour guide who had heard her share of cultural myths, looked impressed.

"It's really more complicated than this. I'm not explaining it well."

Mitzi knew her mother was raised in an orphanage, never had higher education, and probably felt inferior to those filling her head with all this crap. Nevertheless, she was drawn in. After all, here she was in their castle. It was important to know what they believed.

"Let me guess. There isn't room for more than one sun at a time," Mitzi said, the ritual becoming clearer.

"Yes. Only one survives until the next time, and their faction rules."

"Do they mean S-O-N or S-U-N?"

"I don't know. Others have talked about that." Her head cocked as if remembering something. "Your father had sons, but they were killed in battle."

Mitzi looked stricken.

"From other mothers," Susan said, as if that made it better. "One of them fairly recently."

Mitzi nodded for her to continue. What a violent and sad story. Now she had half-brothers she would never get to meet. Mitzi was floored. "Have you been in touch with this world all this time?"

Susan looked away, a sure tell she had something to hide. "I wasn't supposed to, but I had to know what was going on in order to keep us safe."

Mitzi looked at the locked door and asked, "And how's that working out, Mom?"

Susan reddened but continued. "On a certain day at a certain time, the children of the leaders of both worlds must be represented in the circle. It symbolizes the joining that took place the last turning point. There are four people who stand in for the elements for balance, representing the overlap of our and the magical world, North, South, East, and West." She stopped and shook her head, as if trying to sort something out. "When Ehren's last son died, I worried they would come for you. Don't you see? You mustn't be seduced by the magic. You're a human, for God's sake, human! Please say you'll stay with me until after the time for that ritual." She looked into her daughter's eyes. "I'm sorry Mitzi, I'm so torn, I—"

"Which thing are you apologizing for, Mom? Having me kidnapped? Put to death maybe in a couple of days? Not telling me the truth? For letting that bitch judge me for being a lesbian?"

Susan winced. Silence stretched. They both heard the cold wind blowing outside. "For everything I guess. Odilia means well."

"No, she doesn't, Mom. She wants to kill me."

"I won't let that happen." Her weak mother said this with more resolve than Mitzi had heard before. Mitzi believed her mother genuinely meant it. Whether or not her wishes would be honored was another matter.

Mitzi felt a tingling in her shoulders then. Surprisingly, she still had compassion for this very wounded woman who bore her and was trying to do what she believed was the right thing. Her mother was wrong, but she wasn't evil. "Mom, if you love me, you'll help me escape this place."

Susan pulled back. "I can't. It goes against everything I believe."

"You don't get to pick what I believe, Mom." She paused. "Wait a minute, a child of both worlds? Who is Wolfrum's child?"

CHAPTER SEVEN

MERRYVILLE

Hours passed before Alex got Valerie bailed out of jail, and as soon as they got in the car, Val tried calling Juniper with no luck.

"Thank you for getting me out of there. Did my wife call you? I can't seem to get through." She rubbed her wrists where the handcuffs had been.

"I got a call from a friend in Germany who knows your wife and called on her behalf." Alex kept driving. "We need to go somewhere we can talk, other than your house. The news cameras are there."

Valerie went through her purse to make sure everything was still there. "Why is this such a big deal? I don't get it."

"Haven't you been following the news stories?" Alex asked. "They started right after the museum event and haven't died down yet. There are people protesting outside Councilman Smithers' office that he hasn't done enough about the feral cats. There's another group writing letters to the *Merryville Bee* about the homeless problem. Another group thinks we're not doing enough for the homeless. It was kind of a dry-tinder situation, and Fiona Castlebaum lit the match."

Thinking about her client who recently passed, Valerie said "I've been busy and, to tell you the truth, not real eager to read the papers lately."

"Well, somebody's keeping this thing stirred up, that's for sure." Alex pulled into the Fowler's house on Thistle Drive. "This it?"

Valerie nodded as Alex parked her flashy Tahitian Pearl Lincoln. She gave Val a dazzling smile. "While we're here, let's inspect the alleged scene of the crime."

Valerie knew where the Fowler's spare key was hidden, Mitzi and Panda had keys to their house too. God, she missed everyone. Brutus came running up. A neighbor had been feeding him, but he was anxious as all get out with his people missing. "Meow. Meow," he said, telling her all about it. Or maybe he wanted the food from the purple bag.

"What a beautiful cat." Alex leaned down to pet him, but he scooted inside as soon as the front door opened. Alex followed Valerie and Brutus to the kitchen. While Alex captured and pet the cat, Valerie made tea. The familiar routine of boiling water and choosing cups always soothed her.

In the kitchen, Alex continued the conversation. "Another reason I'm on this case is because the mayor and city council were pretty embarrassed by the Castlebaum Floodlight extravaganza. Certain folks in this town are invested in distracting the public from that. Your arrest fits the bill nicely." Alex took the delicate cup Valerie offered. "I've handled many high-profile cases before, and we need to find out who those folks are."

"A conspiracy theory already?" Valerie set down the tea kettle so fast some water splashed out. She felt like she was losing her mind. "This is Merryville, for goodness sake, not Washington DC."

Her initial relief at being bailed out now turned to suspicion. "Hey, who hired you anyway? I'm pretty sure we can't afford you." She remembered seeing Alexandra on TV in more than one news cycle.

"You can afford me. Fiona Castlebaum's got me on retainer."

"That woman? Oh, you can turn around and leave right now." A tea towel was thrown. "Juniper was fired because of her."

Alex ducked as Brutus leaped from her lap. She put her splendidly manicured hands up in mock surrender. "Look, don't shoot the messenger and all that, okay? There are six sides to every story, then there's the real one. Wait until you have all the facts."

Valerie snorted. "Facts? Okay, you want facts? Before last weekend, my life was fine, in fact, pretty wonderful. Then your client torpedoed my wife's big shining moment. Mitzi got kidnapped, my patient died, and I got arrested." She was truly pissed. "Want more facts?" She sat, spent.

"Please, withhold judgment until you talk to Juniper. She should be checking in soon, which is what I'm kind of waiting around for. In the meantime, I'll go interview the neighbors and find out who is friend and who is foe. Open the front door and flag me if Juniper's call comes in, okay?"

Not really having many choices, Valerie agreed. She took her tea and Brutus and sat on the living room couch, petting him. There's nothing like tea and a purring cat when you've been through what she had that week. Her cell was plugged in, and she watched it on the table.

She looked idly around the room, drawing comfort from all the times she and her good friends had sat here, playing Rummikub or watching TV and eating pizza. When Panda's aunt/mom was alive, they all watched *Jeopardy* with her here from time to time.

The pictures and pieces of invitation paper from the previous Sunday were still scattered where she and Juniper had left them. Oh my God, she thought, there's no way I'm going to get to Germany in time. Brutus looked up at her, and she had the strangest feeling he truly understood.

In a tunnel under Schwarzvald Castle, Heloisa moved ahead, with only the lantern held high to light our way. I pondered the stability of the tunnel, which looked to be fairly new. It had stones and sticks piled up, held together by the same putty-like stuff the Hercynian Garden favored for its building materials. The air smelled damp and earthy, and I tried really hard not to let my fingers brush the walls as we moved silently toward our fate.

"This tunnel goes under the walls and will let us out in the castle garden," Heloisa whispered.

Soon, I heard running water. Heloisa turned and said softly, "Wait." Juniper and I held each other's arm and blindly walked forward as far as we could to see what our guardian would do. At the end of the tunnel, we could see Heloisa standing at the edge of the water. A wooden boat shaped like a leaf with sides silently cut through the water. A slender elven woman dressed in white gracefully leaped to the makeshift dock of planks. In one sweeping gesture, Heloisa took her in her arms and gave her a kiss that would make Pat Robertson's head explode. She then turned and motioned us ahead.

Juniper and I remained silent, partially in deference to the seriousness of our mission and partly to give Heloisa her dignity. That was obviously a very private moment. Heloisa said, "This is Lily, my mate."

The younger woman spoke to her in a tongue we couldn't understand, and Heloisa's face looked grim. "Panda, Juniper, I think you two ought to wait here and let me go get Mitzi."

"No way, Heloisa." I looked directly in her eyes. "If you had a chance to save Lily from an evildoer, would you let someone else do the job for you?" Heloisa softened and gave a sideward glance to her lovey.

She tried once more to deter us. "You could get killed."

I shook my head. "No. Fiona lost her husband to this fight, Ehrenhardt lost Frederick, I'm going to get Mitzi back right now or die trying." I turned to my friend and said more softly, "but I wouldn't blame you at all for staying here, Juniper. This is my fight."

Juniper put her arm around me, "Art is dangerous, darling, and so is living. Let's go."

I love my friends.

∾

A hundred-and-thirty-five feet overhead, and oblivious to the intruders below, Wolfrum paced his round war room overlooking the forest. Sconces burned brightly on the stone walls, and a map sat on a rough wooden table in the center of the room. Brother Dieter, one of the chanting monks from earlier, entered, having returned from ground reconnaissance.

"What is their position?"

"The same, Master Wolfrum. They appear to have broken camp by the clearing."

Wolfrum leaned into the map, as if he could see actual figures near the mark that indicated their camp.

Wolfrum's spy looked worried.

"Is that all?" Wolfrum's tone was always sepulchral.

"If I may speak freely?"

"Of course." The white hands lowered the hood, and Wolfrum fixed his gaze on the underling.

"I don't understand why they have been so obvious."

"Obvious?"

"Yes, they know the ravens are listening, and they've even lit a fire. I wonder why they would do that? There must be some purpose."

"Indeed." Wolfrum poured a glass of wine. "Would you like some?"

The young monk stammered. "N-no thank you, sir, I—"

Wolfrum smiled cruelly. "No, I insist."

His face was unreadable as he gave Dieter a glass filled with blood-red wine. "The ravens, don't you think that has occurred to me?"

"Of course, Master."

"Good. When I want your opinion, I will ask you."

"Yes, Master." He took a sip. Suddenly, his throat began to burn.

"You'll be fine in a day or so." Wolfrum dismissed him with a wave. "Get Brother Bruno up here. He knows his role."

Wolfrum hated being told anything spontaneously by an underling. However, it was curious that the scraggly band of would-be rescuers would let themselves be seen, unless . . .

∾

Outside, Heloisa and our motley band exited the boat and slipped through the underbrush to a place as close to the castle as was wise. The young monk had almost discovered us. Lily went ahead, as she appeared to be allowed in the castle vicinity. I tried to follow, but Heloisa's strong hand and maternal arm stopped me. I looked at her to argue, but she shook her head as if to say, "Not now."

The reason soon became apparent. Around the corner came a duo of the meanest-looking dwarves I had ever seen, and by now I was getting to have some idea of what I was talking about. These two were sniffing the air, and Heloisa pulled us back even farther. Unfortunately, Juniper stepped on a twig that snapped loudly. A light shone our way. *Halt! Zeige dich!*"

"Get back underground. Now!" Heloisa fiercely whispered as she drew her sword.

Juniper and I retreated, but not all the way to the boat. I found a tree with holds, and we helped each other scramble up. A raven landed on the branch next to me, and I thought we were sunk. Instead, it flew away as if we weren't even there.

Below, the battle raged. The two dwarves looked strong and were covered in a mix of metal and leather armor. They used shorter knives than Heloisa wielded, but their arms were like tree trunks. She was a thing to behold in action. Two against one, however, was never good odds. Juniper and I looked around for anything that would be helpful and found nothing except branches.

The warrior woman fought valiantly, using a combination of judo moves to use the attackers' weight against them and sword parries when any vulnerable spots were exposed. Then, Heloisa's shield was nearly shorn in two by a direct hit from a battle ax, which had to be a heck of an impact. She staggered. One of the dwarves was bleeding heavily from a blow that she previously landed on his shoulder, pretty close to his no-neck. The other seemed to redouble his efforts, sensing she was off balance.

We knew something had to happen, or our only hope would be finished off. Without thinking too much about it, I broke off the biggest branch I could find, swung it directly down at the wounded dwarf, and rapped the stick on his head as hard as I could. He dropped like a sack of sand. Juniper climbed down the tree and picked up a rock, coming to join the fray with her jewelry swinging. Jewelry! The pendant! Could that be why the dwarf was semi-paralyzed beneath me? While Juniper knocked him out with a rock, Heloisa made a more permanent end to his friend.

She was winded but appeared unhurt. "We don't have much time. Drag them into the bushes."

Inside the castle, Lily walked the halls, eyes downcast when the brothers walked by, as if she were on an ordinary task, her white gown flowing prettily. She stopped behind a column near the retraining room, where Mitzi was about to be taught about her proper role as a woman. All the castle maidens knew this was merely an excuse for

Wolfrum's brutal men to rape, and it was all the more repugnant that they did it in the name of their righteous cause. Two guards stood outside the door. Lily took a deep breath and trusted that Heloisa would do her part.

She was about to walk in front of them and faint, which would be Heloisa's cue to move in quickly for the kill, but Brother Dieter came running through clutching his throat. He managed to whisper to the guards that he was looking for Bruno. Bruno was a beast of a man, who had many kills to his credit. Mitzi's retraining-room guards pointed down the hall, and Dieter went on his way.

The delay was fatal. No less than Wolfrum himself came down the hall, followed by Odilia and his usual sycophants.

Lily continued on and they walked past her without a second glance. Once around the corner and out of sight, she rushed to find Heloisa and let her know what happened.

While that was taking place, Heloisa crept quietly into the castle hallway from the garden, turned around by the maze-like qualities of the place. Lily had prepped her, but perhaps the battle had rattled her more than she thought. Instead of the retraining room, she ended up in the bathing room.

"It's been too long," I whispered to Juniper outside. "Go back. I'm going to help Heloisa bring Mitzi out." Seeing her look of worry, I added, "I've got the pendant. Nothing's going to happen to me."

My dear friend said, "I'm climbing the tree and will keep lookout. If you're not back in half an hour, I'll take the boat back and bring reinforcements."

"You know that's a Juniper tree, don't you?" I said.

"Good to know." She rolled her eyes. "Hurry."

I nodded and took the same route I'd seen Heloisa take into the castle.

I held the pendant in one hand like the talisman it was and opened my mind for direction. Mitzi, Mitzi, baby, where are you? I heard someone coming, made up my mind which way to go, and scooted down a carpeted hallway toward the sound of running water.

MERRYVILLE

Alex returned from her neighborhood investigation and perched on a chair across from Valerie and Brutus.

"Nice cat." Brutus chose that moment to do yoga leg, a move Panda swore he learned from Mitzi. She missed her friends.

Alexandra gave her report, drawing it out on paper. "Okay, Scott and Mary, neighbors to the left, and Rick and Michelle, right of here, are okay, but they both confirmed that Panda did ask them if they'd seen Mitzi last Sunday. Michelle said Panda looked nervous and worried. That's all they had."

"Okay, the neighbor on the right, Michelle, is feeding Brutus."

"Meow." Brutus rubbed his fur on Valerie's legs.

"A few neighbors weren't home, but the one directly across the street was." Alex marked an X. "No one answered the door, but I heard a TV, and there were cars in the driveway."

Valerie put her index finger on the house marked X. "Oh, that's my best bet for who called the police. I can't remember her name, but Panda's had problems with her before. Like when Proposition Eight was happening. They put up a 'Yes on Eight' sign in their yard facing this house, and she and Panda got into it one morning when they were both rolling their trash cans to the street. I think they know our city council person, too. They always put his signs in their lawn at election time."

Alex jotted that in her PDA. "Okay, so she's your average homophobe. I like the connection with Gary Smithers, though. That might be our link." Alex looked thoughtful. "Still no phone call?"

Valerie drew the cat up on her lap and shook her head. "Alex, I have to be in Germany like, now. What would happen if I just left?"

Alex gave her a shocked look. "You don't want to know." She looked sternly at Valerie. "I'm not kidding. Don't even think about it. Besides, you don't have your passport, remember?"

"I'll go some other way. There are consequences if I don't go."

Alex stood up. "Consequences? How does Federal Prison sound? What aren't you telling me, Valerie? Never mind, it's better if I don't know." She left her card on the table with the neighborhood map. "Call me if anything happens. Any calls, any visits, any anything, okay?"

"Will do."

Once the door closed, Valerie heard a noise from the back of the house. Before she could react, Ekk and a female elf walked in holding hands. "We came to keep you company." He nodded at his companion, who smiled shyly. "This is Elsa." Impulsively, Valerie scooped them both up and laughed and cried at the same time. How she could be so happy to see elves she had no idea. It definitely reminded her that all this was real, and that she was either not going crazy or she was so crazy it didn't matter.

"Thank you. I was feeling so alone. Are Juniper and Panda safe? And Mitzi, did they find Mitzi?"

"Yes, safe for the moment, but I won't lie. They're still in dangerous territory."

"I have to go to Germany now. I don't care what the lawyer says." Valerie flew to the keyboard.

"Valerie, stop."

She turned to look at Ekk who said, "We've come all the way *from* Germany to tell you that's no longer necessary. If all goes well, they'll come to us."

"What? How?" She resumed her position on the couch and was filled in on the amazing and magical news of her wife and Panda's Black Forest adventure. After a while, the elves needed feeding, and they all became busy in the kitchen, still awaiting Juniper's phone call.

Meanwhile, Detective Potts was cruising back to the Fowlers' neighborhood after receiving another message their neighbor had called in. Upon arriving at the neighbor's house, which was directly across from Panda Fowler's house, Charlie Potts lifted his hand to knock, but the door opened seemingly of its own accord. Gail, the neighbor, had a narrow face and stuck her skinny neck out, peering left and right furtively before speaking.

Startled, he pulled his own neck back like a turtle. "I believe you called for a detective?"

The older woman looked him up and down, before saying, "With Mitzi Fowler missing, I needed to let you know, the Gooden woman's "wife" (she did air quotes) is over at her house alone."

"And?" He was growing impatient.

"She doesn't live there. Isn't that illegal? Isn't that trespassing?"

He chewed on his pen thoughtfully, studying her. "Maybe, maybe not. Thanks for letting me know. Anything else?"

"Yes. That horrible woman who's always defending scumbags was over here knocking on my door."

He was liking his witness less and less. "Alexandra Stephanovsky?" After Gail nodded, he grunted and asked, "What did she say?"

Gail rolled her eyes. "I wasn't about to answer my door. She left a few minutes ago." Potts looked at her hawk-like face, with her bright eyes and could feel the woman's venom toward her neighbors. It didn't matter, however, because they were focused on the same house. For the moment, their interests coincided.

"Okay, ma'am. In the meantime, keep your doors locked. You did the right thing."

It was getting dark, and he was getting very curious. Why was Valerie Gooden there? What if this Valerie tried to get away using someone else's passport? Maybe she went back to get something in the Fowler house? He moved the car around the corner and walked back. God, he wanted a cigarette, but he couldn't risk anyone in Panda Fowler's house smelling the smoke when he got under the window. He had as much right to be there as Valerie Gooden did, and the house was still technically a crime scene, right? What if she was trying to destroy evidence? He still needed something more to get a warrant and made the decision to spy into the back of the house through the windows.

Potts looked over the backyard fence and saw evidence of recent digging. His heart started beating faster. Walking to the living room window, all he could see was a big, spotted cat draped over the sofa like a cheap scarf, licking himself. What is it with women and cats? He shook his head and moved down a room. Dark, it held only a dining room table and hutch. Light came from the middle of the house that he guessed to be the kitchen. With a bay window, the kitchen portal was too high up for him to peek in while standing on the ground.

He looked around and found a bamboo bench by the trash on the side of the house. He picked it up and moved it under the window. He stepped on it and heard a crack, but it seemed like it would hold. His eyes barely reached over the sill, where he could see Valerie Gooden turning from the sink with a couple of glasses of water. He only got a quick glimpse before the bench completely gave way, but he would swear she was serving sandwiches to dolls at the kitchen table. What a crazy bitch. He bet Mitzi Fowler and Juniper Gooden never left at all. They were probably all buried in the backyard. He walked swiftly down the street to his car and immediately called the D.A. while lighting a cigarette.

ॐ

Mitzi and her mother had finished talking when a key turned and the door opened without a knock. Wolfrum and Odilia entered. "Susan, you can leave now," Odilia said without warmth.

"I'm staying with Mitzi." Susan put her arm around Mitzi's shoulders. Mitzi looked surprised but pleased.

"I see," Wolfrum said quietly. His face was devoid of compassion or any other wholesome thing. "I was concerned about this happening." He glanced at Odilia. "Put them both in the dungeon."

"No retraining?" Odilia asked maliciously.

Susan winced and shouted at Odilia. "The ritual date hasn't even passed yet. How could you?"

Mitzi didn't speak, but her eyes were expressive as she again looked at her mother, thinking "retraining?"

Odilia had ceased dealing with either Susan or Mitzi and turned to leave.

Susan tried again. "You said you cared about my soul. Mitzi's soul."

The old woman spoke calmly. "When Wolfrum and I were young, someone left kittens on our porch." Odilia gave a broad smile. "We drowned them because they were out of order with no parents. God will take you and do with you as he sees fit."

Susan looked at the hooded man and shouted, "I believed in you, Wolfrum. I believed." A moan came from Susan's throat as she was emotionally torn to the core.

Wolfrum glanced at his sister. "Silence her," he said. "You know I hate mewling. Besides, after tomorrow night, it won't matter." He turned to leave the room.

Odilia swished her hand and Susan's lips were sealed. Susan's eyes desperately searched out Mitzi's.

Mitzi hadn't spoken, so the unholy brother and sister didn't know she'd broken the sealing spell Odilia put on her. Her blood was boiling.

"What then, brother?"

He turned back to Odilia "We're going to destroy the encampment of rescuers and get to her later." With a subtle motion of his wrist, the guards came forward and seized both Susan and Mitzi, who resisted futilely. "Put them in the same cell so mother and daughter can have a nice silent reunion before we put them to death." His laugh was mirthless and followed him down the hall.

Dieter found Bruno lifting weights in the torture chamber. "Wolfrum needs you," he croaked out in heavily accented English. "I also think there may be someone hiding in the garden."

The weights crashed to the stone floor, and Bruno flexed his huge hands. "Who? How many?"

"I don't know. I heard them."

Bruno stomped to Master Wolfrum's tower, seeking orders. "Master, Dieter sensed intruders in the garden."

Wolfrum's expression hardened, and his gaze set on the two men as if surprised they were still there. He clapped. "Secure the garden. Throw any interlopers into the dungeon. We are about to march. Hurry. Dieter, sound the alarm."

The bells in the tower began pealing after Dieter ran down the hall and leaped on a thick rope. Bruno blew a whistle in three shrill blasts and was joined by three rough-looking monks. He barked, "To the garden of the keep!" When one of them looked confused, he added in German, "*Der Garten des Bergfrieds!*" Swords and daggers were unsheathed under their monk's robes as the men tromped like rhinos into the overgrown garden of streams, trees, and bushes.

After a few moments, "Bruno!" called a swarthy creature who was neither dwarf nor human. "Garr is dead! And Pardo is barely breathing and cut bad."

Brother Bruno's face went dark, and he looked overhead for guidance. "Wolf-Ravens! Wolf-Ravens, lead us to our enemy."

As soon as she heard the voices and crashing sounds, Juniper struggled to climb the nearest tree. She hadn't climbed a tree at all in years, and this was her second today. She had barely reached the first low branches when a flock of ravens surrounded her, cawing wildly. She held the slender trunk of the tree with one hand and batted at the birds fruitlessly with the other. In seconds, strong hands grabbed both sides of her waist and pulled her back to the ground.

"*Werfe sie in das verlies!*" Bruno shouted. One monk started moving, then he said to the other two the same thing in English "Throw her in the dungeon!"

One of the guards put a meaty hand on Juniper's upper arm and held her there while their fellow soldiers removed the dead and dying dwarves. As the dead dwarf went by, the guard squeezed her arm so hard she cried out. This was getting worse by the minute, and to be truthful, she felt bad someone had died, even the enemy. War is so different in the abstract.

To get to the dungeon, Juniper was marched through the main castle area. Teeming with leather- and metal-clad monks lined up in rows, the scene reminded her of the terra cotta warriors of China. As she watched, row after row of Wolfrum's men marched out the front castle gate, presumably to attack the Hercynian Garden.

She looked up and saw a white-faced specter in his tower, who could only be Wolfrum. He watched his men leave with a sick twist of his thin lips she supposed was his smile. She hung her head in frustration and despair. Powerless against such brute force, she hoped Valerie wouldn't be drawn into this.

As she was being walked down the corridor, one soldier monk said to the other, "Put her in chains?"

The other monk sneered. "No, she's just a woman."

While glad she got the English speakers, they were clearly misogynistic assholes.

Apparently eager to get back to the action, her captors opened a heavy wooden cell door and literally threw her in the cell.

With shock and gladness, she saw Mitzi and her mother. The metal key turned in the lock and secured the door against escape.

Mitzi and Susan huddled together for warmth. When the cell door was suddenly thrown open, Juniper and Mitzi said each other's names in unison. Words flooded out from both women as they hugged.

"Oh my God!"

"Are you okay?"

"Where's Panda? What's happening?"

"Did you know I was kidnapped? It was that awful woman from grad school!"

"How did you get here?"

Juniper realized Susan was silent. "Are you okay?"

"She can't speak," Mitzi said. "It's this thing that both Wolfrum and his sister, Odilia, can do. They wave their hand, and your lips are literally sealed." She looked thoughtful, "Only I was able to undo mine." She turned to her mother. "It might just wear off, Mom."

Susan looked pissed.

Juniper suddenly remembered. "Do you know who your father is?"

Mitzi nodded. "Allegedly. This whole thing is so surreal."

"Do you think—" Juniper started to say.

They heard the jangle of keys and quieted. Soon they heard a whisper. "Mitzi? Are you in here?"

Thinking it might be a trick, Juniper said, "Who wants to know?"

"Juniper?" the voice on the other side of the door said.

Juniper looked at Mitzi and mouthed, "Oh my God," then quietly said aloud, "Yes, who is this?"

"Lily. I've come to save you." A key turned in the lock, and the heavy door swung open. "Hurry, I think we need to go save Panda and Heloisa now," she said, giggling.

❧

CHAPTER EIGHT

MERRYVILLE

After the Elves were fed, Valerie tried Juniper's cell phone again to no avail. The house phone rang while she was staring at it, and this time it was Babs. "Panda?"

"No, Valerie Gooden. I'm house sitting."

"Oh, I know you. When does she get home?" Babs sounded panicky.

"Hopefully, soon. Are you okay?"

"It's my dad. He's not breathing right."

"Give me your address. I'm a nurse. I'll be right over. Give me a minute to find Mitzi's car keys."

❧

Potts hit end on his cell phone harder than he needed in order to disconnect after talking to Debra, his D.A. It hadn't gone well.

"Potts, have you been drinking?"

"I tell ya, she's 'Cuckoo for Coco Puffs' crazy, having a tea party for dolls. Can't we arrest her again for trespassing?"

"I wouldn't touch that with a ten-foot pole. Stephanovsky would come up with something showing permission, then cry harassment."

"Look, my gut tells me there's a lot more to this. I need a warrant to get into that backyard. It looked like graves."

"We've charged her for obstruction of an investigation, if there's even been a crime. Call me back when you have something I can use."

Potts lit another cigarette, thinking about how he was going to get into that backyard when he saw Valerie leave the Fowler house and jump into a car. This might be the break he was looking for.

After Valerie left, Potts called a buddy of his who worked for Gary Smithers' office. "Let Councilman Smithers know I'm at the, ah, scene of the crime and need to go in. He'll know what I mean."

"What do you want him to do?"

"One phone call to a friendly judge and we can have a CSI team crawling all over the yard. Might be a good backdrop to a press conference. Just saying."

"I'll pass that along, Detective."

I entered a room that seemed to be there for the sole purpose of bathing. It smelled faintly of lavender. My steps echoed in the tiled chamber. Suddenly, Heloisa appeared in front of me.

"Panda, you make noise like an elephant," she said. "I could have killed you."

"Well, thanks for not killing me."

She looked worried. "I went up to the room where they were keeping Mitzi, and she's gone."

"Admit it, you have no idea where Mitzi is, do you?" Where was this boldness coming from?

The look I got back shriveled me. "I was just waiting for you. She has to be in the prison. Now follow me and try to walk like a dancer."

I made a face at her when she turned around, but I did try to be quieter as we crept down some stairs.

She dowsed our light. "Someone's coming."

Soon, a light came up from the darkness. It illuminated Lily's beautiful face. "Panda?" I heard from somewhere behind her. "Mitzi?" I exclaimed, beyond happy. She rushed up and held me tight.

Breathlessly, I said, "We need to get Juniper, she's—"

"Present," Juniper said, moving into the light.

"And my mom is here, too," Mitzi said.

I was stunned. "What?"

"Later," Mitzi said.

"All right, let's go." Heloisa was all business again.

Heloisa let Lily, who was far more familiar with the castle, lead. Since most of the men had marched off to deal with their fellow magical creatures, the guards were few and far between. Heloisa and I dealt knockout blows as we encountered them, and the others kept Lily out of sight. Having Mitzi with me as well as the pendant around my neck made me feel I could tackle anything. Even Heloisa gave me a high five.

Lily deposited us outside, near the scene of our recent battle. "Be careful," she whispered to Heloisa, kissing her on the ear before scampering back to her duties.

"I remember her from the cleansing," Mitzi said. "I think she winked at me."

"Lily is able to hear most thoughts," Heloisa said. "It's what keeps her safe. No time for chat now, let's go."

The boat was crowded with Heloisa, Susan, Juniper, Mitzi, and me. It dipped so low, the water came dangerously close to flooding into it. We paddled with our hands and soon made it back to the tunnel. This time, we ran ahead while Heloisa worked to close up the tunnel end. At the base of the ladder was the first time I felt safe to speak. "Susan, how did you get here?" The last time I heard, she was living in Stockton, California. Susan said nothing but looked a tad hostile.

She kept trying to speak, but couldn't. Frankly, I kind of liked it.

Juniper, always fascinated by magic, said, "Apparently Madame Dresser flicked her wrist and made her shut up."

"Long story," Mitzi said, as she petted Susan's hair. "Mom's been holding back a bit." She and Juniper couldn't help but laugh at that.

Heloisa joined us. "Climb. No time to waste."

We climbed. When I lifted the trap on the top, I saw no wagon, only open forest. You could see ruts in the mud where the big wooden wheels had been, as well as ashes from the cold campfire.

Our guardian looked into the distance as if she could see through the trees. "The tent camp is going to be attacked. We must warn them, if it's not too late already."

"Don't you have communication devices?" I asked

"There's no cell reception here, and magic is severely limited."

Heloisa gave a shrill whistle, and soon her unicorn/horse came running. She mounted her steed with a flourish and said, "Wait here."

I put my hand on her saddle. "Heloisa, I want to help. You saved me."

"Yes, we all do," Juniper said, stepping forward.

Mitzi seemed fine to wait. "I'm good."

The guardian surveyed us and said, "No offense, but I can get more done without worrying about you." And to me she said, "Stay put and take care of the girls."

I nodded, feeling important at being put in charge. We huddled together against the cold. Even though Susan wasn't wild about my relationship with Mitzi, I glued myself to my wife and stroked her hair, cooing away the dark experiences she must have endured. Susan leaned in, too, not being dressed for the weather. Juniper went to work covering the trap door.

"I have the strangest tingling in my shoulders," Mitzi said, and broke away from me. "It kind of hurts." I moved to rub them and noticed with alarm she had nodules which grew before my eyes. Susan looked like her eyes were going to pop out of her head, and she was making noises we couldn't understand. Juniper came over to see as wings started to break through Mitzi's skin.

"Oh my God!" I cried. "You have wings!"

Mitzi turned her head to the left and to the right, trying to see them herself. She took a few test flaps and laughed. "I can control them."

Until now, the whole your-wife's-a-half-griffin thing was just part of a tale. Now?

"Can you fly?" Juniper asked, entranced. My friend was so comfortable with all of this.

"I don't know," Mitzi said. She really looked quite cute, like an angel, but the wings didn't look like they could hold her weight.

"Try," Juniper said.

"Juniper!" I said sternly. Truth be told, I was frightened.

"Well, wouldn't you want to fly if you could?" The art diva was smiling.

"I am kind of cold. Maybe this will warm me up." Mitzi took off running and flapping her muscled wings. She achieved a modest lift off the ground, then came down again.

"Mitzi?" I asked, in wonderment.

She laughed and ran and flapped her wings. She also flapped her arms like a big bird, and up she went.

"Ohohoho!"

"Don't go too high!" I called.

"Let me try to see what's going on. I'll be right back." If I could have fainted, now would have been the time. I saw my wife fly up to the top of the trees and hover there like some helicopter.

Juniper squealed. "This is marvelous!"

"What, doesn't your wife fly?" I said with a grin.

CAMP

Morning had broken and the camp inhabitants were packed up and ready to go. Ravens had been circling all night, and there could not be a brighter neon sign pointing to them for Wolfrum to see than that. The dwarves were getting surly.

"She put us here to be a decoy," a heavily muscled warrior said, pacing the edge of the camp.

"There's nothing wrong with that, Chuk," his buddy, Groh, said. "That's how they got in the castle."

"If they got in the castle. For all we know, they could be dead right now."

The elves sat on their horses, noses and ears twitching.

"They're coming."

Chuk climbed on his sturdy steed. "Heloisa or no Heloisa, I'm ready."

"Stand fast," Ernst, second in command shouted, for there was no more reason for stealth.

From the trees surrounding the clearing, monk warriors poured out of the darkness with weapons raised. They chanted gutturally:

"Wolves are always followed by ravens!"

"Scavenging for the kill!"

"Eat fast, ravening wolf!"

"Ravens follow five and twenty!"

"Cleansing the world of unworthy prey!"

"Taking out the weak!"

"Consuming the meek!"

"Wolf-Raven cycles this world to the next!"

The monks outnumbered them ten to one. The morning air was crisp, and Ernst opened his mouth to issue an order. Suddenly, Heloisa appeared, her horse in a sweat. She moved right in front of her motley group and breathed heavily. "Mission accomplished," she said to her fellow guardians. "This is for Ehren's son. Let's go!"

Wolfrum's men should have studied British history in the early days of the colonies, or that of the American side in the Vietnam War. They thought their cause was so righteous no one could harm them. They thought their numbers and frightening visage were enough to win the day. Fortunately for those from the Hercynian Garden, they were wrong.

Elves popped up from the treetops and, with their excellent marksmanship, took out most of the first two rows of horsemen. Others tripped on booby traps between the trees leading to the rebel encampment. Heloisa's group hadn't been idle while waiting.

Wolfrum's men got in their licks, too. The ravens did much of that work, attacking the tree elves. Suddenly, a sight none had seen in a unicorn's age came before their eyes. The woman from America, who should have been in the dungeon back at the castle, literally flew over the skirmish, shouting, "This one's for my half-brother I never got to know." Then she said to the ravens, "You're all eagles now!"

The fighting paused as all looked up in disbelief. Mitzi surprised herself and didn't know where the words had come from, only that her blood boiled, and her fighting spirit came to the fore. "You've already lost, you freaky whackjobs! For I am free and doing magic in your world." With that, she flew away and most of the ravens followed.

Without Wolfrum to explain what that meant, his warriors fled. The elves, dwarves, and other magical creatures were emboldened and chased the Wolf-Ravens from the clearing.

"Enough. They will be talking about this for a hundred years," Heloisa said. She was blood-spattered and muddy but looked triumphant.

"As will we," Chuk said and bowed. "You are my leader." The prevailing Garden folk gave a cheer and sheathed their weapons.

Heloisa raised her arm to get their attention. "Warriors . . . to the Garden!"

They left the scene, with only a few serious injuries, and headed back to the Hercynian Garden. Heloisa went to collect her rescues, although she now knew at least one of them, Mitzi, had joined the ranks of the guardians.

ℭℴ

MERRYVILLE

Councilman Gary Smither's number two man, Brad, met with the councilman behind closed doors and filled him in on the conversation he'd just had with Detective Potts. "He says there's not enough for a warrant on his own, unless you want to make a call."

"What does he have?" Smithers said. He sat in front of a poster that read: *Bringing Merryville Back to its Old-Fashioned Family Values.*

"Well first, your cousin Gail—"

"The neighbor, Brad. Call her the neighbor. Her last name isn't Smithers. Let's make sure any reference to my name doesn't come from us."

"Okay, the neighbor called Detective Potts. He went to the Fowler house because Juniper Gooden's wife was there."

"Very suspicious, but that's not enough. And Brad, call them 'domestic partners.' "

"But the Supreme Court—"

"Our Supreme Court made a mistake, one that will be corrected eventually." He squeezed a rubber stress reliever compulsively. "In the meantime, this Juniper Gooden has brought chaos and shoved her 'lifestyle' down my district's throats. Did you see that GBLT exhibit?" His face was getting red.

"Um, that's LGBTQ," Brad said.

"LGBT, GBLT, please! Give me a BLT! I don't care what these people call themselves. They're disruptive. They're hijacking this community, and that fiasco at the museum was just the latest proof of it. I know there's something going on. Gooden is in the middle of it, and I want to know what it is. Now!"

Gary walked to the window and looked out. Below his office, on the sidewalk, citizens marching all day long carried signs that read "Save the cats!" and "Homeless Lives Matter." He shooed away a blackbird that had been camping on the sill with its friends.

"They've been there since that Floodlight exhibit at the museum." He returned to his desk, sat in his chair, and leaned back.

"Who? The birds or the protesters?" Brad's attempt at humor fell on deaf ears.

"If only Dick Mortimer was still in charge at the museum. It was the crown jewel of my district before that lesbian took over. They used to show such nice art, very classic."

He sat back in his chair, made a steeple with his fingers, and tapped his lips.

Brad hated to see his boss so upset. "He did say the backyard was dug up."

Without looking up, Gary said, "What if an anonymous call came in, saying they saw Panda Fowler and Juniper Gooden digging in the backyard before leaving the country?"

"Boss, no one has—ooh, okay."

"Get me Judge Reed, the mayor's brother. He needs to know about this. Detective Potts needs a warrant."

The light increased in the councilman's chambers as the rest of the ravens flew away.

Elsa and Ekk took full advantage of being alone and off duty and lay with Brutus on the couch sleeping. Their bellies were full, and for once, they had a break in the action. Brutus had told them a few things, and they recharged their batteries, waiting for contact from the Hercynian Garden.

Potts held his cell phone to his ear, and as he looked through the window, he saw the cat sleeping with the dolls. "Looks like she brought in garden gnomes from the outside," he said to Debra, the ADA. "That's kind of a tie-in with the backyard, which, like I said, has been recently dug up. God, they're lifelike."

"Still not enough," Debra said and hung up without further conversation. He could tell he was getting on her last nerve.

ᔕ

HERCYNIAN GARDEN

Heloisa, Mitzi, Juniper, Susan, and I arrived back at the castle after the triumphant cadre of guardians. Word had already spread of the magnificent rescue and rout of the evil Wolf-Ravens.

Ehren himself was in the courtyard with the magical folk under his protection, and he wordlessly embraced Mitzi with tears running down his face. They spoke privately and he shooed us off to get our things. Time was passing quickly, and there was still much to do. Ehren had his healers working on Susan, who had sheepishly entered his presence. He cracked a joke that perhaps he should leave her that way. I sensed those two had some talking to do later. The big news was Valerie didn't have to come here. Hercynian Garden archivists said the ritual could take place in Merryville, but they warned it wasn't ideal.

So much had changed. Heloisa brought a raven back on her shoulder and met with Ehren and his council. With the change of dynamics, Mitzi getting her wings and all, there was a chance for a new treaty with the ravens, who had cast their lot with Wolfrum eons ago. The compound was buzzing with possibilities.

I kept my hands on Mitzi, first, because I missed her, and second, because I didn't want her flying off. It's one thing to have a wife with wings; I didn't want to lose her again. Fortunately, her wings had retracted after the danger passed and were almost undetectable. We gathered our things and entered the throne room, ready to leave for the "real world" of our lives back in Merryville.

"What I don't understand is this," I said to Ehren, my father-in-law—still getting used to that. "Why Mitzi, me, and our two American friends, Valerie and Juniper?"

"I was wondering that myself," Juniper said, fully resplendent after a quick shower.

"You don't know?" Ehren exchanged a look with his chief advisor.

"Know what?"

A scribe-looking fellow stepped forward, an elf with a beard tossed over his shoulder. "Sun dogs appear as a rainbow around the true sun. It's also called a solar halo. According to Hercynian Garden legend, the true sun is truth and peace represented by a raven, but that is hunted from time to time by the dogs of good and evil. Our worlds achieve balance for a time, but that balance can be disrupted by this heavenly phenomenon and greatly shape the way the next millennia will be. The use of the four elements to call this power to the Hercynian Garden is so old its roots are lost in the mists of time. We need a descendant from our world and a descendant of the Wolf-Ravens. We also need the love that those bonded to them generate. It would have been Mitzi's brother, Ulf, but he was killed, and another, also dead. Now we need the four of you."

"We're part of the magic ritual, too?" Juniper looked thrilled.

"But that doesn't answer Juniper's question of why. Why the four of us?" I asked. "I can see Mitzi is your daughter, but who is Wolfrum's daughter?"

"I think it kind of does answer the question for me." Juniper was excited. "Valerie's mother told her a story when she was a child about their ancestors being warriors. Valerie and I met when I was doing a retrospective with indigenous people in Colorado on the reservation. She's Native American."

"Wolfrum's child can be any descendant, however distant," Ehren said. "It's probably magical that the four of you became friends. The wolf people, who were good, many years ago came to what is now known as the United States. Valerie must be a descendent of one of them. The need to have spouses is the balance. Each soul has two parts, you and your wives complete each other. Time is of the essence, however, and the risk of delay is great."

With another hug or two and my promise to "take care of his girl," we took our bags and loaded up the Touareg.

The ride back to the airport was quick, and the driver couldn't speak to us because Elsa wasn't with him and he apparently only spoke

German. He handed us our tickets and left us standing with our bags. As soon as we got cell service, Juniper left a message for her wolf woman, letting her know we were on our way. To say our spirits were high is an understatement.

"Hey. Only you got First Class," I said to Juniper.

"I didn't make the reservations, love. See you in Merryville." She waved her book at us and made her way to the line for First Class.

"I don't care. I've got you." Mitzi hugged my arm and made kissy noises.

I melted a bit. A woman behind me made a face. Ah, reality.

We had more to look forward to when we returned home, but for now, our reunion was sweet and we had many hours in steerage to catch up.

"Sure beats the dungeon," she added.

"I flew Business Class out here," I said, smirking.

She gave me a look. "It was miserable without you, truly."

"Poor baby. Maybe *I* should fly us home."

"Yeah, Air Mitzi!" We laughed and got in the long, twisty line.

Back at Merryville Police Station, the front desk took a telephone call from a man who said, "I need to remain anonymous because I'm scared. I've seen strange goings on in the backyard of that woman on Thistle Drive. Is there a Detective Potts there?"

"He's out in the field. Can I take a message?"

"Yes, tell him to dig under the old oak tree in the backyard. That's where you'll find Mitzi Fowler."

The person taking the call rushed over to the desk sergeant. "What do you make of this?" He relayed the sensational tip.

"It's been in the news. Could be a crackpot, but call Potts and make a printout of the call."

By four in the afternoon, Potts had his warrant based on the anonymous tip, and a CSI team descended on the Fowler residence. Homeland Security confirmed someone used Mitzi Fowler's passport, but they couldn't be sure if it was her. All video from the airport showed a heavily shrouded woman being walked through the airport by another, older woman. Something very fishy about the whole thing. Either she was kidnapped or maybe she didn't leave Merryville at all.

The police chief and Councilman Smithers were on hand for a press conference directly in front of the house.

Valerie was at Babs's house, and had checked over Henry, Babs's father. He had emphysema and was having trouble with his oxygen. Once that crisis had passed, she was able to suggest a good hospice for him so that Babs wouldn't have to keep paying a nurse while she worked. In the background, the local news blared. Henry had the TV on twenty-four-seven.

"Now we're going to a neighborhood in Merryville where we're dealing with a real-life mystery." The camera zoomed in on a young woman with too blonde hair, who stood in the front yard of Mitzi and Panda's house. "This is Wendy from Channel Five. In a few moments, we'll be hearing from the Merryville police chief about the stunning turn of events in this quiet neighborhood."

"That's Panda's house!" Babs exclaimed.

Valerie reached for her cell phone and called her attorney. She knew from a text message that Juniper was still in the air and wouldn't be landing for another couple hours. She opened her mouth to speak, but before she could say anything, she heard Alex say, "On it. If you hear from Juniper have her call me." Click. Wow. Alex was good.

Babs and Valerie sat down side by side on the couch. Babs turned up the volume with the remote.

"Can you tape it, too?"

Babs's dad, Henry, turned up his hearing aid. "What's going on?"

Babs pressed Record. "Done." Then she said to her dad, "My boss is in the news." She looked excited. "Valerie, shall I get chips?"

Henry said too loudly, "What for?"

"They think she murdered somebody."

Valerie winced at hearing that word and prayed Alexandra Stephanovsky could set all this right.

"Oh." Henry pulled up his blanket and seemed ready to go back to sleep.

Valerie just looked at Babs. This wasn't a party, but she couldn't blame her for trying to make it one. Babs's life was pretty much on hold while she took care of her dad and worked. This was a break in the routine. "You never want to see a news van parked in front of your house or that of anyone you love."

"There's that detective that came to ask me questions." Babs squealed as Detective Potts filed onto a makeshift dais with the captain. Councilman Smithers was standing behind them, along with several other people.

The sun was shining, a typical Southern California day, and neighbors stood outside the parameter. Over the shoulder of the newscaster, the front picture window of Panda and Mitzi's house was front and center. You could see Brutus glaring out at everyone. The entire event had a circus-like quality to it. Valerie silently wondered where Ekk and Elsa were.

CHAPTER NINE

SCHWARZVALD CASTLE, GERMANY

Wolfrum didn't waste time licking his wounds. Back at the castle, he called his followers into the courtyard area. "All true believers, there is only one Sun. We have heard that the enemy will try to recreate the ritual of the dog sun in the United States of America, home to our brothers under another name. They are doing this with *women*." The crowd burst into angry muttering.

"Silence!" The talk ceased almost immediately. "Already forces are gathering to see this mockery of a dog sun ritual doesn't occur. None of this could have happened without someone in this very castle helping these inept creatures." More muttering as the monks looked in their midst as if one would be visible. Bruno looked ready to tear that someone apart, limb by limb.

"We'll find the traitors in our midst, and by noon tomorrow, our gallows will be casting their shadows across this very yard. All is going in accordance with our ancient scripture. Let us howl in the name of the true Sun!"

The Wolf-Ravens howled and began their chant.

Ekk and Elsa hadn't been idle. As soon as they awoke, they checked in with their handlers from the Hercynian Garden to find out their next task. The quick holograms were more like text messages, but did the job in an emergency. Thankfully, they were gone from the Fowler house before the hordes of police, news crews, and curious onlookers arrived. Their mission now was to secure fighters for the showdown to come, for Ehren knew that Wolfrum wouldn't let the sun dog ritual proceed without interference. Too much was at stake.

A familiar, late-model Lincoln pulled to the curb, and they hopped in the back. "Thanks, Alex." The attractive woman merely nodded in the rearview mirror. Fiona Castlebaum turned around to the elven couple in the backseat. "Buckle up, kiddies. We've got some work to do."

~

Dick Mortimer was at home, getting ready for the "Alive at Five" forecast. His house was on the bluff, within walking distance of the museum. The house had been in his wife's family for years, and it was exquisitely furnished. The security system was flawless, guarding priceless art of the old craftsmen that hung on the walls. He already had his pajamas, robe, and slippers on, a Sunday night ritual. Blanca, his wife's white, French bulldog, snuffled up to him on his expensive leather couch, searching for treats.

He looked to see if wifey was watching and carefully moved the animal to the floor.

"Dick," his wife called from the kitchen, "did you forget to feed Blanca again?" Her voice often made him jump.

"No, dear." He glared at the dog. "Besides, she could stand to lose a few pounds."

Beatrice Vanderhooven-Mortimer appeared in the doorway, all three-hundred-fifty pounds of her. "Is there a hidden message in there?"

He stood. "No, precious, I was talking about the dog. Can you bring a blanket for Blanca?"

Bea tossed a quilt at him. "What are you going to watch?" She settled in on the couch, which groaned under her weight.

Dick made a face. "There's a press conference about that woman who kidnapped her lesbian partner. Good friend of Juniper Gooden." He couldn't help but smile.

"That Gooden? Ha! I'll bet you can't wait."

"It's not gloating. It's about the integrity of the museum."

"Sure it is."

Beatrice sat on the white, Sunpan Modern Bughatti grain-leather sofa with her chocolate ice cream. With her free hand, she started playing with his hair. Dick looked like he would like to be anywhere else on the planet but there. Blanca farted in his general direction.

Mayor Reed was in the only five-star restaurant in Merryville and was joining his entourage in the bar for pre-dinner drinks. A well-groomed young man with his hair shaved up one side, drying a cut crystal tumbler, looked up when the heavy hitter entered. The mayor flashed his five-thousand-watt smile and said, "Sir, would you be kind enough to put the station on Channel Five?"

"Of course, Mayor Reed. What can I get you to drink?" The TV screen soon showed the Fowler's house on Thistle Drive.

He and his companions ordered single malt Scotch, for this was a memorable occasion.

Mitzi, Juniper and Panda were due to land in a couple of hours. Valerie's lawyer needed that time to set up a press conference of her own.

After dropping Fiona and the elves at Panda's tax office, Alex raced to the airport, her Lincoln chewing up asphalt going north up the I-405 to LAX. She was thinking that Merryville might turn international when traffic ahead of her started bunching up. She applied the brakes, but the luxury vehicle only seemed to go faster. As if in a dream, she pumped the brakes but nothing happened. The cluster of stopped cars was rapidly approaching.

Snapped into that millisecond-by-millisecond attention that such a situation causes, Alex put the car in neutral and turned to the left to the shoulder of the freeway. She hoped she didn't take anyone with her in what was sure to be one hell of an accident.

Our Lufthansa Flight Number 456 touched down on the tarmac after almost twelve hours in the air from Frankfurt. Mitzi and I were holding hands, like we do every time we take off or land. In fact, when I have to fly alone, I put my hand over my heart and say in my mind, "I'm holding your hand in my heart." We had slept, wept, traded stories, and were happy to be alive and together. We waited in the crowded aisle to deplane, unaware of the drama unfolding on our front lawn at home.

"Anything more? The press conference is about to start." Gary Smithers needed just one more thing to add to the announcement about to be made.

The old CSI technician dusted off his hands and snapped his plastic case shut. "Sorry, got some dog bones buried about a year or two ago."

Smithers looked absolutely intense. "Are you sure they're dog bones?"

The technician laughed. "They sure look like it. I'm not a forensic anthropologist, but—"

"But it could be human, right?"

"Well, anything's possible." He picked up his case.

"Thanks." Smithers went to Detective Potts and said, "We got human bones."

After a fist pump, Potts straightened his tie and joined the police commander on the makeshift stage.

Cameras flashed. A uniformed police commander with bars on his collar stepped to the mic. "Thank you, members of the press, ladies, and gentlemen. We've called this press conference to give you, the public, the latest on the investigation."

In the back row, Councilman Smithers stood serious faced, every bit the public servant. He could see his cousin, who had reported the situation, smiling from the crowd.

The commander said, "Here is what we know. Approximately one week ago, the owner of this home, Mitzi Fowler, went missing. Her wife, Panda Fowler, a local tax preparer, fled the country with Juniper Gooden, the embattled curator of the Merryville Museum. Interpol has been notified."

The crowd murmured loudly, and young reporters keyed the story into their hand-held devices. Philip, vegetarian reporter for the *Bee* raised his hand. "How could that be, when—"

"We'll be taking questions in a minute. The Merryville PD was notified of suspicious activity by a concerned neighbor, and this was verified by veteran detective Charles Potts, who also noticed digging in the backyard."

Potts nodded when the commander mentioned his name, like an old cowboy would tip his hat.

The commander went on. "I'm going to turn this over to Detective Potts, who will bring us up-to-date on the results of the backyard search."

Potts took one step up to the microphone and cleared his throat. "At one-fifty-seven this afternoon, a CSI team from the department did a grid search in the backyard of this property. Several bones have been found, which have yet to be positively identified. They do appear to be human."

Now the murmurs turned to gasps. Flash photography lit up the scene, and several stringers ran to their cars to beat the others in writing up the story. Inside and unimpressed, Brutus stretched out his yoga leg and gave the audience a clear view of his asshole, which he licked with gusto.

"How was first class?" Mitzi asked Juniper.

"I mostly slept, but fabulous. I won't lie."

We made it to the curb, but there was no one to pick us up. Not knowing who was supposed to, we decided to take care of ourselves and Mitzi called Uber. Once we got on the freeway, I said, "Sure glad we're not on the other side. The traffic's completely stopped." Emergency vehicles were present with lights flashing. There must have been a terrible accident.

"I want to go home first, do you mind?" Knowing she must be missing Valerie we readily agreed.

"Oh my God! I can't believe this is happening," Valerie said. "Don't the police know they're on their way back?"

Babs was halfway to the living room from the kitchen with more snacks. "Call them."

Valerie was still trying to process all that was happening. "The police?"

Suddenly, Henry barked out a laugh and kept it up, pointing at the screen.

Not seeing anything funny, Valerie turned to the old man. "What?"

"That cat is lickin' hisself."

They looked again, and it was pretty hilarious. Everyone was so focused on the information being given, it took a slightly off-center perspective to see the cat seemingly sitting on the speaker's shoulder and yes, "lickin' hisself" where the sun don't shine. Even Valerie had to laugh.

The phone rang and Valerie picked it up on the first ring. "Juniper?"

"Yes, baby."

"Are you really here? I mean, on American soil?"

"Yes, my love, we're on our way home."

"Did Alex get you?"

"Who? Oh, your defense attorney? No, we Ubered it. I'm so glad you're not in the hoosegow."

"Oh, I thought she, oh, never mind. I'm going to our house right now. Tell Panda and Mitzi—just tell them to go home as soon as they can. There's a press conference being held on their lawn."

After a beat, Juniper said, "I don't think anything could surprise me anymore."

ॐ

Valerie was on the front lawn when the Uber cab dropped Juniper off. Panda and Mitzi gave her a quick hug and went on to their house. Once inside, Juniper and Valerie hugged and hugged, not wanting to ever be apart again. Juniper looked into her eyes. "So, Walter died?" Walter was the man on hospice that Valerie stayed with to the end.

Valerie loved that Juniper was thinking of her and what she'd been through, when obviously she had traveled across the world and been through God knows what.

"Yes. His faithful poodle was right there with him 'til the last."

"What happened to the dog?"

"Walter's niece took him." She held Juniper, who looked thin, at arm's length. "Are you really here? I've been so worried."

"There's so much to tell, but right now we have to get ready for the ritual tonight. Let me fill you in on what I know."

"I have things to tell you, too, but first come look at the TV."

"Alive at Five!" The station's theme music played as the talking head cut back to the press conference.

Those truly paying attention would have seen Councilman Smithers being signaled by his frantic aide to leave the stage. Gary Smithers appeared angry at being torn from the limelight, then, after some whispering, couldn't seem to depart fast enough. The police commander looked over his shoulder then back at Potts and shrugged. "We'll take your questions now."

The place went crazy. Reporters from radio, TV, and online media jockeyed to be heard.

"Is it true that there were sixteen bodies found in the backyard?" That was from the yellowest of tabloids, the *LA Cryer*.

"No. Next question."

"Why isn't Valerie Gooden in custody now?"

"She's currently out on bail. Next."

"Is Interpol involved?"

"We're not prepared to comment, only that wheels are in motion. There may be an international connection in this case. Next."

"Isn't it true that to have a murder you need murder victims?" This from Phillip at the *Merryville Bee*.

"Sometimes it takes awhile to find the actual bodies. In this case, which I remind you is an ongoing investigation, things are developing quickly. Bones have been found."

"'Cause I got a call from someone who tells me that Mitzi Fowler is alive." Phillip said it calmly, while waggling his cellphone. It was a calling out.

Detective Potts stepped forward to the mic. The commander put up his hand to hold him back and spoke directly to the reporter, "Young man, if you have information relevant to this situation, you need to speak directly to the detective in charge, Detective Potts."

Potts elbowed his way to the microphone. "Phillip, in a case like this, there are always psychics, crackpots, and others who turn up and want to inject themselves into the investigation. Why I remember . . ."

As he went on, the majority of the press were turning around and gasping as an Uber cab pulled up and Mitzi and Panda Fowler stepped out. Pandemonium ensued.

The police commander barked, "No more questions!" Then he said to a TV cameraman, "Turn those damn things off."

When we arrived, the crowd in front of our house went wild and several things happened at once. The Uber driver looked wide-eyed as he put bags on the street and quickly sped off. I faced cameras flashing in my eyes and drew Mitzi up next to me. People were shouting questions now.

"Where have you been?"

"Why didn't you call the police and tell them you were all right?"

"Where is Juniper Gooden?"

There were too many questions to answer. Mary and Scott, our next-door neighbors, came forward. They made a protective flank on both sides of us and led us to our front door. "Leave them alone," and "Get off the lawn," I heard them say.

"What the hell?" Mitzi said as the door closed behind us. Mary stayed for a few minutes and filled us in on the recent happenings in the hood, then she left to help disperse the crowd.

Reporters ran to their cars. The commander looked at Potts coldly. "My office, fifteen minutes." And then he left.

TV cameras were being stowed in vans. Phillip clicked off his call to the newsroom. He had quite a scoop. Other than techies wrapping up cords, he and Potts were the only two left on the lawn, which was littered with coffee cups and wires leading to microphones. Potts looked dazed, then he fixed his gaze on the young reporter. "If I find out you knew something and didn't come forward . . ." His tone was menacing.

Phillip was undaunted. "I only have one question left. Who was driving this train wreck? Give me an exclusive, and I'll make sure you don't take the fall in the public eye." He held out a card.

Potts said, "I've got your number," and trudged off. He sat in his old, unmarked Crown Victoria and smoked a cigarette.

∾

Mayor Reed, after watching these things unfold on TV, said brightly to his comrades, "Let's go get dessert." When asked about the stunning turn of events, he said, "Oh, I'm just glad our citizens are home safe. That's what matters." He wasn't called the Teflon Mayor for nothing.

∾

Dick Mortimer was livid. "How did the police screw this up so badly?"

"There there, Dickie, I'm sorry that your Juniper woman is not a serial killer." Beatrice, his loving wife, moved toward him.

Blanca crawled up in his lap as if to comfort him, too, because dogs are generally nicer than people, bad gas notwithstanding.

He was so mad he shoved Blanca, Bea's baby, to the shiny wood floor where she failed to land on all feet and struggled to get up. He gasped, knowing this was the one unforgivable sin.

"Dick! How dare you!" Red faced with anger, Beatrice picked up the pudgy animal and held him close. He thought how alike their faces were, animals and their owners and all that.

"Bea, I'm just upset," he said, but the fight continued into the night. Beatrice ended up with Blanca snoring softly beside her in the couple's Duxiana bed. Dick slept on the white, Sunpan Modern Bughatti, grain-leather sofa.

∾

Fiona, Ekk and Elsa were in the office of Fowler Tax Services. "It's not as big as I hoped," Fiona said, hands on hips.

"How much room do you need?" Elsa moved some of the chairs.

"She's right," Ekk said. "According to Ehren, we only need them to stand in the four spots. Then, whatever's going to happen, happens." He referred to his written notes, which magically had appeared from his cuffed sleeve.

"No, I don't think so. The parking lot is much better." The flamboyant woman walked out the front door and scanned the landscape. "Ekk, do you think we were followed?"

"Nothing on my radar. Why do you ask?"

Elsa said, "You know Wolfrum will do anything in his power to stop the ritual. It would be weird if no one was watching us."

Fiona put her cell to her ear and spoke to Siri. "Get me Alex."

"Calling Alexandria Stephanovsky on cell," came the obedient robotic voice.

To the elves, Fiona said, "She should have picked up the girls and been back by now." The phone went to voice mail immediately. She texted and got no response.

"I'll try Panda." Ekk took out his European model and punched in many numbers. "I need to make sure she and Mitzi are all set for this evening."

Elsa suddenly froze, then she climbed up a chair and scrambled onto the file cabinets to turn on the TV that was mounted on the wall in Panda's office.

Fiona watched it happen so fast. "I would have helped you turn that on. What's up?"

"Something, intuition, listen." Elsa had a strange look on her face.

On Channel Five, an excited blond woman was reading news with an inset showing Panda and Mitzi's house and neighborhood.

"A stunning turn of events is reverberating through Merryville, and many are asking how it could have happened. Here is a scene from earlier today at the press conference."

A news clip showed police on a stage in front of Panda and Mitzi's house and then the arrival of the women by Uber car.

Fiona's slender hand went to her mouth. "They're back. Oh my God, that's not Alex dropping them off. I knew it was too quiet."

"Let me try to sense where she is," Elsa said. The diminutive elf, back on the floor, crossed her arms and lowered her head, eyes closed.

The scent of roses became strong in the room. She pictured Fiona's close friend, Alexandra, and drew upon that woman's love of her good friend to send a tendril of energy out to the universe.

Soon, she wasn't seeing the tax office. Her mind's eye envisioned sky and she said, "Airplanes flying up ahead. I can see them, then asphalt . . ." Images sped by. A scream ripped through her mind. Elsa saw a blinding crash, then blinking lights caught her attention. Alex's Lincoln was suddenly a twisted shape, with smoke billowing from the engine area. "Her car crashed!"

Fiona and Ekk gasped.

"I can see her. Alexandra is wearing a neck stabilizer and was or is being loaded into an ambulance, so at least she is, was, alive—for now." The shock snapped Elsa back to herself. She was white when she opened her eyes, leaving out the worst. "Hospital, she will be at a hospital."

"No!" Fiona screamed, and grabbed Elsa by both arms as if she could shake more information out of her. "What else did you see? What did you see?"

Ekk watched in rapt fascination. Elsa always gave off some of the feeling of well-being from the Hercynian Garden when performing her special skills, but it faded rapidly. This new information was awful.

"It was red and white."

"Which one, where?" Fiona's hair flew around her face wildly as she pinned Elsa with her eyes.

The diminutive seer still looked pale. "I, I don't know. She was being loaded into an ambulance."

"Easy, Fiona." Ekk moved protectively toward Elsa, who folded into him.

"She said she saw airplanes. I'll start with Cedars Sinai in L.A." Fiona walked to the other side of the office and punched numbers on her phone.

Ekk and Elsa were deep in conversation and didn't notice the front door open. Lulu, the Samoan security guard, walked in. Her face was triumphant as her strong arms reached out. "Gotcha!" She grabbed Ekk in her left hand and Elsa in her right. Their feet kicked in the air harmlessly.

Fiona lowered her phone, tears in her eyes, which quickly turned to fury. "Unhand those elves!"

"Hey! Fiona? Weren't you the lady at the art museum with dat big ting the other night?"

"Yes, now put those two down." Her tone brooked no disobedience.

Lulu carefully lowered the struggling couple, who moved close together again. Lulu took a deep breath and hooked her thumbs in her belt, adopting a belligerent stance: "Somebody better splain what going on."

Ekk spoke first. "I was sent here to watch over Panda. You almost caught me several times."

"Dat was you?" She looked off to the side and shook her head. "Knew I wasn't crazy." The big woman sat down, then said, "Where's Panda? I came to tell her somethin' important."

Fiona took charge. "She'll be here shortly. What's up?"

"Oh, shoot," the big woman said in a big sigh. "I don' worry 'bout sounding nuts no more," Lulu said, eyeing the elves. "The Brazilian boys been talking crazy, and it don' sound so good for Panda."

"What do you mean? What Brazilian boys?" Apparently Fiona hadn't noticed their presence in the strip mall.

Turning toward the window, Lulu simply said, "Look."

Fiona, Ekk, and Elsa had been so involved in their own conversation they'd failed to see the jiujitsu studio inhabitants had emptied into the parking lot. There were about thirty-five or forty buff-looking martial arts experts standing in formation. They wore what Mitzi referred to as "white pajamas" but were called "gis," which sounds like gee with a hard *g*. A young-looking, gi-clad man modeled a kick that was emulated down the line, and the visual was that of a rather lethal wave.

"Well, that's a fret," Fiona whispered.

"Isn't this how they practice?" Ekk asked.

"No," Lulu said.

"No," Elsa said simultaneously, her keenly tuned senses on full alert. "They've been enchanted by Wolfrum."

Lulu looked from one to another of the motley group.

"Turn off the TV. I can't reach it," Ekk said.

Fiona turned off the TV.

Then they heard it.

The atmosphere seemed to be compressed, and in the vacuum, the sound of the gi material flapping was scary. The martial arts fighters' expressions were blank, and they moved in unison.

Suddenly, a familiar chant started:

"Wolves are always followed by ravens!"

"Scavenging for the kill!"

"Eat fast, ravening wolf!"

"Ravens follow five and twenty!"

"Cleansing the world of unworthy prey!"

"Taking out the weak!"

"Consuming the meek!"

"Wolf-Raven cycles this world to the next!"

Lulu held the blinds aside, so they could better see the frightening gathering.

Looking closely at the wall of fists and feet moving toward the tax office, they could see the martial arts experts' eyes didn't look normal. "But how?" Fiona said.

"What is Wolfrum?" a very rattled Lulu said. She locked the door and lowered the blinds.

"You mean who," Fiona said absently.

Lulu looked shaken. "All I know is, it's not safe out there."

A chill went down Fiona's spine. "We have to warn the girls. They can't come here." She lifted her iPhone to her ear and had a quick conversation.

Ekk dropped the blinds, where he'd been on tiptoe peeking out. "But we need this space to do the ritual. We only have about an hour. Oh, this is bad indeed."

"I have an idea." Fiona punched in Juniper Gooden's number.

Wolfrum's reach was global. All it took was one person with evil in his heart to open the door to him. Wolfrum could then use dark magic to possess hearts, similar to how a hijacked drone computer is used to infect others.

Fiona hung up and asked, "Is there a back way out of here?"

Lulu said, "No," the same time as Ekk said, "Yes."

Lulu and Ekk exchanged a glance. The security guard had hardly been able to take her eyes off him.

Ekk scratched himself, remembering his uncomfortable two weeks living in the bushes. "While I was here, I made an elf hole. It's going to be tight," he said, looking back at Lulu.

"Let's go." Fiona urged them on.

"Oh, hell to the no, I'm not going down no elf hole!"

Elsa came running in from the back. "We better do something. They're attacking!"

The front window broke and became dark with bodies pushing forward in a surge.

"This way!" Ekk ducked under the desk.

"I hold them off as bes' I can," Lulu said. "You go!"

"No, I'll hold them off," Elsa said in her sweet voice.

More glass splintered on the floor. It was like a zombie attack. "Fiona lady, grab the little one or she be killed!"

Elsa had again put herself in a trance. The scent of flowers was overpowering. This time the fragrance was lavender. Fiona and Lulu couldn't help but look out the window as the beating on the building had stopped. The sight was surreal. Thousands of purple petals were falling from the sky. The jiujitsu attackers seemed confused and diverted from their assault.

"Hurry!" Elsa said, eyes closed, "I can't keep this up much longer." As she said this last word, she fainted. Lulu scooped her up, slipped her into the hole under the desk, and turned to Fiona. "Art lady, go!"

"Lulu, come with us."

"I'll be fine, miss."

"But we need you."

"This my beat, and I don' think I fit anyway." She gave Fiona a shove into the elf hole. Ekk nodded at her and followed the other women.

For those who had never traveled this way, the sensation was that of being in a luge, fast and somewhat disorienting. The trip ended abruptly, seconds later, as the trio landed in the bushes. "This is it?" Fiona asked Ekk.

He looked mildly indignant. "It served me for my purpose. Ehren said never use more magic in the human world than is necessary."

Although at a safe distance, they were still close enough to see the Brazilian boys rally and renew their attack on Fowler Tax Services. Fiona said a prayer for Lulu, then said, "Quickly, this way. I asked Juniper to come get us at the end of the block."

Not having to be told twice, Fiona, Ekk, and Elsa made their way, as silently, quickly, and carefully as they could, to the corner. Lulu had probably saved their lives. Elsa let them know that the enchanted warriors would be able to sense if there was a live being inside the building, and because of Lulu's incredible bravery in staying, they should make it out without being chased.

Juniper's Citroen was packed tight with herself, Valerie, Fiona, Ekk, and Elsa. "Where to?" Valerie asked nervously, seeing the battle going on in the strip mall parking lot.

"Take us to the museum." Fiona and Juniper shared a look and a secret smile.

"Not a great time to look at art, but okay." Valerie put the pedal to the metal and screeched up in front of the Merryville Museum. Mitzi's Miata pulled up a few seconds after. The place was locked up tight, but the security lights made it possible to see the green space between the buildings. Juniper walked to the scene of the great fiasco that got her fired for the "Floodlight!" exhibit.

Fiona walked up next to her and put her hand on her shoulder. "It's lovely at night, isn't it?"

"Yes, as long as some damn cherry picker doesn't rise up from the beach below." They shared a quick laugh before getting to work.

I waved at Fiona, having last seen her at the hotel in Germany. Elsa was in a trance already, with Ekk staring intently at the sky that, to me, looked like any other normal Merryville Spring night. He laid his hand on my arm. "Do you have any food with you?"

I searched my pockets and came up with a couple of Lara bars. "Don't want you two disappearing in the middle of the ritual." Ekk took one and gave one to Elsa, who accepted and smiled sweetly.

Fiona went back out to the parking lot and met several young men with a truck. I walked over to Juniper. "What's she doing?"

Before Juniper could answer I heard someone say, "Don't worry. Be ready to do your part." The commanding male voice came out of the darkness and sounded a great deal like Ehren.

"How is that possible?" I asked. "Is he here?" Mitzi and I strained our eyes into the dark.

"No, but the portal is thinning," Ekk answered quietly. "It leads directly to the Hercynian Garden. Shhh, Elsa needs to concentrate."

Fiona's men, all dressed in black, were well trained to sneak up on the unsuspecting and light it up like the brightest noon. Tonight, they silently unrolled a huge map with what looked like a compass upon it, as well as symbols. In the center was the image of a gigantic octopus.

"And what exactly is that?" I asked.

Rather than answer, Ekk moved forward and tugged gently at my left arm. "Panda, you stand on North. Mitzi, you're West. Valerie, South and Juniper, where's Juniper?"

"Over here." She'd been watching the scaffolding being set up and walked toward the elaborate ritual space. "Looks like a game. Remember Twister?"

Again, the creative artist in her was tickled.

"This is no game, I assure you," Ehren said. Not for the first time, I thought Mitzi would have been under a firm hand in her childhood had she been raised in the Hercynian Garden.

"I'm ready, Father." Mitzi took her place meekly.

With all four of us in place, the moment became denser, compressed. It felt to me like we had entered another two or three atmospheres of pressure. Along the edges of the designated space, I saw blurry images of Ehren and his advisors, but one area was still dark.

Mitzi screamed, "I feel it! Wolfrum's near!" Her shoulders sprouted nodules.

Ekk took control again as the whole place began to vibrate. "It's to be expected. We've opened a portal to the entire area of the Black Forest. Whatever you do, don't leave your spot. Scribe?"

The elf who had explained that we could do this ritual in Merryville cleared his throat. It was so strange that I could hear him clear his throat five thousand miles away. When he first started speaking, his voice sounded underwater, like some of those bad school films in Health class. It slowly became clear.

"The treaty between Wolf-Ravens and Hercynian Garden folk has its roots in the mists of time . . ."

Valerie and Juniper were listening raptly, but Mitzi looked wild-eyed. I couldn't see what she was seeing.

"Every fourth generation, at the time of the dog sun—"

"Wolf-Raven!" The voices broke through, loud and clear.

"Wolf-Raven!"

From the Hercynian Garden, Ehren's scribe spoke louder. "The dog sun is the sign for the change. In modern-day North America, the Native Americans looked to the rainbow."

The ground under my feet rumbled. Fiona's men spread out at the edges of the green space, facing outward. They were obviously there to protect us and were on high alert.

Off to the side, Elsa was as still as stone. I was worried about her. This whole thing seemed to drain her of energy.

Unexpectedly, Mitzi sprouted wings with a force that frightened me, and I almost ran to her. Seeing this, Ekk shouted, "Don't move, Panda!" Then he said to Mitzi "Stay on the ground. Stay on the ground.!" The brave elf ran around us, kind of like my childhood border collie used to do. What weird thoughts I was having. My old collie died twenty years ago.

Valerie and Juniper were amazing. Each held their place and lifted their arms to the sky, as if they'd practiced for this ritual. Valerie was morphing, too, looking darker and, well, Native American. When did she put beads in her hair? I looked up as the sky, for lack of a better term, opened. It was suddenly light and clear as day, and I saw what had been only described to me before. The sun was bright, like an orange ball, but to the left and right of it were arcs of light, like false suns.

The scribe went on. "We call upon great Mother Father God to shift our world into the light, and to stretch the rainbow of peace for all peoples."

My ghost collie ran up to my parents. What? Then I saw them reaching out to me in their hippie garb. "Mom? Daddy?"

"Panda, stay put." A sharp pain on my foot brought me back to the present. Ekk pinned me with his eyes and had poked his bejeweled dagger hilt into my instep through my sandals. "It's a trick. Stay focused," he said.

Back in my body, I noticed a number of cars had pulled up in front of the museum.

The Brazilian jiujitsu boys came streaming across the green space toward us. There must have been thirty of them, far too many for Fiona's men to handle. I stood in place, not sure what to do, with a strange wind blowing from nowhere and everywhere, watching what was surely to be a massacre.

"The false sun dogs the true sun. The rainbow brings together all peoples. The octopus . . ."

This made no sense to me. The arch on my foot still smarted where Ekk poked it. I became very interested in the scene before me and in the battle about to begin. Valerie and Juniper were perfect, smiling and still in their places, arms raised to the sun. Mitzi was scaring me. Seeing her in full wings was still a very new experience. She looked like she was getting the brunt of some very powerful force. It was now so bright, it looked like heaven had landed.

The first gi-clad enchanted warrior took a giant leap toward one of the black-dressed artists from Fiona's Floodlight project. I winced, expecting the skinny, bearded, hipster-looking dude to fold like cardboard. Imagine my surprise when he stood there slack, then lifted his right hand and effortlessly repelled his attacker, who sprawled on the grass and looked stunned. This scenario was repeated again and again as the skinny Eurotrash/hipster art crew used some kind of force field from their hands to meet violence with magic. Cool, very cool. I was encouraged, but this was not to be a slam dunk.

Since our side was outnumbered about three to one, with the jiujitsu folks being under the influence of Wolfrum, there was still some worry. Occasionally one of the men in Wolfrum's dark thrall would break through and Ekk would run up to them and stab at their shins with his stinging dagger, with little effect. I gasped and had to fight the urge to run to him as he was propelled ten feet away into the bushes by a well-placed martial arts kick. Elsa's concentration wavered, and I saw things turning and not in a good way.

The scribe droned on. "The time has now come to reclaim the peace and reverse the spell of evil that has gripped this world."

Reclaim? I guess I had never thought to ask—we'd been pretty busy— but I thought we, the good side, had been in charge. Apparently not. The sun darkened, and ravens poured in from all sides, blotting out the light. The chant of the monks five thousand miles away was joined by the jiujitsu fighters:

"Wolves are always followed by ravens!"

"Scavenging for the kill!"

"Eat fast, ravening wolf!"

"Ravens follow five and twenty!"

"Cleansing the world of unworthy prey!"

"Taking out the weak!"

"Consuming the meek!"

"Wolf-Raven cycles this world to the next!"

This was bad. I could no longer hear the voice of the scribe, and darkness continued to obscure the sun. The ground shook and the wind lessened. That's when my wife took flight. Her head seemed more elongated and her nose like a beak. Oh my God! She reared back her head and let out a war cry like I, or for sure anyone in Merryville, had never heard. "Mitzi?" I said quietly, but she couldn't hear me over the chanting and the otherworldly sounds. Ekk ran forward after disentangling himself. "No!"

Too late.

Mitzi, the avenging griffin/angel took flight and headed to the darkest part of the raven pack. With that weird bird cry, she quickly took control of the area. With a few powerful swoops of her wings, the ravens were disrupted, letting the true sun shine through again. The heavy swoop of her wings brought back the wind, and I could again hear the scribe, although his voice sounded tinny and far away. Each time the ravens were in disarray, the sun shone through again.

The gi-clad martial arts fighters faltered as if their life line had been diminished when this happened. Then their attack would renew. It was so surreal, standing in the open lawn area of a museum in my home town, watching my wife become someone I didn't understand. I felt so useless standing there holding my place and wanted to run to Ekk. Instead, I did as I was told and stood on "North."

The sight of Mitzi flying was scary. Would she ever come back to me? After this, could she be satisfied sitting with me on our couch? Suddenly, it occurred to me the answer was right around my neck. The pendant! I covered it with my right hand and closed my eyes, having no idea how to activate it. In my mind's eye, I saw Mitzi fly back to position. Had I done that?

Down the street, Dick Mortimer heard sirens and peeked out his living room window. "What the Sam Hill is going on?" He cinched his robe and looked back at his sleeping wife. Her snoring had kept him up, and for once he was glad. Slipping his feet into Derek Rose house shoes, Dick called Gary Smithers at his home number. The phone rang and rang. Finally, a very grumpy voice said hello. The call was quick and Smithers made other calls while Dick, chairman of the board of the museum, decided what to wear to a police matter.

Elsa was clearly exhausted, and I worried about her state of mind. Intermittently the chaos would calm, and I even saw a flurry of flower petals a couple of times, but it seemed to take everything she had in her to keep the portal open. I emptied my mind and squeezed that pendant, wishing that good would happen, not knowing what that might look like at this point.

Then I heard sirens. What would the police make of this mess?

Fiona, who had been missing in this pandemonium, suddenly appeared, her men snapping pictures wildly with a camera. Of course she would show up now. I dismissed this thought and turned my attention back to our ritual. As the scribe finished in a language I couldn't understand, Juniper and I shared a look that communicated our concern for our wives. Mitzi was fully griffin and Valerie was fully . . . something Native American. The whole event was surreal. In the center of the mat, I heard a sound like a match being lit, and suddenly a rainbow shot up to the sky from right in the middle of us.

Wolfrum's voice came through then, cold and clear. "Enough."

Ehren's voice said, "Agreed."

Immediately, the Brazilian jiujitsu fighters collapsed like puppets whose strings had been cut. The ravens cleared out quickly into the night sky, and the portal started to close.

"Hold your places just a moment longer," Ehren said. The wind died down. Right about then, Mitzi crumpled in her spot, and Valerie's Native American garb dissolved. Then, it was dark, like a normal nighttime. After a beat, I heard traffic sounds, punctuated by sirens. This is the soundtrack of Merryville. I looked at Ekk, not wanting to mess anything up by going to Mitzi.

"It's okay. Go to her," Ekk said, holding Elsa.

The confused fighters made their way back to their cars and drove silently out of the parking lot. A couple ran down the bluff.

When the last car left, the police moved in, in a comedic ballet of timing. What a scene it must have looked to the police. Fiona's men were expert at melting into the shrubbery, and that's what they did. A coterie consisting of Mortimer, Smithers, and several officers approached our disheveled band standing on a mat with weird symbols in the midst of the green space. I was on the ground stroking Mitzi's hair. Juniper and Val were talking quietly. Elsa and Ekk had disappeared. I hoped it wasn't because of lack of food.

Dick Mortimer looked amused as he walked up to the crumpled mat. Juniper's usual coif was a mess. "Juniper Gooden, you never cease to amaze." He dramatically turned to Councilman Gary Smithers and said, "Most people stop digging when they find themselves in a hole."

Juniper, glassy eyed and tired, said nothing.

The young officer in charge had been pulled from his regular patrol and wanted to get on with his night. "Is this trespassing?" he asked Dick Mortimer, who appeared to be in charge. "There's only the four of them." When Mr. Mortimer didn't answer, he said to us, "Ladies, you need to move along. The museum is closed." A camera flashed from a distance.

"Stop taking pictures!" Dick Mortimer yelled to the direction of the flash.

Officers gave chase, and at least three flashlight beams searched for the source of the disturbance, landing on museum shrubbery.

"Officer, arrest them, all of them!" Gary Smithers shouted.

"For what, sir? I was sent here to check out a disturbance of the peace. Seems like things are settled down." The officer hooked his thumbs on his belt, clearly aware he was being used by the expensively dressed man for his own private agenda. I liked his independence.

Dick Mortimer was having none of that. "It's some kind of weird lesbian thing they're doing, and, and that woman," he said, pointing to Juniper with a shaking finger, "was fired and has no business being here at any time. Arrest them!" A car door slammed in the nearby parking lot. Dick Mortimer looked at his watch, then back at the black-and-white, smiling when he saw Detective Potts.

The old detective was finishing up a cigarette and was ready to flick it out to the street. Upon seeing he was the center of attention, he ground it out on his heel and put the butt in his pocket.

The young officer stepped back and let Potts in their circle. "Let me handle this," Detective Potts said, and moved to the front of the group. "I don't know what this is here, but"—he turned to me, Mitzi, Juniper, and Val—"the museum closed hours ago. You're trespassing. I need you all to come downtown and answer some questions."

"About what? If we were trespassing, we're sorry and ready to leave now."

Mitzi looked at me after my brazen response, I think with a modicum of pride.

"About trespassing. Let's go." As he said this, he put a meaty hand on Mitzi's arm.

"You can't do this!" I was outraged and started toward him. Valerie held me back.

Potts turned to Dick. "You pressing charges?"

"Absolutely. Yes." The director gave his most evil smile. "And I want a restraining order against Juniper Gooden."

At this, she roused and looked straight at him. "Really, Dick, are you serious?"

"You'll have to do that down at the courthouse," Potts said. "This is a misdemeanor, and I'll handle that."

"You work for Dick Mortimer now?" Juniper asked, some of her élan regained.

"No, he works for me," Gary Smithers, city councilman for the district, said. "And I work for the mayor, who works for the city. *Comprende?*"

Dick Mortimer looked at Smithers and nodded.

"Cuff 'em," Potts said gruffly.

Upon his command, uniformed officers moved forward and roughly handcuffed all of us.

Gary Smithers nodded curtly. "You can handle it from here. This is clearly a police matter." He turned to walk away. Suddenly, a spotlight shown on him, and the lilting voice of Fiona Castlebaum echoed off the buildings, eerie in the mostly empty space. "Garrrry, smile for the camera!" The darkened area was bathed in light. Flash cameras photographed the scene from all angles. "This is what you do to the most amazing curator this museum has ever seen?" The men looked around, squinting at the light. Guns were drawn. Gary Smithers quickly got in his car, pulled out his cell phone, and angrily punch numbers.

"Search the area!" Potts yelled at his men, grabbed my arm, and led me toward a car. It felt like paparazzi were present as photo flashes went off.

Mitzi didn't look so good. When the ritual was over, her wings retracted, but she was very pale and limp. "My wife needs a hospital. Call 9-1-1"

"We are 9-1-1," Potts growled. "What's she on?"

Squeezing my pendant tight, I yelled at Potts, "Nothing! This is a medical thing." I kept wondering when that damn pendant would kick in.

"Quit pointing your octopus jewelry at me. What's wrong with all of you? You have no idea how much disruption your shenanigans have caused."

I could see through the smeared back window of the cop car. Police were literally beating the bushes, looking for ninja photographers.

I heard Dick Mortimer say patronizingly to Juniper, "I am positively mystified. You were fired, and now you show up in some drug-crazed lesbian ritual thing? I thought you would be at the board meeting tomorrow. Instead, you've gone completely insane."

She looked at Valerie and ignored him.

He became angry at her silence. "Do you really want to take the museum down with you?"

Juniper now looked at him with an expression that was hard to read. "What time?"

"What?"

"The board meeting. What time?"

"Two p.m. Whatever. You are so done." He walked toward the museum, shaking his head.

The cop car Mitzi and I were put in took off while Valerie and Juniper looked on helplessly. My hands were behind my back, and the car smelled of vomit. I yelled through the scratched plastic to the men in the front seat, "Hey! My wife needs a doctor." The driver ignored me, picked up a mic, and talked cop code into his radio. Mitzi's head lolled on my shoulder, and I was very worried. Is this how it would end? After going to the other side of a planet and completing the rainbow whatever? Oh God. I started to cry.

The squad car pulled up to the Merryville Police Department, and we were led into booking, where we were photographed by a tired-looking older woman in an ill-fitting uniform and put in a holding cell. Juniper and Valerie had still not arrived. I had Mitzi in my arms as I protectively held her. She murmured as if in a dream. They breath tested us, but nothing registered. "Hey, I get a phone call. I need to make a phone call." I might as well have been shouting into a void. Mitzi seemed to wake, but very slowly.

It was now about three-thirty a.m., and we were both still exhausted. A jail cell isn't a place of rest. My cowlicky hair was completely out of control, and we probably smelled after all that travel. There was one toilet in the corner, and I was contemplating having to use it. After all we'd been through, that was one thing too many. I stared at the ceiling, prepared for a miserable night, when the jailer returned. "You must have some pretty important friends is all I got to say." She unlocked the door. Even with a full bladder I was moving pretty good and dragged my groggy wife along with me.

Mitzi and I stumbled down the corridor to the booking area. A dapper woman with her arm in a cast and wearing a neck brace waited for us. Her eyes were fiery under her fashionable glasses. My mouth dropped open. "You're Ms. Stephanovsky, right? Are you here for us? Who called you?"

She looked pale, but determined. "Time for that later. Come with me." We were led back to a desk on our way out, and I was handed a manila envelope with my things in it. Too tired to really study what was in there, and still worried about Mitzi, I gratefully followed our attorney to her rented vehicle outside the precinct station. Alexandra explained that she had gotten to the museum right after we'd been taken in the squad car and was able to keep Valerie and Juniper from the same fate we suffered.

After some argument about going to the hospital, we went straight home. Mitzi wasn't going to spend one more minute away from Brutus and familiar surroundings. Alex looked like she could use some rest herself. Mitzi was coming around a bit more, and I doubted the local hospital had what she needed anyway.

I led Mitzi upstairs, and we collapsed into bed without even showering. We spooned so close that Brutus sat atop both of us, in a show of big cat love. Before I fell asleep, my mind registered that we had traveled across the globe, participated in an ancient ritual we didn't really fully understand, and been thrown in jail. I wondered what my office would look like after being attacked.

The next day, I woke at one p.m., which was really late for us. As I sat in bed watching Mitzi sleep and breathe, I hoped that she'd still be satisfied with our mundane life after the adventure she'd tasted. My finger traced the slight bumps on her shoulders. I got up and went to the kitchen to make coffee. Through the front window, I saw crime-scene tape still marked off our lawn, a piece flapping in the breeze.

A few gawkers stared at our house as they went about their dog walking and lawn mowing. It was time to return to normal. I only hoped we could. I looked in the fridge, which was pretty barren, but managed to find a tin of cinnamon buns. I preheated the oven and poured a cup of coffee, already soothed by the old rhythms of life. I smiled. Did I really punch out a dwarf?

By the time Mitzi awoke, the yellow crime-scene tape was in the dumpster and coffee was waiting. Cinnamon rolls were buttered and iced. She looked at me from the comforter with heavy eyes and yawned. "Smells good."

"It does, doesn't it?"

"Wow. Did we really get thrown in jail last night?" Brutus jumped up on the bed, wanting to get in on the conversation.

"Yep." I kissed the top of her head.

"And the rest of it, could all that be real?" She looked to be on overload.

"Have a cinnamon roll." My go-to heal-all: sugar.

I heard a knock on the door downstairs that led to the backyard. We looked at each other quizzically, but I jumped up and motioned for Mitzi to stay put. "Whoever it is, I'm getting rid of them."

Mitzi found the controller and clicked on the news.

I looked through the glass at the top of the door but couldn't see anyone. Thinking it was neighborhood pranksters, I turned to go back upstairs.

"Hey. Panda. It's us."

This time I poked my head out the window and saw a tired and dirty couple of elves. "Elsa! Ekk! Get in here before someone sees you."

Both of them were half dissolved, and I knew what to do.

"Mitzi. Bring the cinnamon rolls."

She came downstairs with the plate of food, a light-blue robe wrapped around her slender body. "Oh my God, are you guys all right?" She shook her head. "Wow, this is real."

Between shoving rolls in his mouth, Ekk said, "We've been running all night. I don't think anyone saw us come here."

"I'm so sorry. We must look a fright." Elsa tried to tuck her hair in a scarf.

"As soon as we get you fed," I said, "you two take a nap. Any news about the others? And what happened with the ritual?"

Ekk looked uncomfortable.

"Tell her," Elsa said.

"Well, it was a partial success. We showed stronger than anyone thought we would, but Wolfrum still has power."

"But isn't that an epic fail? Weren't we trying to get rid of Wolf-Raven?" Mitzi was distraught. "I thought the idea was to usher in four generations of rainbow peace between all nations, and everything."

The front doorbell rang.

While Ekk tried to explain that the mixed result was certainly not as bad as it could have been, I went to the front door, wishing we were still sleeping.

Juniper and Val stood there looking bright and shiny, with Whole Foods bags. We hugged and they went straight to the kitchen, for that's where we always ended up.

"Tea?" I reached for the electric pot to heat water. After all the events, a tea party seemed a tad weird, but it was a first step toward normalcy.

"Yes!" came from the elves in unison.

Valerie looked at me in my dishevelment and said, "I'll do it." She set about putting hot water on, a comforting task. "We brought you some groceries. Jun and I got in a pretty good night's sleep while you were in the clink. Alex filled us in."

I took the groceries and started stocking the fridge, only leaving out bacon, eggs, and fruit for preparation. All this struggling for good against evil gave me a tremendous appetite. Also, I didn't want our elven friends disappearing on us.

Mitzi took her place at the kitchen table. "So what happened?" She clutched her cup, putting her elbows on yellow 1950s Formica. She looked so sweet in her blue robe against that color. I was glad we were home.

"Oh my God, it was fabulous," Juniper said. "Alex roared up in her rental car with that sling and neck brace. Potts turned white. She was furious and kept pointing at his chest and calling him Detective Putz."

I snorted out some coffee through my nose, laughing. "She got away with that?"

Valerie and Juniper shared a look then laughed. "Uh, yeah." Apparently the sartorially resplendent barrister was a force to be reckoned with.

"Did they arrest her?"

"Oh they tried. Dick was screaming his head off." The two women laughed again. "Her crew caught the whole thing on film. Then she shared some rather, um, personal pictures taken in Merryville while we were in Germany. Pretty soon the officers realized it wasn't a police matter."

"I don't understand. What pictures?" Mitzi leaned in closer, voice dramatically scandalized. She was acting like the pre-griffin Mitzi, and my heart pinged.

Valerie sat down next to Mitzi. "First, there was a great one of Linda Chicolet and Dick Mortimer in an intimate embrace in his office."

"Shut up!" Mitzi put down her cup. "But why would the cops care?"

Juniper said, "There was another of Councilman Smithers meeting with your lovely, across-the-street neighbor and star witness. Seems there is some relationship between them."

Mitzi looked puzzled, and I reminded her about the dug-up yard and Pott's obsession with pinning a crime on me and Juniper.

I said, "The star witness to your murder?"

Mitzi looked stunned. "My murder, wow." After a beat, she said, "Whoa, a conspiracy?" Now her grin was wide.

"Yes, indeed. Apparently Gary Smithers' assistant threw him under the bus when confronted with phone records showing he was the go-between to set you all up."

Mitzi shook her head in amazement. "Who's been working on all this?"

"Alex, Fiona, and Fiona's men. Her guys have been here working while we flew halfway around the world. She's planning a terrific exposé. Everyone's scrambling to be on the right side of the floodlight." Juniper always had a good sense for the social impact of events.

"Including the mayor?" I asked.

"Oh you know him. By the time he announces various resignations, it'll probably all have been his idea," Juniper said.

We all nodded and laughed. "So no charges?"

"Let's just say Detective Potts decided to 'quit digging' at us last night after having a few dots connected for him." Juniper looked like the cat that ate the cream. Speaking of cats.

Ekk was talking to Brutus again.

"Don't hold out on us, Ekk. What does he have to say?" I grinned, this was getting better and better.

"Lots of complaining, but the summary is, he's glad you're home. Don't leave again." The awww moment only lasted while we drained our tea, then Juniper stood up and announced. "Off to the museum, for what promises to be a very interesting board meeting." The girls let themselves out. Suddenly, the kitchen was quiet.

Ekk wandered off to nap with Elsa, and I was left alone, finally, with my wife. "Mitzi," I said. She took my tea cup, put it down, and took me by the hand into the living room.

"I'm so worried about—"

She put a finger over my lips and snuggled into me on the couch. I had so many questions. The phone rang.

"Don't you dare answer it." I didn't.

In the background, I heard my sister Puddles' worried voice. "Sis? CNN, really? What the heck? Call me." Click. My brother, in the same country as me, probably didn't know what had happened. Funny my sister in India would hear about it first. I would email her later. Right now I was on my own couch, sitting with my wife—the phone rang again. In the kitchen, I heard Elsa's voice. Elsa, the elf. "Hi, Babs."

"So much for returning to normal," I whispered into Mitzi's ear.

Mitzi and I looked at each other and shared a giggle. I hadn't thought about the tax practice in a week. This was probably progress.

"Ohh, I'll be right over. Ekk!" She came into the living room with her rosy cheeks, looking for her pocketbook. "Babs found out I do caregiving."

"Um, aren't you afraid someone would wonder who is answering our phone?" I asked Elsa.

She reddened. "I knew who it was."

I gestured with my left arm in a why/how?

"It's a Hercynian Garden thing," she answered,

Mitzi pulled my arm tighter around her shoulders. "Yeah, get with it, Panda."

"Babs needs some help with her dad. Ekk and I are going over for a few hours. Ekk!"

I heard him coming down our stairs and called out, "Hey, I have questions, you two."

He hopped from the last stair to the floor. "Later, Panda. I have a feeling it's time for the two of you to have some alone time." Ekk was more sensitive than I'd given him credit for. "We'll be back later, and there will be plenty of time to talk."

After a moment of sitting and staring at each other, I said, "So, your dad is a mythical creature from a magic realm." We just cracked up at that.

"Yes, and you have a magic pendant."

"You can fly."

"Only sometimes." She nestled into my arm, and I thought she'd fallen asleep.

After the elves left, vanished more like it, she said, "Babe?"

"What?"

"I'm worried about the office. And Lulu."

"Now?"

"Yeah, now. Hope Lulu's okay, she was left at the office with the jiujitsu boys attacking."

My eyes searched hers. "I hate to leave so soon."

"I'm fine," Mitzi assured me. "If you'll go, I'd actually like to soak in the tub a bit."

Feeling torn, I left for Fowler Tax Services.

❧

CHAPTER TEN

MERRYVILLE

I drove my Smart car down Thistle Drive, and the normalcy felt surreal. The last few days had been a dream, right? Baden Baden? Griffins? I literally shook my head. Turning into the parking lot of our strip mall took away all doubt. My windows were boarded up, and there were five or six buff-looking men repairing them. I turned my gaze toward the Brazilian jiujitsu place and saw it was the source of all the activity. Curious, I went there first, not sure if I would be attacked again, but nothing would surprise me now. The martial arts studio was three of my offices wide. The door was painted red, and a chime went off as I opened it. There were mats from wall to wall and mirrors around the room. Gi-clad fighters paired off into groups and were going at it. My adrenaline surged, but no one gave me a look past a quick discernment to see if I was friend or foe.

At the far corner was one of last night's zombie attackers, with his bald head down, working on some papers. I stopped before him. "You're the boss?"

This man, who had looked so crazed the night before, fixed me with calm blue eyes. "Yes. You want to start working out?"

"No. I mean, not right now. Are those your men repairing my office?"

"Oh, you must be P. Fowler," he said. "I got your envelope full of cash, and I gotta say I really appreciate the work for some of my guys. They should be finished soon."

"You do martial arts . . . and construction?"

He looked puzzled. "I thought you knew. We have several groups that meet here. One is for rehabilitation from drugs and gangs. These guys need the work."

I nodded. "Oh, right." What a quick study I am. "Who brought you the envelope?"

"The lawyer. The one on TV sometimes? She was really nice."

"Well, thanks," I said, backing away.

He looked like he wanted to say more, but a call of "Sensei!" drew him away with a nod and an "excuse me."

There was no sense of danger here, and it was obvious no one remembered what had happened the night before.

I left the jiujitsu place and wandered over to my office. "Hi, guys." I pulled out my ring of keys. There was a red-headed young man with unfortunate skin, a kid with what I call "skateboard hair," and another with carefully shaved sides of his head and a tight T-shirt. He appeared to be in charge.

He spoke first. "This must be your office, huh? What the hell happened here? Looks like a freight train hit it." His helpers laughed unconcerned boy laughs, friendly.

"You wouldn't believe it if I told you. I better get back to work." They stood there as if waiting for more. I said "Carry on" and it seemed to break the spell. My smile was one I hoped would convince these guys this was simply another day in Merryville. It was clear they had no recollection that the last time they were here these same folks were attacking my windows like zombies. Again, no tingle of recognition.

The inside of the office wasn't as bad as I thought it would be. In fact, it looked immaculate. I went to my desk and looked under it. Nothing but a recently dusted floor and my metal trash can. No elf hole. I turned to go into the efficiency kitchen, and Ekk appeared in the doorway with his sleeves rolled up and a couple of paper towels strategically tucked into his outfit. "Ekk!"

"Panda!" he parroted, his blue eyes twinkling.

"I thought you went with Elsa to Babs and Henry's."

"She dropped me here. We each have our specialties."

I looked around meaningfully at the source of my income, noting the neat stacks of papers. I reached down and tried to hug the guy. It was awkward, so I simply said, "Thank you."

He blushed a little and turned to pour us some coffee. Over his shoulder, he said, "You might want to look at the Fabishes' return. I found another deduction. Why they buying so much fertilizer?"

"No way, Ekk. I went over that thing twice." I absently reached for my pendant, which had become my touchstone in recent days. "Damn," I said under my breath. "Must have left it in that envelope at home."

Ekk looked up, now spreading out paperwork for me to see. "Left what?"

"My pendant. No worries, I'll get it later." Then we talked about work and the clients, which always calmed me down and put me back to balance. "Have you seen Lulu?"

As if we had conjured her up, my favorite security guard, dressed in a muu muu, opened the door smiling.

"Lulu!" I gave her a big hug. "I'm so glad you're okay! Hey, why aren't you in uniform?"

"Miz Fowler, Panda. This one crazy place." Her eyes looked around the office.

I opened my mouth to speak, but she put her hand up in the universal stop gesture.

"It's okay, but I don't want to talk about it, ever!"

"Okay . . . so—"

"I came to tell ya my application for the Merryville PD finally got approved!" She lifted me up and swung me around.

"That's fantastic! Wow!" A file dropped onto the floor but we didn't care.

Even Ekk was grinning.

She shook her head and said almost in disbelief, "I'm gonna be a cop!"

Back in Baden Baden, Wolfrum turned a pendant in his pale hands as Odilia entered. He looked like he was meditating with his eyes open.

"Wolf, what now?"

He fixed his hollow gaze on her and silently motioned for her to sit by him at the window of his turret.

"It wasn't a one hundred percent win, was it?" she asked.

"Do not waiver in your faith my sister. They only think they've beaten us down into the earth. What they don't know is that we are seeds. In fact, everything went as planned."

Odilia's old face lit with excitement. "Tell me more."

He held up a pendant that started to glow with a cold blue light. In it, she could see dot-sized creatures, like ants, scrambling around in the roots of a tree, except they were octopus limbs, and the ant-like creatures had human faces.

"Is this what allowed them to escape us? A pendant of protection?"

The necklace and chain floated free of his slender white hand, and with a flick of his wrist smashed against the stone wall. "No, that was a child's toy, phony magic."

Cold wind blew through the rectangular slits in the walls.

"Then . . . how?" Odilia's face revealed confusion.

Wolfrum stood, his voice booming. "Do not question!" The heavy wooden door to the hallway was open, his voice could be heard now by anyone in ear shot.

"You are a foot soldier of Wolf-Raven, what do you know?"

She said slowly, : "Wolves are always followed by ravens"

Wolfrum responded passionately: "Scavenging for the kill"

Then together: "Eat fast, ravening wolf," their voices gaining in intensity. Others down the hall picked up their words and the chant reverberated monk to monk throughout Schwartzvald Castle.

"Ravens follow five and twenty
Cleansing the world of unworthy prey
Taking out the weak
Consuming the meek
Wolf-Raven cycles this world to the next."

In the way of their faith, Wolfrum and Odilia howled like wolves, their eyes shining with fanaticism. The castle rocked with energy.

Before heading to the museum for the board meeting, Juniper turned her Citroen into the driveway of her nemesis, Dick Mortimer. Her new, post-exposé-pictures best friend and supporter, Beatrice Vanderhooven-Mortimer, floated out, matching the European car in elegance. It may seem fast, but they had a shared enemy in Linda Chicolet. They were soon joined by Charlotte Windingle, Bea's childhood friend, for what promised to be an exciting board meeting.

"Hello, Juniper," both women said.

"Thank you for coming to support me. I know this is hard." Juniper leaned over and gave her friend Bea a hug.

Beatrice looked sad, actually quite deflated, and Juniper felt a pang of regret for asking her to attend the meeting. Charlotte Windingle must have felt the same way, for she said, "Bea, it's okay, honey, you don't have to come."

The woman sniffled into a perfumed hankie. "I can't believe Dick would do this to me! He didn't even come home last night." She started to wail. "The police are on their way over."

This wasn't going as planned. Although initially it seemed Mrs. Mortimer could be Juniper's strongest ally, she apparently really loved her spineless cheat of a husband. Juniper fleetingly glanced at her retro watch and said, "Charlotte's right. We'll be fine just knowing you support me as curator of the museum. I don't want to destroy Dick. He really does believe in the mission. I know we different ideas of how to get there, that's all."

Beatrice straightened her dress and dabbed her eyes. "Well, if you say so." Blanca, who was trailing her mistress, gave a sharp bark.

"Absolutely. Where is Dick staying?"

This caused another round of tears, and Juniper suspected she would be going to the meeting alone. Bea's mascara was running down her cheeks in black streaks. "He, he's probably down at the Yacht Club, and everyone knows what happened. I was the member there. He's only a member because of me." The floodgates opened. It was hard to know what was worse to Beatrice Vanderhooven-Mortimer—the actual adultery or the fact that her set might be talking about it behind her back. Either way, she was suffering.

In an utterly selfless moment, Juniper looked at Charlotte, and the two exchanged the same thought. "I'm going to stay with you, Bea," Charlotte said. "Let's go get real drunk."

Beatrice let herself be led back into her beautiful home. After hugs and goodbyes, Juniper arrived ten minutes late, and alone, at the museum.

After receiving an epic ass-chewing by the squad commander, Detective Potts found his coworkers wasted no time with their jabs. The

Detective "Putz" comment was making the rounds, and the press conference You Tube video had gone viral. Walking slowly to his desk, he was thinking it might be time to hang it up. Thirty-four years of hard work had come down to this, being made a laughing stock. God, he wanted a cigarette. Imagine his surprise to see the dapper defense attorney, Alexandra Stephanovsky, waiting for him by his cubicle.

"Come to piss on my grave?"

"Of course not. I came to give you a spade so you could dig yourself out."

"Too late for that, lady. It's over. Wanna drink?" He motioned to his deep desk drawer.

She shook her head. "Let's go outside so we can talk, and you can smoke one of your nasty cigarettes." She patted him on the pocket. "I may even join you."

"Oh, so you're a secret smoker, eh?" His eyebrows lifted.

"You don't tell anybody, and I won't tell you're cavorting with the enemy."

"Deal."

The two old enemies trudged upstairs to the precinct rooftop, past the newly remodeled floor for the bigwigs on city council, and up to privacy.

He took an American Spirit out of the pack, gave one to Alex, and lit them. After taking a deep drag, he said, "What's this all about? Last night I was a putz."

She looked so elegant, the smoke curled around her like part of her outfit. She smiled. "That was last night."

"I'm listening."

"The real story here, the people who set everybody up, are on the executive floor."

"And we're done." Potts crushed out his butt on the roof edge.

"Charles, wait." She caught his arm. "Hear me out." The use of his first name got his attention. He got a whiff of expensive perfume.

"When I was called into this mess, it was to defend Valerie Gooden. After interviewing the neighbors and others, it's clear that Councilman Gary Smithers was behind all this."

He shook his head. "Old news. His staff gave him up. He's probably going to resign today—he's toast. That old biddy across the street from the tax chick was his cousin or something. What else you got?"

He looked pleased to know more than she probably expected.

"How about this. Fiona Castlebaum embarrassed the mayor and put a floodlight on the problems Merryville has."

"Yeah, cats and bums, so what? Every city has that. Big deal." He lit another cigarette, a sign he was still listening.

"And, there's been a concerted effort to remove Juniper Gooden as curator of the museum. Don't you see it? When Mitzi Fowler 'disappeared,' you were used to go after the Goodens and the Fowlers. Then, when that plan didn't work, they made you the fall guy."

The wind blew evenly on the roof, lazily lifting the ragged edge of Potts's haircut. His wheels turned. "Connect the dots for me."

"I've read and re-read the search warrant for the Fowler house. It says an anonymous call provided the info."

"Yeah, that happens."

"Why you? And why the Fowlers?"

He smacked his head, suddenly interested in life again. "Excuse me, but I have some digging to do. And, thanks."

"Charles?"

"Charlie please, but anything's better than Putz." They shared a laugh.

She reddened. "I'll take you up on that drink sometime, someplace"— she looked around dramatically at the rusting air conditioner on the top of the building—"more suited to my status as queen of the defense bar."

He smiled, feeling better than he had in weeks. "Okay, but you realize that if I still had a reputation, this could ruin it."

She laughed and reached for another cigarette. "You go first. We wouldn't want people talking, now would we?"

Potts nodded then ran down the stairs like he was twenty years younger.

The first thing he did was follow up on the loose ends of the case. He'd been so busy licking his wounds, he hadn't done his usual tight work. Interesting thing, there was no record of the anonymous call that sent him on a fool's errand to dig up the backyard of the Fowler house. That could only mean one thing: the call came from inside the precinct.

Back at the Fowlers, Mitzi luxuriated in the bath. Lavender scented the water, and she closed her eyes. Her body was not her own anymore. Wings! It was the first time things were calm enough to think of it. She had wings. Her soapy hand felt her shoulder nodules for the thousandth time. She also had a father. Tears loosed from her lids and spilled down her face. Between the two things, it meant more to her to have a father. Her eyes popped open. So much had happened, she had given no thought to Susan. Was she home yet? Did she ever recover her ability to speak? The weirdness factor was overwhelming. She heard a door open below and called out, "Panda, are you home?" There was no response. She started draining her bath.

"Panda?" Now fear set in. Who else could it be? "Ekk? Elsa?" Still wet, she grabbed her robe, put it on, and slipped into the bedroom. Brutus was on high alert, with his hair standing up straight in a ridge down his back. Mitzi grabbed him and went into the closet. Once under the coats and behind boxes, she realized she left her cell phone on the bedside table. Dammit!

While Ekk and I checked the office, he commented, "I'm so glad Lulu's fine."

"Yeah, me too, and I'm glad the building is still standing. Hey, with everything winding up, when do you and Elsa return to the Hercynian Garden?"

"Oh, Elsa and I are staying in Merryville. You got us." He said it so matter of factly.

"What do you mean?" There had been no time to really think of what having a magic wife with roots in the Hercynian Garden might mean. "'Til when?"

"Like, permanently."

"What? I always assumed you would be going back when this was all over." I wasn't upset, just, wow, kind of taking it all in.

Ekk counted off on his fingers: "First, it's not all over, and second, you could use some help at the office. Elsa told me it's something you and Mitzi fight about."

I blushed, wondering what else Elsa had observed. "Where are you planning on living? Elves can't rent apartments."

Ekk laughed. "This is California. I put on my hat," he said and whipped out a Kings ball cap, "and voilà, I'm one of Babs's 'little people.' There are some very low-level spells that work as well. Elsa and I already have a place."

"Okay, then, no more elf holes?"

"Well, if we need them, but Ehren said he will send a stipend and to keep the magic down to a dull roar."

I wanted to tell him he looked like a tiny thug with the cap he chose, but I didn't want to spoil his mood. "Okay, let's go out the front door this time." He went before me and, after I clicked my car opener, got in Sweetpea's shotgun seat. I could barely see him over the dash and shook my head as I locked up the office with my huge set of keys.

I smiled as I turned. It was still a beautiful California day, and I was so glad to be home. This feeling lasted only another instant because Ekk opened the car door and shouted, "Panda, hurry! Mitzi needs us!"

I didn't question and jumped in the driver's seat tearing out of the strip mall parking lot as fast as my three cylinders would take us.

"Dammit, what's happened to Mitzi?" I dared a glance at my new sidekick.

"Elsa called." He held up his cell, which was bigger than his hand and left a huge bulge in his pocket. "She's getting danger vibes from the house. She's on her way, too—back from Babs and Henry's."

I leaned forward, pressed my three cylinders as fast as they would go, and naturally hit every red light there was. I tried calling Mitzi on her cell, but it rang and rang and then went to voice mail.

In the house, Mitzi heard her cell phone ring, but she couldn't do anything to give herself away. Feet pounded up the stairs and a guttural voice said, "*Hier entlang!*" Somehow, her experience allowed her to understand German and knew he said, "This way." From the voices, she pictured at least two huge dwarves.

Why wasn't this over? She wrapped the cat with both arms and scooted backwards 'til the closet wall stopped her. This was the first time she was grateful the closet was cluttered. There were hanging clothes, boxes, and paper grocery bags full of things that were on their way to the homeless shelter, shoes, and even a couple of tennis racquets. Brutus kitty didn't like being stifled, however, and leaped from her arms. He was out the closet door and all she could do was close it and hide. Seconds later, she heard him hiss and what sounded very much like a cat attack. The front door opened again, and she heard a familiar voice. Her sister-in-law?

"Panda, Mitzi, you left the door unlocked, are you home?" The voice got louder as Puddle Fowler, Panda's sister, thumped loudly up the stairs. "I've come thirteen thousand miles to see what the hell is going on with you guys. Tell me you're not having sex."

Mitzi was torn. She didn't want to give her position away, but she couldn't leave Puddle in harm's way—a harm she couldn't foresee or protect herself against. A pain began on the top of both shoulders, and she realized that being discovered versus not being discovered was not going to be a choice. Mitzi dropped her robe as her wings fluffed out and launched her from the closet in time to face two ugly dwarves, dressed in California casual, fighting her fierce Bengal cat. It was an odd scene.

Puddle stood at the bedroom door in her usual colorful tie-dye garb, mouth open, as Mitzi emerged naked from the closet with full white wings flapping. Two dwarves were busy tossing the place, and Brutus was scratching everyone in sight. The smaller one swung around with a lamp and smacked Brutus way too hard with an audible thud. It made Mitzi sick the way he went limp. Everyone froze for a moment, and for sure, it was the strangest tableau Thistle Drive had ever seen. One of the dwarves said something to the other, and they plowed into Puddle, knocked her over, and ran off down the stairs.

Mitzi's wings retracted, and she donned her robe. She said, "Puddle! What are you doing here?" and ran to her brave Bengal kitty.

Puddle got up and looked a bit stunned, as Mitzi heard both the front and back doors open. "Panda?" Mitzi called out, hoping against hope.

I reached the top of the steps with Ekk and Elsa and entered the bedroom only to see Mitzi in tears holding our Brutus, and my sister from India standing with her. I said a lame but cheery, "Hey, Puddle."

Poor Puddle looked from me to Mitzi to the elves and back to me and said, "Somebody better start talking. I feel like I'm watching a movie."

Elsa moved toward Brutus and put both her arms around him as best she could. Puddle looked at me teary eyed, and I gave her a shhh motion. The strong scent of roses filled the room, which felt a bit crowded. Brutus lay still, with his eyes not quite closed. "He's not breathing," Mitzi said through sobs. "He was just trying to protect me." I moved toward her and petted the part of his foot I could touch. Ekk eased us both away and suggested we take Puddle downstairs and let Elsa do her work.

Hours later, Puddle had her fill of explanations and was clearly on overload. We put her on the couch with a comforter and pillow, and after her medicinal marijuana, she was asleep before the light switched off. Brutus' condition was guarded, and he slept between Mitzi and me. I could still smell roses and a wisp of pot and, thankfully, heard the sound of my little warrior's thready breathing. After a couple of sandwiches, Elsa and Ekk retired to the guest room, not about to leave us alone after this visit from Wolfrum's minions.

The next morning, I eased out of bed, excited that my sister was here. She'd moved to India three years ago, and Mitzi and I were only able to make the distant journey once. Speaking of Mitzi, she had an arm curled around our beloved cat, who had a nasty goose egg on his kitty skull. His tongue lolled around his mouth in a way that made my stomach queasy. Pushing out thoughts of brain damage, I suddenly remembered my pendant, or rather, Mitzi's pendant she'd given to me years ago. We'd been distracted by the attack, Brutus's injury, and Puddle's arrival, and our room was still somewhat in disarray. I meant to put the pendant around Mitzi's neck and leave it there. The pendant was in a manila envelope handed back to me by the police a couple of nights ago. My knees went weak at the memory of being thrown into that awful jail with Mitzi.

The envelope was where I left it, in my open nightstand drawer. I upended it to find my wallet and nothing else. I looked into the empty envelope again, like you do, not accepting the fact that the pendant was gone. I looked again and gave a big sigh. Still hadn't reappeared. I sank down onto my side of the bed and looked back at my precious family. Now how could I protect my wife and our four-legged baby?

Puddle was still snoring downstairs, and the elves had their door closed. It was after nine, so I called Juniper.

"Panda. How are you guys doing?"

"Hey, Jun, ready for this? We've had more weirdness."

"What happened?"

"Where to start? Um, Puddle's here."

"All the way from India? I guess that was dumb. Of course, she would be if she's here."

"Yes, she apparently arrived in time to disrupt Wolfrum's men, who were after Mitzi and bashed Brutus."

"Oh, God. Is he okay? We're finishing up breakfast. Can we bring anything with us? Bandages? Food?"

"Actually, I'm not hungry. Wow, I don't say that very often."

"We're coming over as soon as we leave here, no arguments!"

"I thought you might be at the museum."

"Oh, about that. We have some catching up to do. Read your Fishwrap first."

I heard Val say in the background, "You better be sitting down, gorgeous." I wondered at that last statement.

We rang off and I went downstairs, put on some coffee, and made my way to the front porch. The Internet has changed so many things. Getting the paper was still comforting in its certainty. Even though the paper might be wet or thrown into the bushes, a real human tossed it each morning at our porch before we woke. The *Bee* was on the bottom step, and the neighbors got a good look at my portly body in PJs. After all we'd been through, I didn't care. I was the fighter of evil dwarves and had snuck through a castle. That still made me smile. I tucked the paper under my arm and wondered what Heloisa was doing at this very moment.

I slipped by a still-abed Puddle, who had always been a good sleeper, carried the paper into the kitchen, and sat down with my coffee. I opened it, and the headline screamed: MUSEUM BOARD CHAIR'S MISSING BODY FOUND IN BUSHES

I almost spit out some coffee and went on to read:

> Museum Chair Richard Mortimer's body was found in the bushes on the bluff near the museum this morning. Police have not released cause of death, but a person close to the investigation, who wished to remain anonymous, said Mortimer appeared to be the recipient of blunt force trauma.
>
> Ironically, Mortimer was found in the same location as the homeless person spotlighted a week before during a live performance of "Floodlight!" by Fiona Castlebaum, international celebrity. Ms. Castlebaum, who reportedly has left the country, is being sought for questioning.
>
> A source also reported seeing the embattled curator, Juniper Gooden, at the museum last night when there was some police activity. The acting chair, Byron Windingle, said that, until such time as the investigation was complete, all field trips are cancelled.
>
> The museum will remain closed until after Mr. Mortimer's memorial next weekend at St. John's. Juniper Gooden was unavailable for comment.

"Shit!" What else could happen? I felt for Dick's family, but he was a real jerk in life. This could not bode well for our friend Juniper. She had to be suspect Number One.

"I smell coffee." My lovely sister was stretching in the doorway, still in her pajamas.

"I smell patchouli—do you bathe in it?" I said. It was an old argument that was loving, not mean.

We hugged. "What cha reading?" she asked.

"You apparently have arrived in the midst of a story that's still unfolding. Now the head of the museum has been murdered."

She grabbed the newspaper article. "Where your friend works?"

"The very same. Hey, we had so much to tell you, I didn't ask how you are. What brought you home, sis?"

Puddle poured herself a cup of the steaming liquid and took a slow sip. "Oooh, American coffee. I missed it."

I started to speak, but she held up a finger.

"Okay, India was cool. I love the meditation. Whatever it was I needed to work out there has been worked out, though, and a new pathway has opened up."

"A new pathway? You're not here for good?"

She laughed her musical laugh. "Me in Merryville? No, Panda Bear, you're the only reason I stopped here on my way to Peru."

Our parents had disappeared in Peru when we were children. Even hearing the country mentioned still evoked a response from my body.

"Why? So I can lose a sister, too?"

"Don't be so sensitive. No, when in Carolla, India, I met a man named Diego from the South American jungle. We had many conversations about our folks, and he's going to help me find them. In fact, sometimes I wonder if that wasn't the whole reason I was drawn to India."

The sun shone through our dusty kitchen window, and I made a mental note to do some spring cleaning. "You mean, find out what happened to them."

She didn't directly answer, Puddle stretched her skinny tan arms and bent them behind her head, gray eyes looking into the distance. "We were in the same ashram, and he was from Lima. That's in Peru. Outside of L.A. County." She always made fun of the fact that I wasn't crazy about leaving home.

I missed having Brutus in my lap. He always loved a good story.

Puddle continued. "Over the months, Diego and I talked about the bus accident, which doesn't add up. You know, Paititi really may exist."

Again I felt that tingle of discomfort. "I guess them chasing a mythical city doesn't seem so 'out there' after what Mitzi and I have been through. Although our adventure kind of chased us." A minor epiphany.

Puddle stirred her coffee. "Anyway, his home is right outside of the area they were searching. He invited me to stay at his house and launch my expedition."

"You can't be serious." I heaved a big sigh. "Puddle, it's time to grow up."

She pulled her head back, making her neck stretch, and raised her eyebrows, a comical gesture I remembered well from childhood when our mother suggested she do the dishes.

"You know, get a job, settle down?"

"Ooooh, and have an exciting tax practice? No thanks." She got up to rustle through the cupboards for food.

Ekk joined us, looking refreshed but famished as usual. "Good morning, humans." Apparently, he loved saying this, highlighting his status as otherworldly. It also showed more of his sense of humor.

Puddle continued. "Although I gotta say, Merryville is more interesting than it's ever been before." She stared at Ekk. "Good morning, little man. My sister, who is friends with elves, thinks I'm crazy to want to go to South America and see if I can pick up the trail of our parents who disappeared when we were kids."

He was interested immediately. "*Vale do Javari, Brazil?*"

Her head snapped around to face him so fast her dreads flew. "How did you know?" Her mouth dropped open.

Not happy with this turn of conversation, I was getting irritated. "Yeah, I thought you were a German elf. What's all this about Peru?" I frowned. This wasn't good. Puddle was getting support for her hare-brained scheme.

Ekk jutted out his chin. "We have student exchange programs in the magical world, parallel but equal Panda." He was a bit defensive. "I have a distant cousin in the El Chullachaqui."

Puddle was excited. "Seriously? This is awesome. I could use an elf! Want to join me?"

It was hopeless to try to stop her now.

"Actually, I'm on duty here, making sure Mitzi and Panda are safe. I could put in a word for you with my cousin, however."

Puddle looked at me. I knew that look of wanderlust mixed with a bit of defiance. She kind of reminded me of our mom.

Sigh. "How about breakfast first?" I opened the fridge to take out our standard bacon and egg breakfast.

"Eeeww, I'm vegan, sis. You know that." Her dreads quivered.

"Sorry, dear, it's been awhile. I'm off meat now, too. I have a cantaloupe and some toast. Heard from our dear brother?"

"Nope. Is it whole grain?" Any subject that didn't interest her usually met with one-word responses.

I made the tell-me-more gesture with my hand.

"Not the whole time I've been away. Wait, he sent me a cell phone one Christmas."

"That was nice. Did you send him a card or call?"

"Um, no."

"Cause and effect. I guess you're both guilty. You're getting wheat bread." It was hard being the baby of the family and acting more like the oldest. Our doorbell rang out, playing Scotland the Brave, announcing the arrival of Valerie and Juniper. Reintroductions were made with Puddle. It started to feel like a party, although tempered by Brutus' condition. Val poured herself the last cup of coffee and prepared another pot. I was reminded of the headline and said, "Dick is dead?"

Ekk was still stirred up by Puddle, who had him doing Munchkin impressions earlier. He sang out, "He's really most sincerely dead," in his Munchkin voice. We all looked at him, jaws dropped. Until then, I didn't know elves could turn red, but, apparently they can.

He ducked out quickly, smiling. "Sorry, I'll go check on the girls." The girls he was referring to were Mitzi and Elsa, who were upstairs tending to Brutus.

"Let me know if you need me." Valerie chimed in.

I sat down and faced Juniper. "And?"

"Yes. The board meeting was very quick." Juniper shifted to a chair to be comfortable for her storytelling.

"Tell," Puddle and I said simultaneously.

Mitzi came in the room rubbing her eyes. "Ekk and Elsa have Brutus duty. Coffee? I heard Dick Mortimer is dead." Her face scrunched up as she yawned and stretched.

I rose to pour her a cup.

Juniper launched into her story. "Okay, let me tell you what happened. I intended to show up at the board meeting yesterday with both Dick's wife Beatrice *and* Mrs. Windingle."

This evoked a "wow" out of Mitzi.

"But Bea was distraught over the revelation of her husband having an affair with Linda Chicolet, another board member."

"And nemesis," I added.

Puddle, who didn't know any of these people, walked over to the cutting board and started in on her cantaloupe, saying "Draaaamaaaa" in a sing-song voice. I suddenly remembered how irritating she could be.

Juniper continued. "It turned out to be a blessing in disguise that she didn't go because she was so mad at him for cheating. No one knew he had been murdered."

"Oh my God, how sad," Mitzi said.

"Who found him?" I asked.

"Garcia. He was so distraught I thought they'd have to sedate him."

"Where's Fiona and her camera crew when you need her?" I asked. The woman had seemingly been everywhere and was now nowhere.

"I don't know," Val said. "The last time I saw her was as you were being arrested."

Puddle dropped the knife and looked at me. "You got arrested?"

"Yes, your boring tax-preparing sister got arrested. Now, I want to hear this." I turned back to Juniper. "What happened at the board meeting?"

"Garcia called me before I got there and said Dick was dead but come anyway. We went into the board meeting, and the police were already there interviewing everybody."

"They sure seem to have a hard-on for that museum," Mitzi said.

"They do, don't they?" I said. "Did Detective Putz show up?"

"No," Juniper said with an evil smile. "I think he's out writing traffic tickets about now." We all laughed.

"Linda, who had the nerve to show up, was in tears. The rest of the board is somewhat in disarray. We'll meet again in a couple of days. The good news is, I guess I'm not fired."

"Yay?" Mitzi said tentatively. "After all that's happened, do you still want to work there?"

Juniper paused. "I love that museum and the chance to put on exhibits in such a beautiful setting. The grounds alone are so rare—beach-front property that's for the people of Merryville, not cut off in a gated community."

"I'm surprised no one has snapped it up and turned it into a condo complex," I said. My observation hit a nerve.

A dot connected with another dot for me. "Maybe that's why so much attention is focused there."

"Sounds like a Scooby-Doo episode." Puddle plopped down with her breakfast fruit, pleased with herself. "Evil developers want the property so they say it's haunted."

"Life isn't a cartoon, Puddle." I sounded like the aunt who raised us.

Juniper looked at her, puzzled, then back to me. I never really explained our family dynamics to her. "Anyway, how would you prove it? We have no way of knowing who's pulling the strings."

Hard to describe, but I felt it before seeing Elsa came to the door of the kitchen with our beloved cat. Brutus was looking better, if a bit puny, and meowing. We crowded around, and Ekk said, "Can't you hear him? He's starving."

Nothing like a wounded kitty to get a room full of feline lovers moving. Val got his bowl refreshed. I went to haul in another purple sack of his favorite food, and Mitzi, Juniper, and, yes, Puddle, started petting his head.

Ekk cracked up. "Brutus said something to the effect of, 'That's more like it.' "

CHAPTER ELEVEN

MERRYVILLE

Charlie Potts sat back in his chair and thought. He had an erasable board in front of him and was busily diagramming all the info he had. He got into this mess by responding to a call for a welfare check on a slow day. He was the only one in the squad room available to follow up.

1. The Fiona fiasco at the museum. What country is she from?
2. Orig. welfare check call - Inside or outside the precinct?
3. 9-1-1 call, Panda didn't know where Mitzi was?
4. Fowler goes to neighbors and asks if they know where Mitzi is.
5. Fowler and J. Gooden leave for Germany, right after Fowler makes the 9-1-1 call.
6. V. Gooden interview, hiding something, what?
7. Gail Furrows – neighbor - related to Councilman Smithers, connection to mayor?
8. $$$$ defense attorney hired, who is paying retainer?
9. Valerie serving dolls tea. He puts three question marks beside it.
10. Valerie tries to leave the country for Germany.
11. Warrant, based on call from inside the precinct. Nothing in the Fowler yard. (He almost added "career over.")
12. Museum chairman of the board found the day after the weird thing involving the Fowlers and Goodens at the museum.
13. Museum, museum, museum.

Then there was that, whatever it was, last night at the museum, which resulted in the arrest of Fowler and the missing wife, Mitzi, who Alex Stephanovsky got released. Museum, museum, museum, museum! That was the thread that ran through this whole thing.

A light went on in his brain. The surprise visit. Defense attorney, Alexandra, Alex, flirts her ass off and basically says, "Look over there," and points him to his superiors and away from her clients, and whatever they were up to. He had no clue, but Charlie hated having the wool pulled over his eyes and being played. He'd be damned if he went charging into the power floor with nothing but a schoolboy crush for a pretty defense attorney. A man was dead, and Charlie was a good cop. He pushed back his chair and erased everything on the board.

Charlie had his own agenda now and didn't trust anybody. He grabbed his keys, opened the drawer for another pack of American Spirit, and headed out the door. He was off duty and in his own car, the decommissioned Crown Vic. He lit a cigarette and drove, smoking and thinking. It was his best thinking time. What a damn fool he was. Of course a woman like Stephanovsky wouldn't look twice at him, much less have a drink with him. This made him sad and angry. Well, he was tired of being a fool, and his anger pointed him like a laser. Potts accelerated and headed for the one he considered a weak link in the chain of whatever was going on, Fowler's secretary, Barbara. Then he would head for the museum.

A man in security at the police building sat before several blinking monitors. He'd been told to watch Detective Potts and to record anything unusual. He backed up the video feed to before the list Potts had been writing was erased. He took a still photo, emailed it to himself, then to an encrypted address. He didn't know what it meant, but better safe than sorry. His real boss was someone you didn't want to piss off.

Nanoseconds later, a computer on a modest desk at the museum pinged softly, and the encrypted message was delivered.

When Detective Potts arrived at the home address for Barbara, Panda Fowler's secretary, no one answered the door at first. He knocked again. Through the door he could hear the TV on loud, then an old man said, "Hold your horses."

A man opened the door with his walker in front of him, saw the detective, and moved to close it again. "We don't want any."

Potts put his foot in the door and showed his badge through the opening. The man sighed. "You might as well come on in."

"Are you here alone, sir?"

"What?" It was hard to be heard over the television, which was playing the local news.

Charlie Potts went to the TV and manually turned it down. "Mind if I sit?"

"Suit yourself." The man settled back in his Barcalounger and adjusted his suspenders. He pushed his glasses back up his nose and squinted at the detective.

"Sir, I'm here to speak with Barbara." Potts's eyes traveled to a picture of the old man with the woman he interviewed at Fowler Tax Services. "Is she your daughter?"

"Babs? Of course she's my daughter. I'm Henry."

"Yes." He spoke louder. "Is she here?"

"She went to pick up thingamawhumpy, you know, that small girl." He lifted an aged hand to show a distance of about two feet.

"Who is that?"

"My new caregiver, Elsie...something like that. She's German." At that he wheezed and spit into a cup. "My own daughter hardly lets me be alone, like I'm decrepit."

"Your daughter works for Panda Fowler at the tax place?"

"Yep. Has for nigh on seven years or so. She's a good girl, my Babs. What does the po-lice want with her?"

Potts had to smile. "Actually, I—"

He was interrupted by the sound of the back door opening. Babs rushed in, both arms filled with grocery bags. "Pops, sorry I'm late. Elsa and I—" She stopped dead upon seeing the detective in her living room. "We stopped by the store." She looked nervous. "You're that cop."

"Yes, Detective Charles Potts. I came and asked you some questions at your work." He forgot what he was going to say because, right behind

Babs, it appeared a grocery bag walked in by itself. All three heads turned, and the elven woman, with great effort, set the bag on the floor.

The old man laughed out loud. "See what I mean? Never seen a girl so little, but she's all grown." He slapped his knee and knocked over the TV remote.

Charlie Potts closed his mouth and gathered himself. This was one of the dolls he'd seen at the Fowler house. He started again, something he did when he didn't know what to say. "Ma'am, I'm Detective Charlie Potts, and you are?"

The small woman stepped forward and gave him her most charming smile, saying, "I know." The faint scent of roses filled the room. "Elsa Gephardt. I'm Henry's nurse."

Charlie laughed out loud and felt calmer than he had in days. Babs laughed, too.

Elsa said to Potts, without the question being asked, "No, you're not crazy."

Brutus continued getting better, and I suspected him of milking the sympathy for all it was worth. I was sitting with him on our couch. Puddle had gone out for "supplies," whatever that was. Seeing how she was getting ready for Peru, it could be any number of things. Brutus rolled over on his back and showed me his spotty belly. Okay, I rubbed it and tried not to wonder what would happen next. The cat therapy was helping. Mitzi walked into the room with her cell phone to her ear, wrapping up a phone call. "Okay, Mom, love you, too."

I lifted my eyebrows, and Mitzi smoozled on the couch on the other side of our four-legged baby. "Is your mom back?"

"Yes, living in Stockton, you would never know what she'd been up to a short while ago." After a beat she added, "Obviously she has her voice again."

"Wow. Your mom." Mitzi plopped next to me.

"Yeah, your mother-in-law." I patted her thigh. A beat passed.

"Are you pissed at her?"

"I don't know how I feel." She rubbed her face, tired.

"May I make a suggestion?"

"Sure."

"Let's call Dr. Tina. We both need to process this." Mitzi laughed.

"Oh sure." She mimicked making a call. "Hi, Dr. Tina, my mother let me be kidnapped and brought to an evil kingdom in Germany. Uh-huh, there were unicorns, and by the way, I have wings that sprout when trouble is around." She looked deep into my eyes. "You can visit me in Bellevue Mental Hospital." She took both my hands. Brutus looked hurt that he was not the center of our universe. "Baby, we can't talk about this to anybody."

I counted off on my fingers. "Except for Puddle, Ekk, Elsa, your mother, and, I guess, your, um, father, Ehren."

She dropped one of my hands, leaned back into the couch, and stared off into the distance. "It's too much to deal with right now. Ekk said I can make a recording like when we got that one from Heloisa, but there's no direct dial to the Hercynian Garden."

"Imagine that." I kissed her on the forehead. Brutus was tired of all our movement and jumped off the couch. We snuggled closer and held each other.

After a while I said, "Did you ask your mom about the pendant?"

"No, I will though. Did you find it?"

I shook my head no.

Juniper was also getting her head around all that had happened. She and Mrs. Charlotte Windingle were having lunch. The elder woman had invited her to the Yacht Club, and they sat at an outside table to enjoy the ocean view.

"How's Beatrice?"

"Mourning is hard." Charlotte took a dainty sip of her Bloody Mary and fixed her eyes on Juniper. "That woman can cry."

"I can imagine." Juniper picked up her menu. "I'm surprised you wanted to eat here. Wasn't Dick Mortimer a member?"

"And Bea, and me, and a lot of other important people. It's exactly why I wanted to eat here." A lovely woman stopped by the table, and pleasantries were exchanged. Charlotte turned back to Juniper. "My family built this club, and Beatrice and I have known each other since we were children. I didn't really like Dick from the beginning, but he made her so happy—at first."

Juniper looked around the room. There were almost enough city officials to hold a council meeting. "What happened?"

The diamonds in Charlotte's ears sparkled when she laughed, a practiced gesture. "Linda the homewrecker, who is on the board at the museum. At events, she and Dick always were off together talking. It was only for a couple of minutes, but you could tell they had a secret, some special bond."

Juniper started to speak, but another couple came by to pay homage to the *grande dame*. After they left, Charlotte said, *sotto voce*, "I'm rehabilitating you, darling. They're all so afraid of my money, they wouldn't dare go against you."

"I thought my job was safe," Juniper said.

Another musical laugh. "Oh, honey, for the moment. And I wish it was only about one job, even if that one job is yours. That property has been in jeopardy for years, and it's why I donate so much to the museum. It's the last undeveloped beachfront in Merryville."

Juniper felt dense. She had focused so much energy on what went into the museum, she rarely, if ever, thought about the actual land it sat upon. "But you're a developer." She was sure she looked as puzzled as she felt.

"Yes, an ethical one. We Windingles know when enough is enough. Cities need open spaces, art, and pretty views to stay flourishing, in addition to condo complexes. A city on the ocean can be developed out of existence if you let it."

Juniper looked at Charlotte with a renewed sense of appreciation. "I see." They waited as servers placed plates of melon and heirloom tomato in front of them. "Who wants to develop it, if not your company?"

"I'm glad you're better at art than social politics, my dear." She shook her head. "Any number of developers, including the mayor and that Linda woman. That's why she got on the museum board in the first place. She probably snared that weak husband of Bea's into an affair." Another sip on her Bloody Mary. She held it up, and a staffer quickly removed it, presumably to go make another.

"Boy, did that backfire."

Juniper felt lost at sea. Her focus had been on getting another installation at the museum that would electrify the crowds. She felt like the rug had been pulled out from under her. What if there was no museum at all?

Juniper excused herself to go to the women's room. She forced herself to smile. She nodded to several acquaintances on the way, and one stopped her, smiling through red lips. "Ms. Gooden. How interesting to see you here." The woman's face was familiar, but her name escaped Juniper. She put her tan hand on Juniper's arm. "Be smart. You may have fooled that old Charlotte, but we don't want you and your bad press tainting our club or the museum. Why don't you just quit? You're not fit to lead this community."

Someone said, "Jennie!" and the woman waved and smiled.

She said, "I'll be right there!" and gave Juniper's arm a fierce squeeze. "Think about it."

Shaken, Juniper went into the nautical-themed bathroom, entered a stall, and silently cried. By the time she returned her face to presentable and went back to her table, Charlotte was sitting there chatting with a young man who probably sought to be seen with one of the pillars of society.

After he left, and after Juniper took a steadying drink of water, she said, "Wow, apparently my rehabilitation is going to be harder than I thought." She told Charlotte what had happened.

"Dick Mortimer had some friends and some enemies. Some of these people are angry their carefully scripted lives of lunching, brunching, sailing, and shopping have been making it into the paper. It doesn't look good next to the homeless problem we still have."

Juniper chewed silently on a piece of ahi tuna. "Charlotte, what do you think would happen if I invited Fiona back to do a new show? We could expose whoever is behind this other developer's agenda and stir things up."

Charlotte looked at Juniper as if she were a true innocent. "Timing is everything. Fiona did light a match, Juniper. Having her again so soon would stir things up all right, but right now everyone wants to go back to normal. I hope you'll pay more attention to the way the wind is blowing."

Juniper sighed, tired of metaphors. "After the last month, I'm not even sure what normal is. With enough attention, the powers that be might back off from the museum."

"Or, it could accelerate the sale of the place." Charlotte again gave her a sympathetic look and patted Juniper's hand. "I think that your Fiona idea is coming from your hurt and desire to strike back. Let's put our heads together and think of something smart, and I do have some ideas. Besides, I told Bea you and I would figure out who killed Dick." Juniper almost choked on her dish of Eggs Benedict, but she leaned in to hear Charlotte's plan.

Mitzi went to the library to research griffins and the Winters family, her true birth name, and I had some precious alone time—for about five minutes. I went into the backyard to fill in holes, part of my quest to return to normalcy. I intended to ditch a five-foot-tall cat condo in the corner of the yard that Brutus never used, and other things needed to go as well.

Ekk joined me, sandwich in hand, apparently at home now in my kitchen. "Need help, Panda?"

I looked around at the mess in the yard. "Sure." My spirits were low, probably a natural reaction to this sudden cessation of wild activity. Ekk grabbed a spade and, in magic elf fashion, filled five holes to my every one.

The borders we left upturned, hopeful of planting, but the yard was at least level after our exertions. Brutus inspected our work then lay down in one of the remaining holes. Afterwards, we, and the cat, sat on the back porch, looking at the not perfect but hugely better yard. I had gotten us lemonade. "I thought you weren't supposed to use magic here."

Ekk tilted his head sideways, like my childhood collie used to do, and said, "Miss Panda. It's pretty low-voltage magic, filling in holes. I could tell you really needed a hand. What's on your mind?"

So there I was, sitting on my back porch, spilling my guts to an elf. "I don't know. Everything seemed fine when I was trying to find Mitzi, moment by dangerous moment. Now Puddle's here, Mitzi has lumps on her shoulders, and I'm not sure what our life is going to be like." A tear came to my eye.

"Are you crying?" He was way more sensitive than I'd given him credit for.

"No," I said and cleared my throat, "it's allergies. They got stirred up with the dust." He let that alone.

We sat in silence, and a raven landed on the table between us. Ekk and the bird had a quick conversation, and it flew away.

"See what I mean? What was that?"

Ekk said, "I'm not going to lie to you. Things are always as they have been, but now you know there are more . . . layers. Ehren wants to speak with Mitzi. A message will be coming soon."

I sighed and stared at the trees. "It's never going to be over, is it?" I looked down at my white legs peeking out of shorts. At least I'd lost some weight with all the dashing around.

"Woe is me, the Quoon has Sweened!" Then he laughed.

My head jerked up. "What?" My pity party had been interrupted.

"That's what drama people do in the movies."

My look remained puzzled.

"Buster Keaton, 1930?" I was learning about Ekk's fondness for old, human movies.

At that, we both chuckled, and I got more real. "What about the tax practice?"

"You go in Monday, and I help you. Next?"

"What about Mitzi? She has wings, you know."

"Yes, and they'll stay dormant unless an extreme circumstance makes it necessary to deploy them. Then you'll be glad she has them. Next."

"What kind of extreme circumstance?" I started to cry again.

Ekk put down his lemonade and held both of my hands. He stood in front of me, so elven, but his presence was that of a much bigger man. "Stop, Panda. Stop."

"And what about my parents? Puddle seems to think she can find them. I know you said it was a trick, but I saw them when we did the ritual at the museum. I saw them."

Ekk looked sad. "You saw a reflection, from when I don't know. You said you saw your old dog, right?"

I sniffed. "Yes."

"He would be what, thirty years old now, Panda?"

I got his point. "So they're dead?"

"Who knows? When you were so open, the evil forces used what they could to distract you. The answer is"—he adopted a strange imitation of someone—" I don't know, sweetheart. Above my pay grade."

That last bit, probably learned from a TV show, made me smile. We sat in silence. The yard was calming. I caught a whiff of a trumpet flower's perfume.

Something inside me shifted, and I sighed, realizing that acceptance was the only course. "So when do we get this message?" I wiped my eyes with the clean part of the back of my hand.

Ekk looked up, and we saw a bundle drop from the sky onto the lawn. "I'd say, right about now."

The green bundle fell with a thud on the dirt.

I was out of my chair in an instant and tripped over my feet when I looked up to see more of who dropped it. I landed eye to eye with the bundle, which was wrapped in the same green substance the Hercynian Garden was constructed with. Ekk hopped down from his chair and over to where I lay. "Are you okay?"

"Fabulous." I wanted to go back to bed and pull the covers over my head.

He snatched the pouch and opened the seamless green substance with a wave of his hand. In it was a shard of crystal.

I sat up. "Jewelry?"

"No, it's how we store the holograph message like the one you saw of Heloisa at the tax office."

"Open it up!" I reached for it.

"It must be played in Mitzi's presence."

"How do you know?"

He gave me a look I was becoming more familiar with.

I shook my head, got to my feet, and dusted off my legs. "Never mind." We went inside to await her return.

Down at the library, Mitzi was frustrated. The only references to griffins were in fairy tales, hardly helpful. The library in the center of town, built in the Spanish-style, was old, and she always felt comfortable there. This had been such a strange time of discovery. She was disappointed her go-to haven didn't have all the answers. Even though she gave up the search for information on the magical world she now knew existed, she still wasn't ready to go home.

Thinking back to the conversation around the kitchen table this morning, she asked to see microfiche of the museum property, to see if she could find out who owned it. The librarian, an eightyish woman in comfortable clothes, was ecstatic someone was asking how to use the microfiche.

"What with the advent of the Internet, most folks only come in to do Google searches or look for books to help with a research paper."

"Mmm hmm." Mitzi didn't want to be rude, but she needed to see what was on those reels. After more chatter and a couple of misses, she found the following in an old article from the *Merryville Bee*.

> August 12, 1922. Josiah Windingle, builder of the Merryville Museum of Art, today joined city fathers to dedicate the newly built complex to future generations. The project was met with cheers, but it has not been without controversy. The land was once owned by a Spanish family who still claimed ownership of the prized parcel. The family was granted the land and has family ancestors buried there. An agreement between the two factions was resolved barely in time for the ground breaking.

Mitzi wondered where those ancestors were buried, and if there wasn't more to discover. Returning to the chatty librarian, she asked for other ways to dig into the old controversy. "Sure, there's another newspaper, *The Merida Times*. It stopped publishing shortly after the turn of the century, only ninety-something years ago, really not much time in the grand scheme of things." Mitzi loved to research and was like Brutus chasing a mouse, single-minded and focused.

After lunch, Juniper went back to the museum. She still had her key and went to the main gallery. The Fiona Castlebaum exhibit on homeless and feral cats was, of course, gone. In its place, Dick Mortimer, in his last installation to curate, had placed a very safe but completely out-of-touch "Founding Fathers" exhibit. It was clear to her trained eyes the exhibit had been hastily cobbled together from stock photos in the storage basement. Juniper was sure that the current "City Fathers," such as Mayor Tom Reed, gave Dick his marching orders, in order to rehabilitate their reputations after the day her life changed so dramatically with Floodlight. That seemed light-years ago.

She walked from the beginning, as if a visitor to the museum. There were pictures in black and white of the original dig and a piece on the Windingle family. She scanned the stories of how oil changed this beach town from a marshy backwater, and the Windingles' role in building a town from a getaway for Hollywood stars into a sprawling metropolis. There were stories about fundraising for local charities and the new no-kill shelter that actually killed quite a lot of animals. The exhibit was unchallenging and boring and was very selective of which truth to tell.

Now Dick Mortimer was dead.

As she had done before when puzzled by a piece, Juniper sat alone on a cube in the center of the museum, in the enormous space, and let her muses speak to her. She didn't know where they would take her, but she knew the current exhibit had to go, or at least be turned on its dull head. The tinkling sound of her cell phone shook her from her reverie. When she answered, the muses gave her a very excited Mitzi Fowler. She sat in the semi-dark, and a smile slowly spread as she listened to an amazing tale that had yet to be told to a modern audience.

Across town, Alexandra Stephanovsky straightened her purple derby hat and went through three different scarves in her blazer pocket before announcing one perfect. She took her private elevator down to the secure front door and checked for messages at the front desk. "There is one," the clerk said, handing over an envelope with spidery writing. She looked at what appeared to be an invitation, which she chucked in her bag and headed out to meet Charlie Potts for that drink.

She took an Uber to Denny's, on the corner of Briar and Obispo.

Detective Potts arrived at their agreed-upon location, a place at which Alex had said neither of their friends would ever show, not knowing he ate there at least once a week. He played with the mat in front of him, straightened it out several times, and checked his watch again. He knew it wasn't a real date but couldn't help but look forward to seeing her again.

The waitress brought another pot of coffee over, but he said no, hoping his bladder wouldn't burst before she even arrived. He was distracted and didn't notice a uniformed colleague until he eased into the booth. The officer was about five-feet, six-inches tall, with brown eyes and wavy black hair. His name tag had a piece of black electrical tape over it. "I was hoping I could find you here."

"Wow, maybe you should put in for detective."

The younger man said, "I need to deliver a message."

He looked like a cop—fit, trimmed mustache—but his eyes were off somehow.

"So, deliver."

"Stay away from the museum, and don't turn on your brothers."

"Says who? Who is sending this mysterious message? If you have nothing to hide, why worry?"

"I'm giving you some friendly advice. Next time we won't use words."

Potts was up and out of the booth in a nanosecond, blood boiling, "Who's this 'we' business? I'll have your badge, you pipsqueak. You've already crossed the line by threatening me." He reached across to rip off the tape.

The young man stood up and evaded his moves. "You need to retire, old man. Haven't you embarrassed the department enough?" Alexandra burst through the door of the diner, impossible to miss. The young cop looked at her, then back at Potts. "Apparently not." He bolted.

A mom with her crying toddler in tow moved in front of Potts, her stroller blocking the way. The stranger was out the door in a flash and disappeared around the corner. Charlie motioned for the check, frustrated.

"Let's get out of here," Alex said, correctly reading the situation. Potts threw a ten on the table and followed her out. She looked over her shoulder and batted her eyes. "Got a car? Let me guess, that old decommissioned Crown Vic."

Charlie felt pretty low. He was so easy to read. "Sure, outdated, exactly like me."

"Let's change it."

"What?"

"What kind of car do you like, not what kind of car you accept." They got into the car, with her trying not to touch the insides. He grinned. "Sounds like Zen bullshit, sure, gimme a Porsche Carrera." He backed the old car out and headed for the Pacific Coast Highway.

"Seriously, what do you make? Seventy-eighty grand a year?"

He pulled his head back into his neck, making the frown that says, "That's nunya. As in none of your business. Where's this going?"

She sighed. "Sometimes you have to stir things up a bit, Charlie, to get a fresh perspective."

The feeling of being the center of her attention was uncomfortable but in a good way. "What are you, my fairy godmother?"

She smiled and her eyes looked up and to the left.

He had worries about the case, and hated being in the dark, but really enjoyed the presence of the dapper defense attorney. What the hell. "Where to?"

"Let's go to the Auto Square." She put her hands together in her lap, obviously pleased.

"What?"

"We need to swap out cars. If we go to the Mercedes dealer, they have donuts and cappuccino."

"You're crazy." He was smiling, driving like a cop does, eyes constantly roving, edging the car in traffic toward the freeway leaving for Los Angeles County.

"Probably. Just drive. Indulge me. Now, what happened in there? Who was that cop?"

"I don't know. I'm not even sure he was a cop. He had tape over his name."

She was all business now. "You know everybody in the precinct?"

He didn't answer and checked the rearview mirror. He patted his pocket for cigarettes. "Not the new recruits necessarily."

She fingered her pearls then opened her purse and shook out one of her Virginia Slims. "It looked like you two were going to start throwing punches." They drove in silence.

He lit the skinny cig and took a deep drag, finally saying, "Sounds like you think we're being followed, or are going to be followed. Why?"

"Sit tight. I'm going to tell you a story." Alex proceeded to tell him about her involvement in the case, from the initial call from Fiona to represent Valerie to the present time, and her suspicions about who she believed was pulling the strings. She brought a manila folder out of her satchel and, when they hit the red light, showed him photos that sealed the deal. Potts listened, and even though a bit past his shelf life, he was a good detective. He saw more clearly what, until now, had been obscured.

It only took twenty minutes or so to get to the Auto Square, just like the commercials promised, but in that time Charlie had heard so much his head spun. "We've got to take this to the mayor. If someone at the precinct is involved, I want our butts covered."

"Are you sure we can trust him?"

They got out of the old Crown Vic, and he went around to open Alex's car door. "You should talk. Why should I believe you? Defense attorneys are paid to spin tall tales."

She fixed him with her serious face, but it softened, and she said, "Because I'm working for good and against evil, nothing less." She left him in a swirl of her soft perfume and walked toward the tall, glass-and-chrome entrance to the fanciest car dealer Charlie had ever been to, except one time when he had to question a witness. "All-righty then."

At the Mercedes dealer, they acted like regular shoppers, checking out all the new and used cars. Charlie was drawn to a Chrysler 300 that looked like a Bentley, as Alex tried to convince him of the many charms of a German automobile. Potts started to think it was time to update his ride and said he'd had enough of Germany. When they returned from a test drive, he put the car in park, looked straight at Alex, and said, "You sure about all of this? Cuz if you're wrong . . ." He pawed his pocket but decided not to light up and ruin the new-car smell.

After what he'd seen at Babs and Henry's with that Elsa, his mind was open to possibilities.

"I don't have every single piece of the puzzle yet," Alex said, "but, yeah, I'm sure."

He playfully rested his cheek on his fist and said, "When you said we were gonna have a drink, I thought you meant a drink." His thumb and pinky mimicked tipping a beer. He was smiling now.

"There are all sorts of drinks, right?" I like caffeine. If I'm right about a few things, we're going to be up awhile." The young hipster salesman came over to them and gave them a quote on taking the old Crown Vic as a down payment on the impressive-looking Chrysler 300.

∾

Back at the house, Ekk and I waited for Mitzi, but Puddle made it home first, both hands full of department store bags. "Hey, Panda Bear. Hey, little man." Ekk was heading to the kitchen, and I could see him cringe. He didn't like being called that.

I put aside my own worries and was glad to see her. "How did your shopping go?"

"Fabu, but ohmygosh things have gotten so expensive! In India, I could have spent a fraction for the same things."

"Why didn't you?"

"Honestly, I was ready for some American R. E. I.," referring to the sports store. She loved to spell things out. "Sometimes I do miss California."

"But you're taking off again."

"Let's not talk about that." She flung herself down on the couch, and a wave of patchouli drifted by. "Where's Mitz?"

I sat down in the overstuffed chair near her. "She should be home any minute from the library."

As if on cue, Mitzi's keys turned in the door. She came in very excited and talking. I nearly tripped over Brutus as Puddle and I raced Ekk for the door. Mitzi fell into my arms. After all we had been through, our romance had definitely kicked up a notch. After a kiss, I said, "How was your research quest?"

Her brown eyes shimmered with excitement, "I found a piece to the puzzle . . . actually a couple of pieces."

Ekk, who'd been waiting patiently, said, "We have a message from Ehrenhardt." He turned to Puddle and said, "Mitzi's true father."

Puddle beamed. "I love this." She pawed through her bags.

Mitzi sat on the arm of my chair, and I took my place in it. Ekk made sure the blinds were closed and then touched the new stone on his dagger. As before, a hologram about the size of a Barbie doll took form, but this time, the king of Hercynian Garden, Ehren, the proud griffin, appeared, dragging his broken wing.

Puddle stopped crinkling her bags and turned to me. "This is awesome, sis, better than a movie." I shushed her.

Ehren spoke, his voice strong and commanding as usual. "Darling daughter, and my new daughter, Panda, we at the Hercynian Garden owe you a debt. You are both worthy and brave. Word has come to me that, for now, the evil of the Wolf-Raven coalition has been halved. The ravens are now neutral and have been a great help in this endeavor. The truce is uneasy at times, but the world is more in balance than when I first sent Heloisa to you."

Puddle started to ask a question but was shushed by everyone. Ekk whispered, "It's a recording that only plays once."

"Eternal vigilance is now part of your life, and I'm sorry for that. Ekk and Elsa will stay until I feel you're safe, but that may be a very long time, even in your world. We will send someone for Valerie, but when and who, has not been decided. Communication between worlds is dangerous, but if you have great need, you will learn the ways from Elsa to get in touch. Panda, keep my daughter safe. I'm counting on you." The image faded.

Puddle's eyes were huge. She turned to me with new respect. "That was rad." Seriously, I had to agree with her.

We all sat silent for a moment with our thoughts. I was puzzled. "Ekk? Can you explain a little bit more? It almost sounded like he was saying goodbye."

Ekk cleared his throat, moved in front of Mitzi, and took her hand. It was a very gentlemanly gesture. "Mitzi, Panda, this place and the things you have seen must not be shared. That goes for you, too, Miss Puddle Fowler. You must forget it and go on about your ordinary lives. Our parallel worlds weren't meant to overlap like this. But, as you've experienced, it was necessary. You may see Ehren again, or even visit the Hercynian Garden, but it will be rare and may not ever be possible."

Mitzi's eyes turned glassy. "I just found my real dad, and I've lost him again."

"No, but keep the octopus pendant near. That's how you will call him if you need to." Mitzi looked at me, and I looked at Ekk and then cast my eyes down.

"What?" Puddle said.

"Ekk, it's gone," I said. "The dwarves took it."

"Are you sure?" Upon seeing my expression, he said, "Of course you are. It's probably back in the Black Forest by now. Mitzi, did you talk to your mother about it?"

"We've only talked once since I've been back."

All eyes looked at her expectantly, and she sounded defensive when she said, "The topic didn't come up."

"Let's give her a call."

The house was crowded and messy, with Puddle camping out in the living room and the elves in and out of the kitchen, needing constant snacks to literally keep from disappearing. I found my phone in a jumble of TV remotes. "I'll call."

I dialed the number, and after two rings, Susan answered.

"Hey, Susan."

"Panda, is Mitzi okay?"

I paused, thinking, I'm fine, thanks for asking, but I said, "Yes, are you okay?" Ekk and Mitzi sat around me in the living room and stared at me. I turned away. Their eyes were distracting me.

Susan said, "It's been a time of remorse, of analyzing." I inwardly groaned. Mitzi's mom could go on for quite a time in a poetic vein. I cut her off as gently as I could.

"Susan, I have a question—well a lot of questions, but we'll save those for a face to face sometime."

"Don't blame me."

"I don't blame you for anything, Susan." Now I felt bad. I called for information and had given no thought to her fragile, if self-centered, state.

She sniffed. "What do you want to know?"

"The pendant you gave Mitzi, the one with the octopus? How did you get it? What's the story on that?"

I punched the speaker button and let her talk.

"Which one?"

All three of us at my house looked at each other. "How many are there?"

"Two. They were given to me by the seer at Ehren's palace for protection. When I left with you, they were worried about your safety. Ehren gave me one ceremoniously, and this kind old woman gave me the other."

Ekk zeroed in. "Susan, this is important."

"Who is this?"

"Ekk. I'm a guardian elf." This had all started to sound so normal. "Who was the woman who gave you the twin pendant? Can you describe her?"

"So many questions. It was ages ago." She started to cry again.

Mitzi jumped in and said, "Mom, hold it together. No one is blaming you for anything. I don't have time to explain, but it's important. Can you please try to remember?"

"Okay, I was on my way out to the carriage to leave, and a woman approached from the shadows. She seemed to know everything that had happened and said I must always keep you safe. I was touched by her gesture. She didn't tell me her name but handed me a package with a pendant in it exactly like the one Ehren gave me."

I tried not to get irritated. It was just like Susan to take a magical item and not get details. Aaargh. "Was there anything on the wrapping? What did the woman look like?"

"So many questions! I don't know. The two necklaces looked alike to me. I threw away the wrapping. The one did have the picture of a raven on the front, come to think about it."

I asked the most important question that was in all our minds. "Do you still have the other pendant?"

"I think so. Let me look."

We all talked softly about the implications of this while she was away from the phone. "Yes, it's here."

Ekk's ears quivered, and he said, "I'll be right over." By the time I swiveled my head at this, he had run out the back of our house at lightning speed. I wondered if he knew she was four-hundred miles away, or if that even mattered to an elf.

Mitzi continued to talk to her mother in reassuring tones until Susan said, "Excuse me, someone's knocking at the door."

We could hear her in the background. Suddenly, Ekk's breathless voice came through. "She's got it."

"Mitzi, shall I give it to this elf?"

Why did Susan always make me want to scream? "Yes," Mitzi and I said in unison.

"Now if you don't mind, I'm very tired."

"Okay, Mom, thanks. We'll be up to visit soon." Mitzi swatted me as I made a face. We rang off and sat waiting for Ekk's return. It was several hours, and he came in very hungry. "That took way too much energy. I flew back commercial."

Mitzi jumped up to get the sandwiches she had prepared for this eventuality, and I patted the seat next to me. "More elf magic?"

He blushed. "Yes, there was no time to waste. I used our emergency elf hole to Northern California." He reached into his pocket and pulled out a duplicate of the pendant I'd been carrying until recently. Mitzi entered with a tray of grilled cheese and root beer, Ekk's favorites, and looked in wonder at the pendant I was holding. "It looks like the one that got stolen, but it's different somehow."

Mitzi was very sensitive.

"I know," I said. "First off, it's tingling. The other one didn't do that. Ekk, are you sure this is safe?"

He paused between bites and said, "More than safe. This is a very powerful protection charm."

"Then it belongs here," I said as I looped it over Mitzi's lovely neck, taking care to make sure it didn't get tangled in her beaded braids. It looked perfect.

Mitzi smiled at me, and I had a sudden thought. I turned to Ekk. "So was the other one *not* a charm?"

"Apparently, not at all." He chuckled.

"Ha! Those thieves got nuthin'. Wait a minute." A thought was dawning on me.

Ekk grinned. "You remember when you decked the evil dwarves?"

"How could I not?"

"All you." I noticed for the first time how the skin around Ekk's eyes crinkled merrily when he smiled.

Puddle was, for once, silent, and Mitzi seemed to be having the same thought I was.

My eyes couldn't have been bigger as I sank back into our couch. "Holy shit."

"I knew you had it in you, babe." Mitzi encircled my head and kissed the top of it.

"You rock, sis. I'm going to go chant." Puddle lifted herself effortlessly, the result of years of yoga, and headed out to the backyard.

I thought about our adventures in Castle Schwarzwald and how safe I'd felt with the chain around my neck and I laughed. Ekk laughed, too, and soon we were all in tears, telling stories and remembering.

"But a raven landed next to me and then flew away! When it didn't give me away, I was sure that was the protection charm."

"You know what happens when you assume, darling." Mitzi collected our dishes and sauntered back to the kitchen.

Ekk responded seriously. "I wasn't there. Who knows what bird brains think? They've waffled back and forth for ages and now seem to be staying out of the Great Conflict." We pulled apart other details, and I sat a little taller, feeling like a bad-ass.

Brutus sauntered in and meowed in that serious way he had lately acquired, now that he apparently knew a message might be understood.

Mitzi returned, picked up our boy, and said she wished we had a miniature pendant to hang on his collar.

CHAPTER TWELVE

MERRYVILLE

Mayor Tom Reed was getting nervous. On the ninth floor of City Hall, he looked out at his city. Six weeks ago, his reelection was a done deal. Now there were citizens' groups at every city council meeting beating the drum about the homeless and those damn feral cats. People also wondered about a murderer being loose.

He had nothing against the homeless. But even Jesus said the poor will always be with us, and a mayor can't solve every problem. The embarrassment at the museum in Councilman Gary Smithers' district started all this. Richard Mortimer died in Smithers' district, too, and then there was the press conference fiasco.

He looked down through his window at District Seven as if he could see Gary actively working against him. Maybe a call to the press was in order. His office was big and airy, the walls covered with awards, pictures of himself with well-known politicians and celebrities, and accolades from civic groups. He really did love his city, almost as much as he loved himself. But there was work to do. He turned from the window and sat at his heavy oak desk and buzzed his secretary.

"Margaret, where's that coffee?"

"I'll be right in, sir, and you have two visitors, an Alexandra Stephanovsky and a Detective Potts. They say it's urgent."

"No appointment? Send 'em in anyway, but make sure the city attorney stops by."

"Done."

A few minutes later, a rap came on the door and Margaret led in the unlikely duo. The mayor knew who they were, and his face held a puzzled expression.

He stood up and shook hands with them then took his steaming mug of coffee from Margaret. After pleasantries and a similar cup placed in the defense attorney's hands, they got down to business.

"This is a surprise. You remind me of the way a lot of jokes start—a cop and a defense attorney walk into a bar." He laughed heartily." When his joke didn't rock the room, he set his coffee down. "You said it was urgent?"

Alex spoke first. "Yes."

He chose to turn to Potts as if it were he who had spoken. "Detective, it's unusual to see you in the company of the enemy." Big white-toothed smile. "No offense, Ms. Stephanovsky."

She gave a fake laugh. "None taken. I think you meant to say 'defender of the constitution.'"

It was an old argument.

Mayor Reed sat back in his chair and was winding up for his typical political response, but Potts's patience with small talk was exhausted. "Mayor, you've known me for years, at least by reputation. Have I ever come to you?" The mayor opened his mouth, but Potts answered his own question. "No, I have not." He pointed to Alexandra and himself. "We're here together to show you that there's a problem in this town, and we believe you're the person to make it right. It cuts across lines."

Reed leaned forward, folded his hands, and waited for them to say more. Abruptly, there was a knock on the door, and the city attorney poked his head in. "Bob," Reed said, "join us." Then to Alex and Charlie he said, "I asked the city attorney to listen in. Saves time. It sounded important."

Bob and Alex exchanged nods, obviously familiar with one another.

Potts was literally risking his career, saying the words he next said. "I'm not sure who killed Dick Mortimer, but I"—he looked at Alex—"we know City Councilman Smithers is involved."

The mayor paid rapt attention. "Look, I know he was involved in bringing our police over to that house on Thistle Drive. His cousin lived across the street from them. That's a big leap to committing murder."

"No, no, we're not saying he killed Dick Mortimer, but he's definitely involved in police corruption."

Reed was all seriousness now. "Do you have any proof?"

Alex opened her Louis Vuitton bag and brought out an envelope with a stack of pictures that she tossed on the shiny desk. "The call used to justify the search warrant came from inside the precinct, and this is from the night your officers arrested Panda and Mitzi Fowler."

She pointed to Panda and Mitzi, who were in the forefront of the pictures. Mayor Reed had heard about their arrest, along with the curator of the museum and a woman he assumed was her wife. The pictures were in the floodlight the Castlebaum woman made famous. They looked like stills from a graphic novel. The women appeared to be tired and bedraggled, and his officers were handcuffing them. In one picture, a woman with her hair sticking up looked ready to rip somebody's head off. It was Panda Fowler.

"So these lesbians are behind it?" He was puzzled. "What am I looking at?"

Alex moved in, irritated. "Look over here. Gary Smithers was unintentionally caught in the frame. Fiona uses infrared photography in addition to regular film, so she can pick up details like this, even in the dark."

In the edge of the picture, Richard Mortimer was walking away and Smithers had his wallet out. He appeared to be handing money to a police officer in the dark of the parking lot. A shadow was following Richard.

"How did you get these?" Mayor Reed fanned them so Bob could see.

Potts said, "Fiona Castlebaum sent them to Alexandra. Sometimes side issues present themselves in her art pieces, and this is a big side issue."

"I'm surprised," Bob said, "she didn't decide to do an exposé on corruption in Merryville and finish the trash job she started the other night." He clearly wasn't happy with the visitors.

Alex jumped in. "Juniper Gooden, has had a chance to talk to her. I don't think Fiona is our enemy here. She's really trying to help."

Bob grunted. "I'm going to need those pictures."

Mayor Reed squinted and put on his glasses, something he didn't do in public. "And who is this cop? Why is he after me?"

"We don't know yet," Potts said, "and this is what concerns me. I don't know how infected the department is. I wanted to make sure this went all the way to the top so you know we're all on the same side before I start rattling cages." He pointed to the officer in the photo. "This is the same cop that tried to warn me away from the museum." Potts relayed the story of what happened at Denny's.

"Wait a minute," Reed said. "Gary Smithers knows this cop. Have you asked him about it yet?"

"No, *in casa* as they say. There's a bolo out," Potts answered. "We already knew Smithers was related to the woman who pointed the police department to the Fowlers. This is a whole 'nother deal. His council office was my first stop after seeing this picture where he's giving this guy money after the arrest of these women."

"Find that cop and Smithers. I'll deal with the police commissioner."

Alexandra started to speak, but Potts grabbed her arm. "Yes, sir."

The door closed on the detective and the defense attorney, and Bob launched into his questions. "Shall I make a few quiet inquiries?"

Mayor Reed sat seething. He and Bob put their heads together. "If they're right, we need to move now."

"Agreed. What do you need?"

Reed called for Margaret. "Call the police commissioner. Hell, get everybody on the Commission for Pubic Corruption. Get them in here now."

❧

Alex and Charlie walked silently to the town hall parking lot and got into his new Chrysler 300.

"You're a good cop, Charlie. It was a big risk going to the brass."

Potts wheeled onto the street and sighed. "I'm ready to retire, anyway. Shall I drop you at your office?"

"Please." She needed to get to work. "And thank you."

Charlie patted his pocket and decided not to smoke. "For what?"

"Trusting me."

When they stopped at her office parking lot near the courthouse, she got out and started to open her car's door, then she ran back to Charlie's window.

"Did you forget something?" he asked, puzzled.

"Hey. . . be careful, Charlie. It's okay if you call me sometime." She patted his arm, jumped into her gold Mercedes, and drove out of the parking lot like a shot. He sat stunned, feeling his feelings.

The next day, the *Merryville Bee* printed the following:

MERRYVILLE MUSEUM TO HOST NEW EXHIBIT

In honor of former Chairman Richard Mortimer, the museum is featuring a retrospective of his work, including selections from his final exhibit, with commentary by family and friends.

The former FLOODLIGHT! exhibit has also been reinstalled and will present exciting new information, kept strictly secret for now. Fiona Castlebaum was interviewed in Sweden and would only say it "pulls the camera back for perspective, not only in scale, but over the arc of time." She did not further explain her comment and said she has no plans to attend the re-launching of her work. "Been there, done that," she said. "I'm not sure the mayor of Merryville is in any hurry to see me again."

A source close to the investigation of Richard Mortimer's death, who wished to remain anonymous, said Castelbaum probably would not return because she was a person of interest. Juniper Gooden, acting curator, commented only that "Art should be fearless."

Linda Chicolet and others on the board tried mightily to block Juniper from her plans.

"Dick Mortimer hasn't even been buried," Linda said. "This is a slap in the face to his family. You know how he hated the Floodlight exhibit."

"Linda," Juniper said, "you haven't even seen it. You left that night, right? We decided to get this out there right away. Also, there are two exhibits."

"Give her a chance," someone said. "Besides, it's already been in the paper."

Juniper stood up and nodded to Garcia, who stood by the light switch in the corner of the board room. He looked haggard. "Lights, please."

The video shown was new to everyone in the room except Juniper. It showed the original Floodlight exhibit that had apparently been filmed secretly.

The board members gasped. One asked, "How did you get this?"

Juniper turned to them and said, "Did you think Fiona Castlebaum would let her greatest California showing go undocumented? Please."

The film was, oddly, without its own sound. As if made from a 1920s reel-to-reel, the background music was from a circus or carnival, but it seemed appropriate to the strange events as the cherry picker arose from the beach with Fiona on it and the crowd started to panic.

"This is the opening film clip that will introduce the new visit. Commentary by Fiona, who is being interviewed about it in Sweden, is coming up next."

The film switched from fleeing patrons to Fiona, sitting in a chair on a set, being interviewed by a young man. "*Unterbauch*" was written in anarchic spray-paint letters across the backdrop. A rolling hand-graphic translated it to mean "Underbelly." The clip started mid-interview.

"Brilliant! Now let's turn to your work in the United States. What did you think of this," the interviewer said and looked down at his notes, "Merryville town in California?" He was hip looking, all in black with round, black glasses. He had some sort of accent that indicated English wasn't his first language. "I understand some of the locals were not so pleased." He giggled.

A clip was shown of angry groups outside Councilman Smithers' office, chanting and bearing signs. Afterwards, Fiona turned her face directly to the camera and said, "It's time to make this project clear. It was never my intention to harm anyone, only to throw light on their local problems of feral cats and homelessness."

She looked old in the set lighting, but her blue eyes were sparkling and intelligent. "There is not a city in the world that doesn't have problems. I want to make sure there's balance about what I found. My next exhibit there will show the amazing resilience of the people of Merryville."

"Oh, that sounds dull." The interviewer wrinkled his nose and looked confused.

"It's okay. I made several friends there. One was named Panda, who showed me that ordinary, so-called dull people are the salt of the earth."

The film faded to black, and statistics with snapshots of volunteers and soup kitchens rolled, showing the efforts of the Merryville Homeless Coalition, the "Cat Ladies" Coalition, a Merida Shore resident who dedicated hundreds of hours to cleaning up the beaches, and other noteworthy organizations and individuals. What made it cool was the music turning from circus to some Snoop Dogg rapping (Fiona touch), then some Beach Boys, ending in a rousing cheer led by Mayor Reed.

"PARIS! LONDON! NEW YORK! MERRYVILLE!"

Juniper said, "Lights, please."

Garcia wasn't there; it was an odd time to leave, but one of the other board members switched them on.

Lucas Windingle, member-at-large on the board, sat back in his leather chair and removed the pencil eraser he was tapping against his white teeth. "I must say, I'm impressed."

Maribel, sitting next to him, said, "It's an olive branch. I think."

Juniper turned to the rest of the board. "It's about the closest thing to apologizing Fiona Castlebaum has ever done. What do the rest of you think?"

"You know what I think, but I guess that doesn't matter now," Linda Chicolet said. "Dick hated that woman. Be honest. We all did—even you, Juniper, after the event. Why bother with Floodlight 2.0?"

Juniper sat down at the head of the table, Dick Mortimer's seat. Linda shot her an evil glance. "Linda, Dick's gone. It's an epilogue. The past is past. I was pretty pissed at her, too. But this is bigger than our egos or personal feelings. In fact, it's the one way we have of achieving closure after the problems she highlighted—showing the community that we're telling the narrative, that we're not afraid."

Linda's face showed rage. "We have reason to be afraid. There's a maniac out there killing board members!"

Lucas, a millennial, leaned forward. "One board member. We have no information that any of the rest of us are being stalked."

"I've had enough of this. You all can do what you want to do. What else have you got?" Linda folded her notebook with a snap. "I have a funeral to attend."

A few board members looked up at the ceiling. They were all going to go as fellow board members, but everyone knew Linda Chicolet had been involved with the now deceased board chairman and had to be hurting. Thankfully, no one said anything.

Juniper continued. "The rest of the show is the history of the community that Dick started. My additions simply dig deeper into the same subject matter."

"Well, let's go see it," Maribel said. Others nodded. "We have about a half hour before the memorial."

Juniper stood and crossed her arms. "First, I need to know right now if you all trust me. This is an exhibit that is under my artistic purview. Garcia's helping me, and I won't show anyone else until the opening. If you don't want me as your curator, now's the time to say so."

Juniper looked from face to face and saw ordinary people who were only trying to do the best they could. They looked tired and had been through hell after Fiona's "Floodlight!" exhibit.

"Oh, what the hell, it's kind of nice for a museum as old as ours to be edgy." This, from Lucas. "Did you see the article Phillip wrote for the *Bee*? A lot of folks are saying it's about time we took the lead on social issues."

"Do it, Juni," Maribel said.

Juniper noted she had started putting green highlights in her hair, something she never would have done with Dick Mortimer at the table.

She also noted that Maribel usually voted with Lucas Windingle, and today was no exception. Juniper hoped the young man realized someday that Maribel had a crush on him.

Lucas looked around the board. It was silent.

It was a little over the top when Maribel then added, "I vote yes. Art should be fearless!" but Juniper appreciated the support.

"Let's get T-shirts that say that," Juniper said. "Linda?"

"Do you need to ask?" Linda looked like a grumpy cat.

"Okay, one no. Anyone else?" This was the fish-or-cut-bait time. Juniper was ready to walk out, but she really wanted to stay. The board had the power.

In the end, it was ten to two to go forward on Juniper's terms. The exhibit would open the following Saturday.

∞

The Episcopal Church chosen for the memorial was over a hundred years old and had the most handsome, wood, gingerbread over the marble surfaces. The Vanderhoovens and others who'd been in town for generations had their names on brass plates at the end of certain pews. There was no Fowler pew, alas. Mitzi made me laugh sometimes when we went to a wedding pretending to look for it. She was surprisingly funny for such a pretty woman.

The memorial was well attended, as one might expect for such a notable, who was—whisper—murdered. The front row held Beatrice Vanderhooven-Mortimer, who was swollen-faced and holding her precious Blanca. The Windingles shared the pew with her, and Lucas, the youngest, kept handing tissues to his elders.

Father Bennington, often referred to as "Father Benadryl," for his sleep-producing sermons, presided. I saw him in the back, speaking to the ushers as the service was about to begin. A huge picture of Richard Mortimer beamed his famous smile from an art easel near his coffin.

Gigantic sprays of daisies, lilies, orchids, and roses decorated the steps that led up to the altar. Valerie and Juniper had donated their prize orchids, and my heart warmed at the gesture. The crowd, I noted ironically, was about the same as the crowd who came to the Floodlight exhibition. There were some extras, however. Detective Potts was in the back of the church watching everyone who entered. This time, mercifully, the police didn't form a ring around the audience.

Saint John's Episcopal Church had an original, real, pipe organ, and the bellows wheezed out "For All The Saints, from Whom Their Labors

Rest." The verger led in the choir. Lay ministers and priest followed with great ceremony. A thurifer swung a pot with incense. Yes, all the bells and smells were out for this important man.

Funerals are funny that way. I really didn't know Dick Mortimer, and he'd had my wife and me arrested the same night he was killed, but we were here. Thankfully, that factoid about the arrest hadn't been in the press.

All in all, affair and arrest notwithstanding, he was part of our Merryville community and local parish. I wondered what people would say and think about me at my funeral, and I squeezed Mitzi's hand.

Most folks were already seated when Linda walked in, and there was a bit of a murmur in response. She was alone and wore a hat that covered most of her face. She made her way to an empty spot in a pew a few rows in front of ours. The woman she sat next to scooted farther away. Mitzi looked at me and silently mouthed, "Wow." I noted it was the Vanderhooven pew and hoped Beatrice Vanderhooven-Mortimer didn't see that.

The service was nice: Old Testament readings, a comforting sermon, and even communion. Linda didn't go up for communion, and I was grateful for her tact. The last thing Dick's widow needed was a scene.

Finally, there was time for remembrances. Dick's brother from out of town went to the front and said something appropriate and bland, followed by an old fraternity brother and various pillars of the church. Notables of the community then went up, as well as museum members, including Juniper, who spoke about Richard Mortimer's longtime commitment to Merryville and the arts.

It was warm, and my attention was drifting when Garcia made his way to the podium. Garcia? From what I knew, he was a fairly new museum guy who adored Juniper and didn't care for Dick at all. At his approach, Beatrice Vanderhooven-Mortimer gave a look that could kill to the usher, who tried to stop the young man, but he was having none of it. Garcia was younger and quicker. He ducked around the coffin and went to the waiting microphone. He held a can of spray paint and put a red X on the picture of the deceased. The congregation gasped, but nobody moved. He moved quickly to the podium.

The microphone squealed at the loudness of his tirade. "Dick Mortimer was an asshole and a racist who betrayed my mother, an artist who died in poverty. He was a big phony. He was my father," he sobbed. The ushers and Detective Potts broke their seeming paralysis and subdued him. As he was led away, he said again, more quietly, "Dick Mortimer was my father." A hundred spontaneous conversations ensued. The vicar woke up from his glassy reverie and nodded for the organist to play. Caught by surprise, the drowsy musician launched into "Hail Thee Festival Day" which, although not appropriate for a funeral, is a favorite of Episcopalians everywhere.

Dick's widow, Beatrice, was livid, and Charlotte Windingle was doing her best to hug the upset widow and simultaneously keep her in her seat. Lucas wanted to help, but the whole thing was so awkward, and after all, he was only twenty-four. Tackling a three-hundred-pound-plus female was no easy feat. Detective Potts returned to ask everyone to stay seated for a few more minutes.

Juniper looked stunned. She was sitting in a pew with other board members, as Valerie had to work. She fanned herself maniacally with the program.

Mitzi and I searched out Linda Chicolet, who was gathering her things and preparing to bolt. Stunningly, someone had already pointed her out to Beatrice, who was making her way laboriously to the younger woman. I saw the exact moment when it registered upon Beatrice's face that Linda was in the Vanderhooven pew. *Her* pew. Linda was sobbing, and ushers rushed to intervene in what surely would be a train wreck.

Reverend Bennington took the pulpit as strains of the hymn died down and said, "Let's all please calm down. A reception is set in Vanderhooven Hall. Please join us there to celebrate this man's life." Then he said, "Go in peace to love and serve the Lord." Again the organ cranked up, and people reluctantly filed out, encouraged by six ushers, their necks craning back to see the fireworks.

Mitzi and I left, too, but not before I saw Blanca run ahead, barking and growling, and leap on Linda.

The crowd drank punch and ate cookies as the they shared remembrances, along with some cheap shots, as people are wont to do in situations like this. Garcia and Detective Potts were nowhere in sight. In the reception hall, pictures of special moments from Richard's life were displayed. "The Dash," the famous funeral poem, was projected onto a white wall. An art enthusiast, Dick's career as a painter of still life was chronicled, as well as his sterling teaching career at the local university. There were pictures of him addressing the State Senate to promote decency when the NRA flap was the big thing in the Eighties, as well as shots of Dick and Bea at their fabulous Saint John's wedding, many years and a few hundred pounds ago. It was sad for her that her husband's final public appearance was marred by this outburst. Was Garcia really Dick's son?

Board members and nosy questioners surrounded Juniper, presumably asking what she knew about her devoted sidekick's outburst. She looked distraught and seemed to be saying she didn't know. We gave her space, and Mitzi and I drank our punch and coffee from the sidelines.

An hour later, when Beatrice still hadn't made an appearance, the crowd was dwindling. Finally, Father Benadryl, I mean, Bennington, arrived to say, "The family needs peace now. Thank you all for coming." We didn't know that at the very same time, the paramedics were taking Beatrice, Linda Chicolet, and Charlotte Windingle to the Emergency Room. Apparently, we missed quite a brawl.

Mitzi and I drove home and thanked our lucky stars we were lesbians. Not that lesbians don't have drama, but usually children from former relationships don't show up that no one knows about. We just have griffins and elves and evil empires to thwart, Mitzi reminded me, which made us laugh.

Tax season was over, but I still had bookkeeping to do. So the following Monday I parked on a side street and entered Fowler Tax Services. Mitzi stayed at home to spend some time with Puddle while Babs and I were back in our orderly kingdom. Routine can be a good or a bad thing. Today it felt marvelous.

"How are you, Babs?" I asked, coming from the mini-kitchenette with my coffee.

"Good, boss. BTW, I love those little people you hired."

I almost spit out my coffee. "Ekk? And what's BTW?"

"BTW means 'by the way' and Elsa, too, is amazing. You know they're a 'thing,' right?" She smiled conspiratorially.

"Yes, right. In fact, you should know Ekk may be helping here from time to time. We need to get him his own desk."

"How fun—we need to find him a mini desk!" Babs was already Googling.

Things were what passes for normal again, and I smiled as I checked my email and returned messages.

AT HOME

Mitzi's wings hadn't unfurled for quite some time. She stood in front of the mirror at home and caressed where her nodules had been. She didn't know what to think about the whole thing. Did she really fly? Was it all a weird fantasy?

No, she knew it happened. All she had to do was put her hand on the pendant she now wore 24/7 and feel it tingle. Nothing would ever be quite the same.

She collapsed on the bed and hugged a pillow. Panda seemed to be doing fine, her work always grounded her. Elsa was busy with taking care of Henry.

Mitzi didn't know how to move forward.

How could she shop for airline tickets and plan tours for regular people to go to Europe when she knew Schvartzwald Castle was nearby, still occupied by Wolf Ravens? The unknown was too much for her and she started to cry.

Brutus hopped on the bed and nuzzled Mitzi with his soft furry head. She wiped her eyes as she replaced her pillow with the warm creature, who exhaled a mighty purr. Although still troubled, deep inside she knew something she did not understand had brought them all through this so far, and for now, that would have to be enough.

❧

At the precinct, in the interrogation room, Detective Potts sat down across from Garcia at the scarred metal table.

"That was quite a show you put on at Richard Mortimer's funeral."

The younger man picked at a piece of missing paint on the table with a chewed fingernail.

Potts went on in a kindly tone, no stranger to recalcitrant arrestees. "So, you believe the board chair of the Merryville Museum was your father? How did that come to be?"

"My mom . . ." Garcia's lip trembled, then he looked up. Clear brown eyes peered from his Latino features. He composed himself and spoke again. "He was a guest lecturer for Art History at Merida University, and my mom was a student. He was pretty famous in the art world, and my mom was young. Do you have any water?"

Without taking his eyes off of his suspect, Charlie Potts got up and rapped his knuckles on the two-way mirror. "Can we get some water in here?"

In a couple of minutes, a uniformed officer came in with a Dixie cup full of water and set it down in front of Garcia. He took a sip with shaky hands, put it down, and continued. "When she talked about him, she would never say his name. She died without telling me his name."

"When did you find out about the relationship?"

"You mean, how did I find out he was my dad?"

"Yes."

Garcia hesitated and rubbed his face with both hands. "After my mom died, I found letters from him. They had broken it off, but she never told him about me. She still followed his career and his marriage to that Vanderhooven woman. My mother loved him, and he used her like a piece of disposable trash."

"How did you get the job at the museum?"

"Merida University has always had a strong relationship with the Merryville Museum. Merryville used to be called Merida, you know. I was an art student, too, like my mom."

Potts was getting restless. "Can we fast forward a bit?"

Garcia shifted in his seat. "Sure. Linda Chicolet—"

"From the museum?"

"Yes. She was liaison with the university and hired me. Before you ask, she didn't know about all this."

"So you're his kid, you find that out, then what happened?"

He took a deep breath. "I worked at the museum for Juniper Gooden. I really like her. Linda, not so much. It was clear that she and my father wanted Juniper out. Then Floodlight happened." He smiled. "Fiona Castlebaum was so over the top."

Then his face turned to a frown. "He was so mean! After the Floodlight exhibit, I followed him out onto the greenspace. Everyone had pretty much left, but he came back for some reason. Maybe I had a few drinks, I don't know, I was yelling about him not appreciating what Juniper Gooden had done for the museum."

Tears welled in his eyes. "I wasn't going to tell him he was my biological father, but he laughed at me and called me a faggot. He told me the board was on his side, and Juniper was as good as gone. I got in his face and said, "You think you're such a big man. Well your board's not around now. I wonder what they'd think of you having a faggot son?""

A tear rolled down Garcia's face. "He sneered at me and said, 'I don't have a son.' "

The young man pointed a thumb at his chest. "I said, 'Do you remember Elena Garcia from Art School? I'm her son. And yours.' " Garcia wiped at his cheeks. "At first, he looked puzzled, then I could tell by his face that he'd put two and two together and didn't like what it meant."

Garcia finished drinking the water. "He called me a faggot again. I said, 'Then you have a faggot son, and I deserve to be acknowledged' "

Garcia mangled the Dixie cup in his hands and set the crumpled remnant carefully on the table. "He blew me off and tried to walk away and I grabbed his coat. He turned around and hit me in the chest with both his hands. 'You'll never be my son,' he said. I shoved him back. I don't know what happened, maybe he slipped, but he went over the bluff."

He covered his face with both hands and broke down into tears. "He was a bastard to my mom, but I didn't mean to kill him, I swear. I didn't mean it."

Potts didn't do the judging, only the arresting. But he figured the kid had a good chance to beat a murder rap.

ᔕ

AT THE BAR

Alex had a glass of white wine at an outside table, watched the street, and waited for Potts to arrive. She dug through her purse and came across what she had thought was an invitation chucked in there earlier. It was in strange script, and read:

DEAR MS. STEPHANOVSKY,

IT IS WITH DEEPEST GRATITUDE THAT WE THANK YOU FOR YOUR RECENT SERVICE FOR THE HERCYNIAN GARDEN. WE ARE BUILDING YOU A RETREAT IN PAYMENT AND HOPE YOU FIND IT SATISFACTORY. WHENEVER YOU NEED TO RECHARGE, COME TO SEE YOUR OLD FRIEND.

EHREN.

She smiled, lit it on fire in the ashtray, and watched it burn like flash paper with green wisp of smoke. She sat musing and watching traffic until a meaty hand scraped a wrought-iron chair noisily away from the table and Charlie asked, "This seat taken?"

Alex looked up to see Charlie Potts in, what she gathered, was his church best.

"By you." She bestowed her electric smile. "How did it go?"

"Sang like a bluebird, though it sounds like an accident. And guess what? That cop at the restaurant? It was Garcia's boyfriend, who works, or worked, in security at the precinct. That's who was at Denny's. He risked his pension to make me think there was a conspiracy of our officers, and it almost worked. It was a conspiracy of exactly two—him and Garcia—to hide Garcia's part in it. We're still checking out whether Councilman Smithers was in on it, but I don't think so. We caught up with Smithers, and he claims the money he gave the cop was for a charity the two had been involved with. Right."

"It still doesn't explain why he would call 9-1-1 about the Fowlers."

"No it doesn't, does it? He says he didn't do it."

"He probably needs a good defense attorney," she said with a mischievous grin.

Charlie lit his cigarette and gave Alex a side glance. "You would, wouldn't you?"

AT THE VANDERHOOVEN-MORTIMERS.

The scene was surreal. After a trip to St. Boniface's E.R. and some stitches, the ladies had time to talk. Beatrice poured herself another vodka and tonic.

Although maybe not drunk, they were definitely loosened up.

Bea fixed Linda with a gimlet eye. "You hired that man who killed my husband."

"We said we weren't going to do this." Charlotte dabbed at what was sure to be a hell of a shiner.

Linda waved her away. "No, let's get this all out. Dick was my friend—only," she said with the vehemence that comes with alcohol. "He was a good man. It makes me sad, too. I'm so sorry." Linda played with the olive in her glass. "Now the museum is in the hands of that woman."

"Why aren't you taking your friend's side?" Charlotte asked.

"Now who's stirring shit," Beatrice asked and laughed. Beatrice had come out best of the three, but red marks were still visible on her neck.

Linda looked startled. "Garcia? There is no side to take. It happened. Whether it was a mistake or on purpose, it never should have happened." She looked down at her bandaged hand. Blanca retracted her head almost all the way into her collar in a parody of guiltiness. Bea stared at her beloved pet.

The women sat in silence until Beatrice blurted, "I hated you because I thought Dick was cheating on me with you." Her words slurred.

"I know. I know, and I didn't know what to say. That picture of me and Dick hugging? It was like, after I told him about my sister's final days with cancer. I really liked Dick, but he was so proud. He was honorable to give me a job at the museum. He didn't cheat. I don't even think he knew Garcia was his son until that night."

Charlotte uncorked another bottle of champagne. "So you see, you both lost someone you loved."

Linda said, "Garcia has always been high strung. He hated Dick because of his conservative views on art and other things." She began to cry. "It's all so pointless. I'm so sorry you lost your husband. I'm sorry Garcia was involved."

"Gay-as-a-goose Garcia," Bea added. They all knew Richard wouldn't have wanted the world to know he had a homosexual son.

Blanca sniffed Linda's bandage. Linda looked so miserable, it pulled Bea out of her nosedive.

"Blanca's sorry she bit you, aren't you, Blanca?" Bea said it in the high-pitched baby voice she used for her four-legged darling.

A knock on the door brought sympathetic visitors to Beatrice. While they were shocked to see Linda there, it was only a matter of time until they got the real story. Knowing Merryville, it would make the rounds by noon the next day.

The following Saturday, a line snaked out of the front of the museum and trailed down the block. Hawkers were selling "Art should be Fearless" T-shirts in bright yellow, and more than a few were putting them on over their regular garb. Juniper was on the second floor, looking out at the crowd.

Maribel, her new, fully green-haired assistant stood next to her. "You miss Garcia, don't you?"

"I do. But you, missy, are a wonderful help." Juniper put an arm around her. "Look at that crowd."

Mitzi, Puddle and I were in the first group to be let in. After watching the Fiona video, we entered into an area with live cats for adoption, mixed in with pictures of the plight of the feral kitty. Puddle was all about animal rescue and soon found a bearded millennial to walk around with. Interspersed with the pictures were faces of locals with their words about the problem and suggested solutions. It was wonderful and interactive and healing for those who had felt slammed by the earlier exhibit.

Farther into the museum, the "Founding Fathers" story had been tweaked until it was merely a framework for the real story. This was what Mitzi had been so excited about. Interspersed with the original "Founding Fathers" pictures were subversive interstices, recording the same events from the views of the original indigenous people, the Spanish land-grant family, and commentary about manifest destiny. Even though the museum would remain in the hands of the board, this history made this land untouchable for any other commercial purpose.

Finally, before exiting, a "talking head" of Richard Mortimer played from a 1950s Zenith television. It clearly showed his views were old fashioned, but a clip was chosen from earlier days when he was fresh on the art scene. The three phases of the installation were well received, and even the mayor showed up, once he was convinced it was safe.

Back at the Fowlers' house, Ekk and Elsa sat on the couch watching television with Brutus. Ekk had put on *Turner Classics*, and was enjoying "Darby O'Gill and the Little People." A knock came on the door, and Ekk put down the popcorn, his favorite food, to answer it. The knob was pretty high for him, but he managed. Looking up, he was surprised to see Gary Smithers, councilman for the district. Elsa sensed all was not well and hid behind the couch. Gary pushed his way in and closed the door.

"You can come out from behind the couch, Elsa." From the moment he spoke, they knew he was part of Wolfrum's crazy religion. Both of the elves, caught unawares, had relaxed their vigilance. Smithers put up his hands, forced them both back to the couch, and turned up the TV.

Ekk said, "It's over, Smithers. The ritual is complete."

Gary sat, face expressionless. "Not exactly."

Elsa tried hard to bring flowers into the room, but she was bound by some kind of dark magic. She focused with all her might on Brutus and pictured the museum.

"If you recall, the ritual was imperfect. You made some gains, but Wolfrum's still a force to be reckoned with." Brutus, ignored by the intruder, slunk out the back door, hopefully heeding the magical call.

"What are you going to do with us?" Elsa asked.

"When your friends return, they will find their protectors strewn about the room in pieces. That should do it." If he had laughed a villain's "bwahaha," the scene couldn't have been more terrifying.

Ekk was so brave and stood in front of his Elsa. "Take me, not her. There must be some decency in you, man."

Smithers laughed. "You both have managed to do quite a bit of damage. I would've thought your elf girlfriend would get the message when we mercifully let her starve instead of killing her. No second chances." He reached into a briefcase and brought out a sharp-looking machete. "I think I'll put your heads on the bannister. Cute, yes?"

❧

At the museum, Puddle, Mitzi, and I were walking out, arguing about Peru. "Are you really going through with this?" I asked Puddle, for the twentieth time.

She replied, "Done talking about it. Done!"

I opened my mouth to answer but instead was shocked to see my cat running toward us in a gallop, meowing loudly.

Mitzi and I said in unison, "Brutus?" The poor guy was exhausted. Mitzi said, "Take the car. Something's wrong." I was about to ask her how she was going to get home, but her wings sprang forth with great force. It was a good thing we were outside. Her blouse ripped at the shoulders, but she had a sports bra on. Funny what we seize upon in times like these.

Puddle just stared. "Holy . . ."

I scooped up our little Paul Revere, grabbed Puddle's arm, and dragged her to the car. Traffic leaving the parking lot was heavy, and I went up on the sidewalk in my Smart car. Where were the cops when you needed one? A siren whooped behind me. I put the pedal to the metal in my three-cylinder car and hoped we would get to Thistle Drive in time.

A minute later, I rounded the corner and stopped in front of our house with the police in hot pursuit. Everyone jumped out of their cars. The front door was open, and Puddle and I pointed inside. "In there!" A policewoman grabbed me, and I struggled to get free. Puddle, always faster, had made it in, and she told me later what she saw.

"It was like a scene from a Renaissance painting, man. That city council guy was advancing with a machete, and your wife was flying in the living room with these huge-ass wings spread between him and Ekk and Elsa. She looked like an angel. There were roses flying everywhere, too."

"Once Mitzi showed up," Elsa said, "I was able to generate some of my flowers, and we were able to slow him down." She was still trembling.

What I saw was two cops run into my house and, moments later, lead Gary Smithers, in handcuffs, to a waiting car. By now, the neighborhood was lit up with red, flashing lights. I held Brutus and kept telling him what a good boy he was.

The police accepted that somehow I had gotten a message that my friends were in danger, although they looked askance at the cat explanation. I think some of Elsa's magic rubbed off, because they finally left without arresting any of us. As I held Mitzi, whose wings had retracted, Puddle asked Ekk and Elsa if we were safe now.

Elsa took her hand gently in both of hers, and said, "I think we need to make sure Ekk's cousin joins you in Peru." She turned to all of us. "It may be over for a while, but not forever. I hope you don't get sick of us."

I started crying, and we ended up in a group hug. Brutus meowed loudly again, and I immediately became alarmed. Ekk and Elsa giggled. Mitzi said, "Purple bag?"

They nodded yes. Elsa told them, "He said hurry up, he's earned it!"

❦

EPILOGUE

A party was in process, both a "Going Away" for Puddle, who was headed for Peru, and a celebration for our brave Brutus who had saved our elven friends from death by machete.

"Our ride is going to be here soon." Puddle put her glass down. "Sis, it sure has been great, and I really mean great, visiting." I looked at my dreadlocked and beaded sister—Mitzi had added the beads to her hairdo.

As if on cue, a horn honked in front of the house. We helped Puddle and Ekk and Elsa with their luggage, and all said their goodbyes as the sun hung low in the sky.

Ekk took me aside. "I got word a few minutes ago Ehrenhardt is sending Twyla, his late husband's niece, to watch over you while I'm gone. She should be here any day."

"Is she an elf, like you?"

"No, a fairy." He sighed and looked at the buckles on his Doc Martens.

We knew each other too well to hide things, and time was fleeting. I stared into his clear blue eyes that I'd come to love and said, "What is it, Ekk?"

"Well, fairies are. . . fairies. You'll see what I mean when she gets here. She'll have been properly trained, however, so don't worry. It shouldn't take more than a few weeks for us to settle Puddle in and make sure she's in capable hands for protection. We'll be back."

The car honked again as everyone else was now inside the vehicle. Valerie reached through the window. "Puddle, here's our address, email, and cell phones."

"Thanks, I'll send you pictures!" Puddle was always happy when traveling.

Mitzi added, "Promise you'll send us an alpaca sweater, oh, and some of that tea they give you when you get off the plane for altitude sickness. Coca leaf!" As a tour guide, Mitzi was very curious about South America in general. I could tell she had been reading.

Puddle laughed. "I better make a list."

I put my arms around Mitzi. "We'll go someday, baby." I kissed her on the cheek.

Before ending our goodbyes, Ekk said, "In any event, it's good Elsa and I are getting away. Our apartment isn't working out. Finding a new place is number one when we get back."

"Why?" I asked.

"People stare, the upstairs neighbors must wear tree trunks on their feet, and a collection of little things." He grinned at that, becoming quite the pun master.

The driver honked yet again.

Holding Ekk at arm's length, I said, "I'm sorry about that, and, Ekk, please be careful."

"I will, Panda." We hugged one last time. I leaned in and kissed Puddle's cheek and waved to Elsa in the backseat, all but lost in the overflow of Puddle's "jungle gear."

As they pulled from the curb, Valerie said, "I'm going to miss them."

She had put into words what we were all feeling.

~

AUTHOR'S NOTE

The Hercynian Forest is an actual place, as are the Schwartzvald Castles. Wolfrum and his deranged monks do not actually live in the Black Forest, and no reputational harm regarding evil, evil religions, cults, or dark magic should be attributed to the area castles. Also, rumors of a hidden Garden Castle in the Hercynian Forest where magic dwarves, elves, unicorns and griffins cavort, although not disproven, has never been substantiated.

[For those who wish to dive deeper: *The Curious Animals of the Hercynian Forest* by Walter Woodburn Hyde, University of Pennsylvania, is intriguing.]

~

ABOUT THE AUTHOR

Reba Birmingham is an award-winning lawyer and author of The Hercynian Forest Series. In 2018, the City of Long Beach, California, inducted her onto the Harvey Milk Wall for her work championing LGBTQ causes. She lives with her wife in a town very much like Merryville, with a collection of beloved pets. Reba's website is at www.RebaBirmingham.com.

Launch Point Press
Portland, Oregon
www.LaunchPointPress.com

Lightning Source UK Ltd.
Milton Keynes UK
UKHW010628020622
403888UK00001B/104